KARMIC LUST

EVERNIGHT PUBLISHING ®

www.evernightpublishing.com

Copyright© 2020

Nikki Prince

Editor: Marie Medina

Cover Art: Sour Cherry Designs

Jacket Design: Jay Aheer

ISBN: 978-0-3695-0143-1

KARMIC LUST

DEDICATION

First of all I would like to give my thanks to God the Father from whom all my blessings have come. I am so happy for the gift I have been given to create characters and worlds that everyone loves to read. I want to thank my family for all their support without it, I couldn't have gotten to this point. I love you all.

My dear, dear friends who went above and beyond to help me by listening to me whine, encouraging me, supporting me, editing, beta reading for me: Shyla, Valeree, Mahalia, Eden, Tari and my critique group Rom-Critters on yahoo. Thank you. I love and appreciate you all. Also a special thank you to those who may not have read, critiqued or edited this, but still encouraged me: Eden, Louisa, Kim and Savannah, Delilah H and Avril. You're all loved and appreciated. Please forgive me if I haven't named you outright, but know that I love each and everyone of you my dear friends so thank you with my whole heart.

I want to also thank Evernight Publishing and my fantastic Editor Marie, for taking a chance on a girl with a dream. A dream I've had since the age of twelve when I found my father's Johanna Lindsey Western Romance book on his dresser and was forever hooked.

To the readers, thank you for your love and support. I'm forever grateful and hope to put out stories that you will love and talk about for years to come.

KARMIC LUST

DEMON MINE

Karmic Lust, 1

Nikki Prince

Copyright © 2012

Chapter One

Liliana Jackson sat on the bed in the darkened room. Her breath was ragged as she eagerly waited for her lover to arrive. The need she felt was always instant when she thought of him. The slightest movement of cloth from her sundress scraping over her hard nipples tortured her as her bare pussy dampened. She glanced at the small clock on the wall opposite her bed. It would be only a matter of minutes before he stepped across the threshold.

She tried to be patient and wait. She let out a whimper, trying her best to wait for him, but failing. Slowly, she slipped her dress up her thighs, baring her shaved pussy to the air in the room, parting her legs while she leaned back onto the pillows; her fingers teased along her slit in one smooth stroke. She slid two fingers around her wet entrance, and then leisurely teased her clit. Liliana inched one, then two fingers inside of her drenched folds with a moan. She rocked her hips to push them in deeper as her head fell back against the pillow.

She groaned once more as she neared orgasm. *One without him.* He'd want to punish her, and she'd welcome it. She loved it when he acted all badass around her. In fact, she wanted it. Even as independent as she had always been, she needed his commanding presence, lust and strength. It fueled all of those things within her as well. His needs fed her needs. Her eyes moved to the door. She grinned. There he stood, leaning against the doorjamb, arms crossed over his muscled chest. He looked angry—the edges of his mouth turned down and narrowed eyes fixed on her undulating body.

"Hello, lover" Her words were a raspy purr of arousal.

Samael, her lover and the object of her lusts, filled the doorway with his presence. Samael, with his lithe, muscular body, tattoos on his arms, long, dark hair that fell past his shoulders, and when angry, eyes so dark they were fathomless against his paler skin. He was her dark demon, the possessor of her very being, her soul. He continued to stand there, arms crossed over his chest. Samael's dark eyes turned hazel as they slowly traveled her body to focus on her fingers, which continued to thrust in and out of her pussy. The change in eye color was a sure sign of his rising lust, a hue she was well acquainted with and wanted ... no, craved to see.

"I ordered you to wait, Lili." She heard the impatience in his voice.

Biting back a small moan, she arched her back up off the bed, her eyes still connected with his as her fingers curled to stroke her g-spot.

"You order me to do a lot of things, Sami. I don't always listen."

He gave a low warning snarl. A groan from her was the response he received. He hated when she shortened his name from Samael to Sami. Her eyes moved down his body with leisure, exploring every nuance that made up the fabulous male standing before her. The black t-shirt fit his muscled form well, along with the black jeans that did little to hide his huge hard-on.

"You protest, yet your cock is enjoying the attention I'm giving myself. Seeing as you were late, I thought it would be okay to start without you. Honestly, do you think I would rather have your cock or my fingers?" All the while, her fingers continued to plunge into her tight core, her legs bent on the bed as she arched her back. She splayed her legs out before him so that he saw every thrust.

"Lili, you're just begging to be spanked." She shivered and ran her tongue over her bottom lip. His words sparked more need than fear. His approach was leisurely as he watched her continue to pleasure herself. She moved her free hand between her spread thighs and tugged at her clit. "Stop your fingers now. Remove them or you'll not get what you want from me."

With measured deliberation, Liliana pulled her fingers from her pussy. Keeping her eyes on Samael, she slowly, teasingly licked them clean. His eyes narrowed, and Liliana smirked. "You didn't say I couldn't taste."

"Remove the fucking dress, Lili. Do it quickly, or you will not get a chance to come as you need to. Then get your pretty little ass on your knees and hold on to the headboard." His words quickly wiped the smirk off her face. She didn't say anything as she got to her knees and slipped the sundress off, tossing it to the floor. With one last look of feigned defiance, she turned to settle on her knees with her hands clutched to the headboard. The rustling of his clothing filled the otherwise silent room, and then they were skin to skin. His cock, hard and throbbing, pushed against the crease of her ass as his body pressed close to hers from behind.

Her breath caught in anticipation of his touching her as she craved. She did not say a word. If Liliana tested him, he would follow through on not letting her come. That could not happen; she wanted him bad. A soft mewl slipped from her lips as the head of his cock stroked along her dripping entrance. Her hands tightened on the headboard when he pressed into her. His lips were only an inch from her ear as he spoke with what could only be devilish delight.

"You're dripping, Lili. So wet for this cock, aren't you?"

"That's a fucking understatement." Cheeky. It's what he was used to receiving and what she was used to giving. Teeth nibbled along her earlobe, and then he bit down hard, only to suck the lobe into his mouth. She shuddered. He pressed in. The head of his cock entered her, though he did not move an inch more. One of his hands cupped her hip, while the other stroked into her hair and tugged her head back, causing her body to arch as he pulled her to her knees. She groaned in pleasure as this angle pushed him in deep, and each thrust pressed against her g-spot.

"I could always leave you like this, Lili. Needy for my cock and not allowed to come." She whimpered in protest; she couldn't help it. He had her, and they both knew it. She shook her head, the tug causing a bit of a sting as his fingers still held her hair.

"No. Please, Samael. I need you."

"Are you sure just any dick won't do? Or any fingers for that matter?" He thrust heavily into her. Every solid inch of him filled her completely. Then just as quickly, that full feeling was gone as he pulled almost completely out. Only the head of his cock was inside of her, teasing her overly sensitive entrance.

"No other cock, Samael, but yours. Only yours, my demon lover." She hummed in pleasure as he thrust into her, this time not stopping. Their movements were in accord, and the emotion of it all caused her to sob as he leaned in, pressed fully to her back, to lick along the back of her neck. "Oh, please more, give me more."

"I love it when you beg, Lili."

She knew, just as she knew begging him was something she loved to do. Even with the defiant part of her character, she always acquiesced to what he willed. The strange thing was she felt like she had known him in a past life and that he had been someone highly important to her. Somewhere deep within her soul she felt their connection. Not just because he was inside of her that very moment, but there was a deeper, more meaningful realization that they were meant to be. Each thrust within her fogged her memory. It was hard to think when he touched her. Her body knew him even if her mind had forgotten. Her soul and his were linked together.

He pressed her forward so she was holding on to the headboard again, and then pulled back slightly so his body wasn't flush against hers. That was when she felt a stinging pain as his hand came down on her ass. She screeched in pain and pleasure, not having expected him to spank her. Pain turned to pleasure, radiating outward from her smarting ass, straight to her clit, causing it to throb. She felt he always knew when her mind was drifting, and that smack to her ass was her proof.

"Focus, Lili, or I'll stop."

She heard the serious tone in his voice, and with a ragged sob, she nodded her head frantically, afraid to speak, only wanting to feel. His thrusts sped up, the hand at her waist moved between her thighs. Deft fingers tugged at her clit, rubbing over the extended bundle of nerves making her back arch as she pushed back against him, rocking gently and causing his fingers to give her more pleasure. She gushed around his cock and groaned as her legs began to tremble.

"Mmm, you are close, Lili. I can feel it." In response, her body tightened on him. Her inner muscles convulsed about his cock as she came hard, crying out. His hand moved from her hair to wrap about her waist and tug her close to his body so his strength supported her as she shook. His face nuzzled into the side of her neck as her orgasm continued to ebb and flow.

Tortured breathing sounded through the room, hitting her ears. She realized it was coming from the both of them and then he was shouting as he released within her, filling her with his seed. His cry muffled against her skin as his cock shot threads of his thick cream into her tight recesses.

It was almost too much, too much pleasure and need. Her orgasm left her overly sensitive. She moved against him, but his hands stilled her. "No, baby, stay right here with me." His voice sounded desperate. His words calmed her and made her press even closer to him. She could never comprehend the underlying pain and nervousness she heard in his voice at times like these. The urgency she felt in him made her wonder. What could possibly be worrying him? He was so strong, but then there were situations like this where he showed his vulnerability.

"I wasn't going to, Samael. I never want to be apart from you. You know that." His hold loosened from her body, the death-like grip relaxing once more. He stroked his fingers up her body, capturing her breasts, squeezing and pulling at her nipples as he thrust into her, his cock still hard and pulsing even after his orgasm. She gasped then whimpered as he pulled out of her slowly, leaving only the head of his cock buried within her for just a moment longer.

"Oh, how you love to tease me." She moaned.

"I am not done with you yet. I will never be done with you." He thrust in slowly, inch by incredible inch until he was fully in. With a groan, he pressed his lips to the side of her neck, kissing and nipping at her skin, his thrusts within her nice and shallow. Those movements gave pressure only sufficient to tease and bring her to the brink, but not adequate to allow her to come. She felt his teeth nip her throat, and then he was sucking that flesh into his mouth, marking her. She gasped in pleasure from his love bites, his teasing setting her whole body on fire with need.

"You're mine, Lili. Do you hear me? Mine."

She shuddered, nodding at his words even as his tongue laved over the skin he had just bitten. She knew there would be a mark there, a mark given by him that would show the world she was his and his alone.

"Get on your back." Samael moved away, and she quickly flipped to her back, her eyes on him, waiting to see what he would do next.

Her eyes wide, she watched him as he moved his hand between them to grab his cock as he teased it along her lips, wetting his cock completely in her juices as well as his. The head of his cock circled her clit, and she whimpered, arching her hips off the bed.

"What do you want, Lili?"

She hissed as he smacked his cock against her clit. The pain was exquisite, and her pussy gushed with her juices. She felt it coating her inner thighs. Her hands moved to grip the bedding as she thrust up against him.

"You. I want you, and only you." *Smack.* His cock hit her clit again, and she gave a low, fervent cry.

Her eyes closed. "Puh-lease, Samael, fuck me!" Frantic. He made her so damn needy.

He took her legs, placing them over his shoulders, as he positioned himself once more between her thighs. "Baby, I'm going to fuck you. Nice and hard like we both desire."

The urgency returned. She could see it in his eyes. They were wild, and he again acted as if they would never see one another again. "Fuck me. Move with me, Lili." He pushed in deep, until his cock was hitting her womb, and then stopped.

"Put your legs around my waist, and hold on tight." She did as he asked, locking her feet at the ankles, and held on for the ride. As soon as her legs locked at his hips, holding him into place, he began thrusting in and out of her at a furious pace.

Their mouths met, and her lips took his in a fevered kiss, her tongue thrusting into his mouth. Her tongue fucked his mouth, just as his cock did her cunt, mimicking the same action they both craved. She rolled her hips in time with the swirling of their tongues, anxious mewls of pleasure emitting as his hands cupped her breasts and pulled at the sensitive nipples. His lips moved from hers to trail down her throat, nipping in between his words. With each nip to her skin, she groaned and arched her body in reaction, small whimpers escaping.

"Such beautiful breasts you have, baby. Nipples as hard as diamonds and they are all mine, only mine." He buried his face in between her breasts, nipping her skin there. She found herself chanting that she was his with each nip to her skin causing a ragged groan to escape her parted lips.

"I'm all yours, only yours, Samael."

Their breaths matched each other's as their bodies

collided repeatedly in a rhythm they'd memorized. They both gave a shout, shaking through a mind and body shattering orgasm. She fell against him, panting and trying to regain order to her breathing, trying to calm herself. He held her close, her face buried in the side of his neck. She didn't want their moment together to end. Neither did he; he didn't let her go.

"Why can't I ever get enough of you?" Liliana whispered against his neck, not truly looking for an answer but wanting one just the same. Samael's hands stilled against her back.

"It is the same for me, Lili. It's always you that I want and need, Lili. No one else will do."

"But I feel it goes deeper than that, Samael." His hands resumed stroking along her back.

"Don't analyze this, not right now. Not while we still have the night before I have to go again, my Lili." As if on cue, she felt him stir within her again. He was hard. As rigid as his cock was, her pussy was drenched. Samael was her other half, made for her, just as she was for him. More proof that they could not do without each other, they were insatiable. Their bodies synchronized to each other's. He set a fast pace that had her legs wrapped about his waist, her pressing up into him, moaning his name in that sinfully sweet way that only she could.

It was the same every night. They met and pleasured one another, only for her to awaken in the early morning hours to find him gone. No explanation given, nor was it asked for. It just was. Though, the more she thought of it, the more she hated it and wanted to know why and if there was a way to put a stop to it. Throughout the night, they reached for one another, seeking solace in each other's arms.

She automatically reached for him in the early morning light, though she knew he had already gone.

"Samael," she whispered softly, as if he could hear her.

Tears filled her eyes and slid down her cheeks as she lay on her stomach, her hand rubbing his place on the bed in an attempt to soak up the last bit of his heat he had left behind.

How was it possible to feel so much for one being? Eyes held shut tight as she fought back more tears, her thoughts turning to when they had first met. She had been out at a bar seeking something, anything, to stop the ache she felt. The need to touch him and for him to touch her always ran rampant through her. Her relationships with other men had always fallen flat.

Hell, she had even tried being with a woman to make sure the reasons for her failed relationships with men weren't because she wanted women. She felt arousal with those she was with, whether it was a male or female, but that was all. The consequence of her searching left her aroused and frustrated. She had been unable to gain pleasure by anyone else's touch. Enter Samael.

****

Two years prior

Standing in the back of the club, Samael watched her body swaying to the music. Every eye in the room had zeroed in and locked on her form as she moved effortlessly. Long, dark hair swaying around her shoulders in a silken mass, her body wrapped in a black sheath, and black boots that made her legs seem endless. Her apple-shaped bottom was smackable; his hand itched to do just that, and her breasts, oh man, did he love to look at them.

As he moved through the crowd, the patrons parted like the Red Sea as if sensing he was not what he should be. She looked up at his approach. The sad fucker with her squared his jaw and clenched his fists as if he was trying to warn Samael away from the woman standing next to him. If he was looking for a fight, he could have one. Samael scowled at him. He dropped his fists and skulked back into the crowd.

A grin spread across her face but then she looked fully into his eyes. He watched her shiver and as she tried to move, he shook his head, stilling all movement from her. It was his Lilith. He would know her anywhere and had to stop himself from smiling when she squared her shoulders in defiance. As the music slowed, he pulled her close with one hand slung low on her back. Her sharp intake of breath moved through him.

Her face nuzzled into the side of his neck, and he groaned softly. It was definitely Lilith. She had always placed her face there, telling him she loved his scent. Even if she didn't know him, her subconscious mind did. His hand smoothed down her back to cup her ass, pulling her even closer, while his other hand crept up her side to cup a breast as if he owned her.

On a ragged breath, she spoke, "What are you doing?"

"I'm dancing with you. Isn't that evident?" He inserted his leg between hers, pulling her flush against him, allowing her to feel every hard contour of his body. She felt his cock pressed firmly against her.

She moaned softly. "This isn't dancing."

"Oh, but it is," he whispered against her ear. "It is a dance that is as old as time. This is a wild and passionate dance that your body is lusting after, baby. I can smell how badly you wish this dance." He licked her earlobe, and she shuddered, a small groan tumbling from her lips.

"You're up to no good." She whimpered.

"Fucking right I am. But what I want to do to you will be good for us both," he said.

She arched back to look into his dark eyes, her

mouth moving as if to speak, yet no sound escaped. By the end of the dance, she was panting against him, her eyes wild. She didn't speak, just allowed him to take her hand and lead her off the dance floor to a darkened corner of the club.

He quickly took control, pressing her up against the wall and leaning in to take her lips in a kiss. Their lips melded together, and he was home. Her taste and touch were everything he remembered, and he wanted more. He knew he had her attention when he heard her soft moan, and she pressed her body against his, her hands moving to cup the back of his head.

"I could take you right here, and you would let me. Wouldn't you?"

"Yes, I would, in a heartbeat," she stated simply.

He rubbed himself against her cleft, a low groan of pleasure escaping their lips as the need continued to build. Instantly he knew that even if she didn't know his name her body knew his and would always feel the answering need that they had for one another. He'd show her what mattered, even if that was only with his touch. He'd teach her to love him again and to need him, perhaps then her memory would spark.

Nibbling gently at her lips for a moment, he heard her whimper as his tongue suddenly thrust into her mouth. He kissed her, devouring her lips. He would overload her senses and keep her off balance until he was all she thought about.

****

Her eyes slid open as she heard her sister Eva's ringtone blaring from her cell phone. Buzz kill! The annoying sound from her phone brought her quickly out of her memories of her beloved demon, her Samael, and back into a stark and very cold reality. Like clockwork, Eva always called at the same time of the day.

Sometimes it felt odd, and other times it was comforting to know her sister cared. Then there were the times that the help she gave her seemed a bit cloying and heavy handed. One would think Eva was the older sister as much as she liked to try to run Liliana's life. It was the other way around; Eva was the baby and Liliana was two years older.

She picked the cell up, holding it to her ear. Her sister didn't even wait for her to speak. "So, let me guess. Mr. Dark and wonderful is gone already?" Her tone dripped with sarcasm.

"Yes, Eva. Samael is gone. Please. No more lectures on how he isn't good enough for me and how I deserve better."

"He isn't, Lil. You know it, and I know it. Why do you let him do this to you?"

"E, when are you going to realize that he is in my life? Albeit only at night, but he is in my life to stay until I say otherwise. Neither you nor anyone else has a say in that, Eva, only me. Now please tell me what you called for this morning."

"Just making sure you weren't going to be late coming to work. We have many orders to fulfill. You're the other half of *Two Sister's Sinful Delights,* after all. I need you here, but most of all, I need you to be here." Liliana heard the emphasis on the last here loud and clear.

"I know, and I will be. I just need to shower. I am coming in this morning."

"Girl, you need to drop his ass like a bad habit."

"Not dropping him. No matter what you say, E; it isn't going to happen. Now, I will see you at ten." She hung up the phone quickly before her sister could say anything else. Flouncing back against the bed, she let out a huff. She had a few hours before she had to get to the store to help her sister open up their sex shop. It was going to be a long ass day. Her sister would keep at it. She didn't know what it meant to stop giving her opinion when it wasn't needed or wanted. Of course, it was done in love, right? Well, hell, what did one do with a demon who didn't take no for an answer? She grinned to herself. She knew what her answer was to that. Anything he asked for.

Chapter Two

Samael watched as Eva hung up the phone, turning with slow, deliberate movements towards him, a smirk on her face. She was perched on a nightstand next to the bed of the hotel room he had rented. As beautiful as she was, she in no way compared to his Lili. Her long, red nails tapped against the wood, the only sound in the room. He didn't speak for a few tension-filled moments, only watched as she visibly prepared herself to go on her tirade.

"No matter what you do, Lili will still be with me. Every time we come back, we find one another. It was destined to be this way from the beginning. When are you going to learn to stop? Every time you go after us, you're only making things worse for you. He leaned against the wall next to the bathroom. He had been coming out of it when she suddenly appeared in his room, talking on her cell phone with Lili.

Times like this made him feel it seriously sucked to know other demons. Most especially, powerful ones like Eva Jackson. Eva Jackson was proof that if you gave a demon an inch, that demon would take a mile. He looked at her and couldn't stop thinking she had taken more than her unfair share of miles from the both of them throughout the years.

Eva gave a shrug of her slim shoulders. "I will never stop, Sami." She smirked as his lips turned down, and his eyes darkened in anger. "Liliana needs to learn that what she did to me was wrong."

"What the hell did she do to you? She left Adam, which made it possible for you to exist." Why was he even trying to speak to her on a level she wouldn't understand? As many centuries that had gone by, she hadn't learned her lesson. Why would she learn it now?

She didn't want to learn anything, nor did she want to move past old hurts and wrongs. Stubborn, that was what she was, plain and simple.

"No, she made it so the man who should have been mine pined away the rest of his days over her! Instead of wanting me, he wanted her!" The venom in those words was like icy talons dragging across his skin.

"So you spend every waking moment, every time she is reincarnated, trying to sabotage Lili and me." The only proof of his annoyance was the shifting of his stance.

"Yes, it's what I live for, after all."

"Drop the curse, Eva, please. Free us. We have been punished enough." His words were meant to entice her into agreeing to free them from the curse.

"No, I can't." She sniffed as if to dismiss his words.

"Can't? It's more as if you fucking won't. You're the key that keeps us in this holding pattern." He rumbled cynically.

"You're right. I fucking won't. So how about you pull up your big boy panties and get the fuck over it. You leave her and have something better." Samael watched as Eva stroked her long, crimson colored nails through her dark tresses. She preened and primped herself as if she didn't have a care in the world.

"And what the hell would that be?" He knew exactly what she was getting at. She had been after him forever. It angered her that he didn't want her, and that he only had eyes for Lili. It was a reminder for Eva of what occurred with Adam. The thing about the curse was that though he couldn't tell Lili who she was, it also made it impossible for Eva to allow him to forget Lili.

"You're life back and me. A sweet little packaged deal." She gave a wicked sounding giggle. She had everything all tied up in a neat little package in her mind. Damn, she was fucking crazy. However, that was an issue with all demons: they were inherently mad.

"I already have my life, and it is one with Lili. That's your whole problem, Eva. Every time she's reincarnated, you always try to take what Lili has. It hasn't worked in the past, and it won't work now." There was a smirk on his face. He wasn't scared of her; she knew it, and it pissed her off.

The growl she gave would have crushed a lesser man. His skin was thick when it came to her. It did nothing but mar her beauty. His eyes narrowed as she moved close, trying to make him back up. He didn't. Her eyes became narrow slits as she brought her hand up, using a finger to jab him in the chest.

"If I thought you were right, I'd give up. But one way or the other she will break, and you will, too." Then with a flounce, she disappeared, leaving him alone in his hotel room. Eva had another think coming if she thought he would give up so easily and let her win. Hell would freeze over first. The curse wasn't going to be removed today. He would have to find another way. There was no way he was going to let Eva win again. Time was running out, but he would be damned if he would go out without a fight.

****

Liliana looked up from her desk in the back office of the business she ran with her sister, trying to focus on the numbers before her. It was hard to think of crunching numbers when all she could think about was Samael. Her sister was right. She wasn't where she should be, mentally at least. Lately, it was harder for her to focus. She couldn't stop feeling as if time was running out. This really didn't make sense when she thought about it. She was only thirty-two and still young with plenty of time.

She should be in the here and now and not worried over the fact that her lover was a demon who only visited her at night. She wondered how many women had to deal with being in love with a demon.

At the rate she was going, everyone figured she would be an old, unmarried woman selling dildos and the like way into her eighties. She chuckled at the thought, thinking to herself that at least she would be one hip old woman.

Not to mention the fact that her being in love with a man she knew to be a demon would be disconcerting for most. From the time she could remember as a child, she had always felt there were unworldly things out there. It had gone beyond just believing there were other beings beyond humans when she was a young girl and had visits from her *imaginary friend* that she would play with when Eva was not around. A friend who'd help her when she needed help and even go so far as to protect her.

He would never present himself so that others would see him. He had always told her he was there for her and that there were others like him. He had said she would have an affinity for those like him and would now have her eyes opened to such things, as she was a natural. She would only not sense a being strong enough to block such things from her.

When she had asked him what his name was, he had told her Adam. For years, as a young child, Adam was always there. Then when it came time for her to grow up, he came to her and told her that he would have to stop coming around, that she was big enough to deal with life's issues, and perhaps, someday they could meet again.

She heard the clearing of a throat and groaned. Of course Eva would catch her daydreaming. Why in the hell was Eva always in the wrong place at the wrong time? Every time she was thinking about Samael, there was Eva. If it weren't absurd, she would think Eva knew what she was thinking and had come to disrupt those thoughts. She was being silly. Her sister loved her. She was a little overprotective. Yet, she loved her. She turned towards Eva, who was standing in the doorway taking a huge bite out of an apple, the scowl on her face all-knowing.

"Want a bite?"

Eva moved over to her holding a big crimson colored apple out. It looked delicious. For some reason, Liliana didn't think she could even stomach it. It felt so much like a trap. Shit, what was she thinking, a trap? God, she was truly losing it! Her sister loved her. She wouldn't do anything to harm her.

"No." Liliana shook her head vehemently. "Thank you, but no, I ate an hour ago. Not even hungry yet." Eva shrugged and perched her ass, clad in tight black jeans, on the edge of the desk and looked at her.

"So let me guess. You're pining away for a man that is afraid to meet you in the daylight. A man, I might add, that's probably married with the white picket fence, two perfect children and a dog. Which, my dear sweet sister, would make you the mistress. Are you so desperate, Lil, that you will take another woman's leavings?"

The pen that Liliana had been holding dropped onto the desk as she pierced her sister with a look of incredulity, her lips forming an O. Liliana fought the anger that was bubbling forth. This was Eva. This wasn't just someone off the street talking trash. It was her sister. She was so crossing the line, a very thin line that would be backing Liliana up against a wall if she kept it up. As much as she loved Eva, she needed to stop getting so close to that invisible boundary of what one didn't say to someone about her man.

"You don't know him, Eva, like I know him." She knew she sounded like a broken record. Eva just didn't get it, and perhaps she never would. God, she hoped that wasn't the case.

"I don't have to know him to see what he is like and what he is doing, Lili." Eva took another big bite out of the apple. "You and I have always stuck together. Since the foster homes we bounced around in, who kept you safe? Who guided you through all the mess that happened to us and kept you from some of the shit that could have happened to us? Me! And this one time I tell you that someone is up to no good, you doubt me?"

"You don't know him like I know him!" Her voice rose with agitation. To calm herself she took several deep, calming breaths and then looked at Eva who still sat on the desk with her hand on her hip. "Please. Stop. This isn't the place for this. We need to get to work. I am almost done with the totals, and then we can go over the new items that have come in and figure out how we want to display them."

"We aren't done with this conversation by a long shot, Lili. I will give you your reprieve, as I know you are right about us needing to get things done today. So in that vein, I suggest you stop dreaming about *Mr. Fuck'em and Leave'em* and focus on the task at hand."

Liliana felt her lips tighten as she fought back the angry words that were so close to the surface. She gave a huff and a nod towards her sister, watching as Eva got up off the desk and made her way back to the office door to head out. She turned back to leave another parting shot.

"You'll thank me later." With another bite of the almost gone apple, Eva winked and left the room.

Thank her later indeed. Eva acted as if she didn't

know Liliana loved Samael. This wasn't just a passing fancy of some young girl. No, this was the love of a woman who knew what she wanted, how she wanted it and why she wanted it. Samael spoke to her on every level. The pain of being without him was a physical hurt, not just a mental one. She felt so empty without him.

Yet if she were honest, it did chafe a bit that she only saw him at night. However, in truth, she knew why he did it. How could she tell her sister, or anyone for that matter, that the one she was in love with was a demon? She couldn't. She would just swallow the hurt and pride and made it seem like the situation was okay. Made herself feel it was okay to be alone half the time and only with him when it was nighttime. It all seemed so convenient. A nice little present for Samael without any of the baggage that came along with being in a fully committed relationship.

The pull towards him was something she couldn't deny. Besides, they didn't just fuck like rabbits all night, not as Eva thought. There was more to their time together than that. He held her and comforted her when she needed it, too. He let her talk about her day. He listened, and he told her he loved her. No, they didn't have a conventional relationship by what society considered normal by any means, but that didn't mean he wasn't perfect for her. Samael was not a typical man. Hell, he wasn't a man at all; he was a demon. He was a demon with a curse. A curse he didn't like to speak of other than to tell her that it was his torment. The only thing he would tell her was that the curse was keeping him bound to the nightly visits. She believed him. Why would he lie?

A thought filtered into her mind that maybe he was lying because he was spending time with someone else when he wasn't with her. No! She wouldn't think like that. This was all Eva's fault. She had put that little niggling of doubt into her mind and made her question the relationship she had with Samael.

Her reflections returned to how Eva had offered the apple and how flippant she had seemed when she knew that Liliana loved Samael. Eva always had to be right about everything and always wanted to tell Liliana how to act, and this instance was no different. Her dismissive attitude spoke volumes of how little she thought of their relationship. The bond she had with Samael wasn't just a fling for her. It was love, something that Liliana had told Eva on many occasions. She laughed aloud, shaking her head. Eva really wasn't one to talk about relationships. She had scared off every man who was interested in her.

The plain fact of the matter was, Eva needed to find love herself, and then she would understand. She hoped. Her mind started working overtime, and she smiled. If she found Eva a man, then perhaps she would let up. Then Eva would understand Liliana. She would understand that what they had was meant to be and a forever kind of love. If anything, she hoped it would at least get her off her back for just a bit. She giggled.

She was startled out of her daydream when Jess tapped on the door, holding a large box in her arms. "Oh!"

"Sorry, boss. I did make my presence known a few times." The shapely blonde, in her skinny jeans and t-shirt with the company's logo emblazoned in hot pink on the front of it over her ample chest, smiled apologetically. Jess was their stocker and cashier extraordinaire.

"It's okay, Jess. I was lost in thought. What do you have there?" One way to forget about her issues was to get back into work. She had to. It was the only way to keep centered because once in his presence, the axis of her center had the habit of shifting off kilter. Being with him did that to her, always left her off balance. She chuckled softly. Not that having that unbalance happen around him was a bad thing.

"It's the new vibrators you ordered a week ago. You know, the pink mini love bullets." Jess grinned, pulling out one of the small boxes from the big box that she set on the edge of the desk. Reaching across the box, Jess handed the item in question to Liliana with a smile.

Liliana took the small box and settled back in her chair, as she looked it over. "Ah, yes. I have been waiting for these. They need to be on display at the front counters in the glass case. These hot little numbers will sell really quickly."

"There are some other things that I need your help figuring out where to put them. Eva said that is your job. She is better at the schmoozing, and you're better at the marketing." Jess chuckled.

"Yeah, Eva is pretty good at convincing people to do as she wishes, that's for sure." *This is the exact reason why I need to stick by my guns about Samael when Eva starts in on me about him.* "Go ahead and fix the display up. Once I am done balancing the books, I will be out to help you figure out where we want the other items." She held out the little box to Jess.

"That sounds really good, boss." Jess grinned and took the small package from Liliana, then placed it back in the bigger box. "Is there anything else before I go?"

"No, that is all. Thank you, Jess."

Jess nodded her head, picked up the merchandise and left the back office. Liliana stood, stretching her arms above her head to work the kinks out of her body from sitting at the desk all morning. It was now well into lunchtime, which was actually their busiest time of the day, and she still hadn't gotten much done. Which she welcomed as it would make the evening come quicker and soon it would be time to be in her lover's arms. The one thing she wanted the most right now was to feel his arms around her. The stress from worry was taking its toll, and she needed the strength that he alone could give her.

Chapter Three

Eva sat in a darkened corner of Diego's bar watching the sinfully handsome man with skin the color of the richest cappuccino. She was sitting on a barstool and talking to Diego himself. He wore a pair of dark colored jeans and a nice silk dress shirt that clung to his abs. Damn, he had a goatee with a military haircut. There was nothing sexier to her than a goatee on a man. He was sin on two legs. He had long tapered fingers that gripped the beer bottle and made her long for those hands to be gripping her. She picked up her brandy and took a quick drink, then gasped as it burned all the way down. She felt tears prick the corners of her eyes from that lapse in judgment. What was it about him that seemed so familiar? She felt this invisible string pulling her towards him, and she couldn't even begin to understand why.

Just as she was about to get up from her table and make her way over to him to introduce herself, she saw Liliana stop right next to him and begin talking as if she knew him. A deep frown developed on her face, and she settled back down in her chair. *What the fuck? How did Liliana know him? As wrapped up in Samael as she was, she couldn't see past his dick.* Not that she could blame her. He was something delicious to look at. But this fine specimen was definitely all that and more. At least, he seemed to be.

The ugliness of jealousy, as usual, began to rear its repulsive head, and she couldn't stop herself; she had to go and investigate. With a toss of her head, she stood and made her way to the bar, standing right next to Liliana.

"Ah, there you are, sister dear. Leaving me all by my lonesome at the bar is quite naughty of you." She gave a sidelong glance at the man Lili was talking to and then looked back at her sister. "Going to introduce me?"

Liliana laughed softly. "Oh, yes. I am sorry. Clay, this is my sister Eva. Eva, this is my good friend, Clay Quinones. He's actually one of the delivery men from the company where we buy most of our merchandise, C&C Inc."

"Oh yes, I remember them. They do supply us with some fun items." Eva looked back at Mr. Sexy and gave a nod of her head. He smiled back at her and she almost melted. That was until her sister said delivery man. Wow, really? If anyone had ever said the cards she held were lucky, they were in for disappointment. She could hear the sarcasm playing in her own head. She gave a small gasp as Clay gave her a soft kiss on the cheek, before pulling back with a devilish grin. She felt her pussy dampen and hated how her legs shook.

"Buenas noches, Eva; a kiss on the cheek is how we greet one another in Puerto Rico."

"You're not in your country, Clay." She rolled her eyes, her hands moving to her hips. She would have made some other retort, but Samael interrupted.

"Aw look, the gangs all here." Liliana giggled at Samael's words, and Eva once again rolled her eyes and gave an unladylike snort. Samael wrapped his arms about Liliana's waist from behind and kissed her softly on the neck.

"Can I buy you a drink, Eva?" Caught off guard yet again, she turned from looking at Samael and Liliana back to Clay.

"Um, I guess, why not?" Hell, the drink would help her deal with the touchy feely shit from Lil and Samael. She had to stand on her tiptoes to tell him that, making sure she whispered in his ear. His hand automatically encircled her waist as he leaned down. Her hands spontaneously pressed against his chest to steady herself, and it was like an electric current shocked her. She stood back quickly.

"Why so skittish?" The look in his eyes spoke volumes. He knew exactly what his touch did to her. Was she imagining it or were his fingers making her feel all sorts of naughty?

"Never you mind. I have a table if you're still buying that drink." With a quick turn on red designer heels, she turned back to the table she had vacated, expecting him to follow. She heard him chuckle behind her, and then he was grabbing her hand and pulling her towards him.

"Oh no, my dear. I will lead, and you will follow."

She was speechless but found herself following Clay Quinones to the table.

****

"Well, that went well." Liliana chuckled and gave Samael a jab in the ribs at his teasing.

"She was fascinated by him. I could at least tell that."

"Oh yeah, she wants him; that much was obvious. But … he doesn't fit her profile of the kind of man she wants."

"You mean rich?" Liliana covered her mouth, trying to stop the laughter that bubbled forth.

"Hmm, my baby has claws." She nodded her head to his statement, grabbing his hand and pulling him towards the small dance floor

"Come dance with me. The night is young, and I want to spend it in your arms." Once on the dance floor, she had her arms about his neck and pressed herself fully against him, placing her face into his neck. She felt his strong arms wrap about her as he pulled her close, and they began to dance slowly to a hauntingly beautiful love song.

She curled her fingers into the hair at the nape of his neck, sighing softly as his arms wrapped around her.

"Haven't we been here before?" she murmured against his neck. He pulled back slightly and looked down at her, though he didn't miss a step as they continued to dance.

"You mean here at Diego's?"

"Yes and no. I mean like this, holding one another, being with one another in all ways. It feels like we have done this over and over again, in another time, another life." She sighed again and laid her head on his shoulder.

"This, meaning the dancing we are doing right now, Lili?" She could feel him probing as if there was something else he wanted to ask, to say. Yet at the same time, it felt as if he were being evasive. She arched back to look into his eyes.

"No, it's more than that, as I have always said. It's as if we know one another. It's as if we have known one another before, in the past; it's like Déjà vu. Don't you see it, Samael? Tell me you see it, not only that, you feel it."

He pressed his lips to hers, hungrily; it seemed to be the only answer to her question. Not just a kiss filled with lust, but one that not only curled her toes but also warmed her heart. He ended the kiss, only to kiss her again repeatedly, seeking entrance into her mouth as he slid his tongue along the crease of her lips. She groaned and drew him into her mouth, tasting him with her own tongue. She felt her heart flutter in her chest and sighed when he stopped, her eyes holding his for long moments.

"It's times like this I know I knew you before. When I sense I've loved you just as strongly as I love you now. I feel like I need to remember something, but it seems foggy and too late to do so." His strong hand cupped her chin, and he caressed it softly. Peering into her eyes, he smiled, and speaking softly to her, he said, "Some love is timeless, like our love for one another."

So caught up in the beauty of the moment and mesmerized by his eyes, Liliana didn't notice Eva standing there until she was tapped on the shoulder. She groaned and turned to look over her shoulder.

"Okay, how long are you going to leave me with that infuriating man?"

"You mean Clay?"

"Yes, Clay. He is exasperating. I refuse to be left with him any longer."

Liliana exhaled noisily and then looked to Samael. "Hold on, baby, let me take her to the bathroom to get calmed down. Please go over and talk with Clay?"

Samael nodded and leaned down to kiss her quickly, giving a nip to her bottom lip. She squeaked and pushed him towards the table that Clay was sitting at and then grabbed Eva's arm, pulling her along towards the women's restroom.

Once in the small bathroom with its pristine white walls, she made sure that no one else was in there before she turned to look at Eva. "Okay, what gives? I can tell you are attracted to him. Tell me what the hell he did to have you so pissed."

"He's forceful." The look on her sister's face was almost comical. Since when did Eva pout?

"Um, come again? Forceful? How do you mean? Did he hit you?" She knew that couldn't possibly be it, but why else would her sister have her panties in a bunch over someone she was obviously attracted to?

"No. He hasn't hit me. But he is domineering." When Liliana laughed, Eva rolled her eyes at her and glared. "What the hell is so funny?"

"So he is forceful and domineering because you finally have a man that won't do what you want him to?" Liliana grinned at Eva as her sister continued to scowl at her.

"Oh! You would never understand because you follow Samael like a puppy dog!" She threw her hands up in the air, still standing there glowering.

"If you don't want him, I am sure there are plenty who will, E." Liliana watched as Eva's frown deepened. "Hmm, I can see you don't like the thought of that. Go back out there and have fun. Let him take care of everything if he wants. It will be a nice change for you. Clay is a very nice man. I knew you would be attracted to him. That's why I invited him here tonight to meet you."

Eva's eyes widened, and Liliana could tell that her words had fully penetrated her artificial anger. "You did what?"

"I invited Clay here to meet you. He's a very nice guy, and you, my dear sister, are single and need some distraction." She held up a hand as Eva began to protest. "No. Go out there and have fun. If you don't want anything to do with him after this you don't have to see him again." With a grin, she turned, leaving her sister there to either stay or follow.

"Lili, you can't do this to me."

She continued walking as Eva rushed up to her side as they walked back towards their table. As usual, the patrons filled the place to the brim, so occasionally they would have to wait for people to move to keep going.

"Can't do what, make sure that you have some fun for a change? You spend excessive amounts of time worrying about me. This is your time. Enjoy." With that said, Liliana hurried on, smiling as she spotted the men still at the table nursing beers and chatting. When she stopped at the table, Liliana grinned and winked at Samael then looked to Clay.

"Clay, Eva told me that she would really love to dance. Care to take her out for a spin around the dance floor?" Eva gasped behind her, but Liliana did not turn around. She just settled in her seat next to Samael.

"Dancing sounds like a plan. Come, sweet Eva." He held out his hand, and with one last fleeting look at Liliana, Eva placed her hand in his and moved off with him towards the dance floor.

Chapter Four

Samael stood on a hill overlooking the city, the very city that held the love of his life, Liliana. The sun was out but not at its highest point. There was still some hustle and bustle that could be seen going on down at the city level. It was early yet, not time to go for his nightly visit to Liliana. Being the type of demon he was had its uses; he could be anywhere at any time. Though it was days like these that made him feel it wasn't worth it. Eva trapped them in a never-ending cycle. Captured by a curse set so long ago that he himself had almost forgotten the reasons for the curse Eva put into place. To think this was all because of Eva's insecurities and jealousy. His mind turned back to centuries before when it had all begun.

****

Somewhere Near the Tigris River

He pulled her close to him, wrapping his arms around her as she sat just as naked as he was on the lambskins. They'd settled at their encampment after a small supper of fish, fruit and bread next to the beautiful Tigris. The sound of the water was as pleasing as it was musical as they whispered softly to one another and enjoyed each other's company.

Samael stroked his fingers gently through Lilith's hair, the dark locks so thick. He loved how it felt against his skin. He had been in love with her since the moment he had seen her there in the Garden, but she hadn't been his to take. The love he shared with Lilith was forbidden. She'd been made to be with Adam. It wasn't until she'd left Adam that she truly became his.

"Samael, what if today is the day my judgment comes? I have not only defied Adam but I also changed the way things were supposed to be. He has already made a substitute in your place. She will be all that you could not be for Adam. We have spoken of this before. He has his other half. Do not worry that he will come looking for you or that you have to go back. You and I were meant to be."

"You're right. It has been a long while since I have been gone. If he had wanted to find me, he could have."

Samael nodded, bringing his lips to hers, kissing her soundly as his arms wrapped around her naked torso, pulling her fully across him as he lay down on the lambskins.

"You're mine, forever, Lilith."

"Yes, I am yours, forever, Samael. This is where I belong, here with you." His lips took hers, at first gently, and then there was the need to mark her as his own. He nipped and tugged on her bottom lip with his teeth. She groaned and pressed her full breasts to his chest. Her nipples were hard nubs pressed into his flesh, filling him with a yearning to taste them, her touch burning into his memory.

"I love you, Lilith. I would risk everything to be with you." She smiled down at him.

"I love you too, Samael. You have given up so much for me."

"And he is about to give up so much more." With a gasp, they both pulled apart and stared up at Eve who was standing there with her arms across her chest.

"Who's this female, Samael?"

"I'm Adam's new wife, Eve. And you must be this Lilith he cannot stop talking about." Eve spoke before Samael could.

"Eve, what are you doing here? Why aren't you back in Eden with Adam?" Samael grabbed his robe that he had discarded earlier and covered them both with the cream colored cloth, hiding their bodies from Eve's gaze.

"Making sure you both get what you deserve." Liliana frowned and looked from the other woman back to Samael.

"What we deserve? Why are you speaking such foolishness? Leave us be, and go back to the Garden of Eden."

"Oh, I will be going back, but not before I do what I came here to do. That would be imparting a gift to you that will ensure my happiness and give me much pleasure."

"Eve, stop before things get out of hand." Samael's words were spoken softly, yet they held an underlying warning that came across loud and clear.

"What will you do, Fallen? That's right, Samael, you will not do anything. You've been left bereft of your power for the choices you've made. So what'll you do?" Eve's head went back as she laughed, her dark eyes filled with what Samael recognized as anger.

"I curse you both." Lilith gasped and buried her face into Samael's neck. "I curse you, Samael, to be doomed to walk this Earth with knowledge of who you were and the awareness of the love you have for Lilith."

"Is that all, Eve? That isn't a curse; it's what's already in place."

"Oh, don't rush me. I've only just begun." The smile on her face did not show in her eyes.

Samael heard Lilith whimper and whisper his name against his neck. He held her even tighter against his chest, trying to soothe her; he knew he was failing miserably.

"Now let's see. Where was I? Oh, yes. You, Samael, will know Lilith and love Lilith throughout eternity. All the same, she will never know you. You can't remind her either. The knowledge of what she has done has to come from her." She giggled and then looked directly at Lilith.

"And you, dear, get the worst of it. You will not know who you are, and Samael can't tell you. You will die, and every time you die, you will come back and be that much further from the truth. This curse will last until you remember your name and what you did to me."

Tears fell from Lilith's eyes, and she looked at Eva.

"Why are you doing this? What did I do to you?"

"Do you know how hard it is to live with a man who doesn't love you? Who pines after another woman and compares everything you do to what she did? No, you don't, because everyone wants Lilith! Lilith even has an angel choose to be fallen just for the pleasure of being between her thighs. I was the one taken from his rib, made to be his. The perfect fit for him and yet he pines for you!"

"You must be mistaken! Stop this! Go back to him, please, Eve. This is madness!" Liliana was pleading with Eve and her words ignored.

"Oh, I am going back, but I'll not stop it. The curse stands." Though she laughed, no humor filtered into her laugh.

"Eve, no good will come of this." Samael continued to hold the crying Lilith.

"Maybe you're right, but I feel better already."

****

He was brought out of his reverie by a male voice behind him. Turning, he smiled as he looked at Clay Quinones.

"I knew I'd find you here, bro."

"Yeah, it is the one place I can come and think." It was a nice lookout point down into the city. Yet, strangely enough, he found that no one really visited it.

Which made it a nice escape for him when he needed to think things through, and today was one of those days when he was in need of such an escape.

"I understand completely. Eva has put us in a bind. She can't find her way to me until what she's put into motion is undone."

Samael nodded his head, half a grin on his face as his fingers stroked over his goatee. "That's one hard headed woman you have there, Clay. By visiting Lili and I with a curse, she doomed the two of you as well."

"You're right, she is hard headed, but she will eventually see things my way. We just need to get things in motion so that your Liliana can remember."

"How is the wooing going by the way?" Samael could not help himself after he said that to Clay, he had to laugh.

"She is as skittish as hell. On the other hand, her body and subconscious remember my touch. So it is well worth the pouting and the like."

"You do realize she thinks you're just a delivery man, right? And that she doesn't know you are part owner in C&C?"

"Oh, I know that. I want her to realize that money is not as important to her as she thinks it is. That what we feel for one another is. You will have to do some damage control in your own relationship. Liliana doesn't know you are the other half of C&C as well."

"Yes, you're right. I do have to tell her that. On the other hand, I am hoping she will understand the reason behind having to keep everything a secret from her. Is Eva aware of the other secrets that you hold?"

"No. I haven't told them to her yet. When the time is right, I plan to. Getting the curse removed is the most important thing now. The rest of the issues can wait."

"Clay, Eva isn't going to take kindly to us

manipulating her. You do realize this could backfire, right?"

"You're preaching to the choir, bro. I already know that. She is going to be very angry. In order for us to break the curse, we have to do this, as she won't willingly break it herself. I will deal with Eva, and she will see that in my arms is where she was meant to be." He sighed and looked down at the city for a moment then looked back to Samael. "What was set into motion was partially my fault. I have to make it right, one way or the other."

"Then, if you're sure, we will proceed."

"I'm very sure."

"Okay then, I will proceed with the plan to have Remie enter Liliana's dreams and get her to remember her past. There is always a loophole with a curse. Eva never said that we could not manipulate Liliana's dreams. She only said that I could not tell her who she was."

"Just think if we would have thought of this earlier in the game." Clay nodded.

"I know. I don't believe any of us went beyond feeling the moment. We've all been too wrapped up in the emotions of it all. I have been too blind with anger and everything else to see past it, until now. Time to end the pain and reclaim what was lost. Besides, looking back at what could have been isn't going to help. Let's move forward."

"I will keep Eva distracted."

"Liliana and I are forever grateful."

"It's the least I could do. This all started because I could not get over what I thought I had lost." They both knew he meant Liliana.

"It will all be over soon. Go now. I need to call upon Remiel." Remiel, otherwise known as Remie now, was the archangel of dreams and hope. He was the only way that Samael would be able to get around the rules that Eva had attached to the curse. Remie would be able to get through to Lili and once she remembered, the curse would end.

"Good luck, bro." Just as quickly as he had arrived, Clay was gone.

Samael closed his eyes, centering himself as he began to call on the archangel whose help he needed. Soon, he heard the whisper of angel's wings, and Remie was at his side. His large wings folding against his broad back were impressive, disappearing as he became more human-like. If anyone had happened by they would've only seen two men chatting on the rise.

"Remie, thank you for answering my summons so swiftly. I know it has been a long time. But the task that I have for you is urgent and must be kept in the strictest of confidence."

"Samael, my brother, it has been a long time. Everyone knows what has befallen you and Lilith. So what is it that you wish for me to do?" The fair-haired Watcher had a very commanding presence. Remie's light blue eyes were brilliant and piercing, making one feel as if he could see into one's very soul. If Samael had not been what he was, he would have fallen in supplication. He was one of his fallen brethren, the keeper of hopes and dreams. He was as magnificent as Samael had remembered.

"I have found a loophole in Eva's curse, Remie, and I am in need of your services. I need you to visit Liliana, nightly in her dreams, to get her to remember her true self so that we can break the curse." Samael smiled as he watched Remie's face, noting just when understanding came as to what task was being set before him. It was like their days of old. To have a task was what they lived for. It was something to do, like centuries before when more people believed.

A smile was on Remie's face, and he nodded his head. "Yes. That would definitely get you around the fact that you can't tell her who she is. Though, I am sure my being the giver of divine visions was meant for a higher purpose." He chuckled. "But I am sure I was given these gifts for more than just one reason."

Samael laughed. "I am sure you're right, Remie. As the humans like to say, things happen for a reason."

"Right. I have to warn you." Samael knew that it was serious as a somber look came over Remie's features. "There is always the possibility that this won't work."

"What do you mean?" Samael turned to his friend to look at him fully, wanting to make sure he heard everything he had to tell him.

"The memories may be buried too deep. I will have to sift through centuries of memories to get her to a place where she will remember her beginnings. Even with my divine suggestions, it doesn't mean it will work. I want you to know from the start. No false hope."

"I appreciate your candor, and I still want to proceed. I have faith in you, brother, and in your abilities."

Remie nodded. "I will begin tonight. Do not prepare her. Her mind must be clear of any outside influences. The next thing that you must do tonight is make sure she is in a deep sleep, and I will take care of the rest."

"I have my ways of keeping her exhausted enough so that she will be in a deep sleep. No worries there."

"I would say too much information, but then I totally understand the allure." Both of them chuckled.

"Thank you again, my friend." He clasped

Remie's forearms with his own in an old greeting of the Watchers, and Remie returned the favor. "I am in your debt."

"I may have to call on you sometime myself. No thanks needed. It feels good to have something to do, a purpose. Besides, who knows, perhaps you will steer me in the right direction of my own happy ending."

"You'd be giving up your wings, my friend."

"Warning heeded and acknowledged. But as you know, some things are worth the loss." Samael smiled and then nodded as he let Remie go from the clasp.

"'Til later on this evening, my friend." Remie grinned and bowed with a flourish, and as he came back up, his wings formed and spread out impressively. His departure was only a whisper on the wind. Samael let out a deep, healing breath to clear his mind of thoughts that what he had planned wouldn't work. He knew he could not think like that. He had to believe that everything had a purpose and that it would all fall into place. This would work. It had to.

Chapter Five

In the aftermath of their lovemaking, Liliana lay in the bed, her head lying on Samael's chest as she drew small invisible designs. She loved the quiet moments with him. It made her feel emotionally closer to him. She felt his fingers stroke into her hair, and he gently massaged her scalp. She groaned in pleasure, her eyes falling closed. She could hear him whispering softly against her hair, but she found she was too tired to ask what he was saying. It all sounded like mumbo jumbo to her now, anyways. She felt so lethargic. Not a way she normally felt. What was wrong with her?

"I am sorry, Samael, I just can't seem to keep my eyes open." He chuckled and kissed the top of her head softly.

"Go to sleep, my sweet. We always have tomorrow."

"But that's just it, Samael. Who says we're promised tomorrow?" She covered her mouth as she yawned.

"I do." It was her turn to chuckle.

"You are always so arrogant, Samael." She was tired of fighting and closed her eyes.

"Perhaps," he chuckled.

Kissing the top of her head again, he stroked a hand gently down her back as he continued uttering words she could not make out. His words were lulling her to sleep; she sighed then snuggled closer as she drifted off.

****

He waited for her breathing to even before he untangled her limbs from his. Once he had removed her body from his, he got up from the bed to place a sheet over her naked form, staring down at her for a few more moments before settling on the floor across from the bed. He sat cross-legged on the deep burgundy carpet waiting for the whisper of wings that would signal Remie's appearance. He didn't have long to wait. Remie was always on time.

"Lovely. She is in a deep sleep and relaxed, which will make it easier to delve into her subconscious." Remie stood off to the left side of him, staring over at Liliana's prone form.

"Yes, I had to speak in ancient Aramaic so that she wouldn't realize what was happening. It's a good thing to know that my abilities haven't completely left me."

"Some things only the originator can take away. Eva isn't powerful enough to even come close."

"Agreed." He stopped talking as he saw Remie move from his side, and then moved closer to the bed and sat at the edge closest to Liliana. He brought his hand up and pressed it gently to her forehead, closing his eyes as the beautiful dead language tumbled from his lips. Samael stayed where he was; this was Remie's show. Unless Remie asked him to help, he would not interfere.

"Her memories are buried deep. Eva did a good job with this curse. I don't feel like it cannot be undone," Remie said.

"Why do I feel like there is a *but* somewhere in there?"

"Because there is one, just pausing to make sure all that I have said sinks in first." He removed his fingers from Liliana's head and turned his attention fully on Samael, though he stayed where he was. "She has had centuries of not remembering who she is, which in turn has dampened her ability to see the truth for what it is, and every time, who has been there to stop her?"

"Eva," Samael whispered.

"Yes, Eva, the same person who's important in Liliana's life. As far as she knows, Eva can do no wrong, and Eva would not purposefully hurt her. She loves Eva. It will be hard for her to believe that Eva did harm to her. She may take some convincing, which means this may take longer than you would like. You also may not get the desired effect." He knew that Remie meant that Liliana could decide not to be with him or to love him. She could be hurt enough to make that choice.

"I understand, Remie, but I will not let Eva win. If I quit now, she has won. As I said before, we need this settled before time has run out for the four of us. No more limbo for Lili and me. I will accept whatever consequences come my way with this as long as the curse is broken and Lili is whole again."

"Okay, my friend, as long as you are sure. I will continue." Remie looked back at Liliana, closing his eyes again as the Aramaic flowed from his lips. Samael bowed his head and closed his eyes as well. Samael felt the ancient words wrapping about him, filling the room, blanketing them all.

****

Some Weeks Later

"I have been having the strangest dreams, Samael." Liliana looked at him as they sat at a table at the all-night diner they often frequented after a night out dancing. He looked up from putting creamer in his coffee as they sat in the quiet booth, and he hoped his face was neutral and she wouldn't be able to see anything was up.

"Talk to me," he said.

Her hands cupped her latte, and she looked nervous. She took a sip before continuing.

"Well, perhaps I have just been thinking of our situation too much because now it has manifested into dreams. In the dream, I was this other person. An individual who I knew was me but didn't look like me." She paused, and he waited for her to carry on.

"You were there as well. I knew you as this other person, and I loved you then, too." When her words came to a halt for a moment, he spoke up.

"Tell me why you think the dreams are odd."

"I guess it's because I have always felt we have known each other before. From the very beginning, that is how I've felt, and the dreams seem to validate that feeling."

"Yes, you've said that plenty of times." He wanted her to feel comfortable and to remember without him having to add to it. He took a sip of his coffee as she fidgeted with her drink. She watched him for a moment and then nodded.

"I just find it strange that the dreams I am having aren't in the present time. A particular one I just had last night was in the 1920s. I know because in this dream I was wearing a flapper dress and my name was Lila Flynn. I was a redhead and white. I knew it was me—I just looked different. I knew you as well, and in fact, you ran the Speakeasy where I worked. But you looked like yourself, though of course your clothing was period." She heaved a sigh and then went on. "You were just as handsome as ever and just as devilish." She chuckled at that small joke. He grinned and gave her a wink.

"And these dreams bother you because it seems familiar? Or because of...?"

"The dreams seem so real, Samael. I know I'm dreaming, but it feels like it is real, or that it was a real point in some other lifetime. I mean, I felt as if it had truly happened! I guess the dreams don't really bother me on a level of fear, but it is a level of why in the hell am I now dreaming about this constantly, night after night. I have also started daydreaming about the dreams. No matter where I am, the dreams have been constant in my thoughts. It feels like Déjà vu all over again and instead of a dream, this feels like a vision."

"Are the dreams interfering with your everyday life so much that they are a problem?"

"No. They aren't that bad, though I find myself wishing for something that I can't define every morning when I wake up. I feel as if I am searching for another part of me. I actually can't wait to go to bed so I can dream to see who I am next and where you are. I just feel like this is important for some reason and that I need to figure it out."

He reached across the table and grabbed her hand, giving it a gentle squeeze. "What does Eva say about the dreams?"

"Eva?" She rolled her eyes. "Eva is nowhere to be found lately as she is so sprung over Clay and has been spending time with him every chance she gets. Her attraction to him is obvious, but if you ask her, she can't stand the man." She laughed gently. "So, no, I haven't talked to her about it. Besides, it seems silly to do so."

"It isn't silly, baby. Not silly at all, in fact, I am happy you came to me with it." It was good to hear that Clay was keeping Eva occupied as he said he would. He really didn't need Eva coming in and stopping the progress that was happening with Liliana's memories.

He brought her fingers up to his mouth, kissed the tips softly, and watched as she smiled brightly.

"It's just strange, Samael. I mean the dreams seem to flow right after each other in sequence. I can go about my day, but once I close my eyes and start dreaming again, it's as if I'm watching scenes from a movie. It feels like snapshots out of my life."

"Then I'd say don't worry about the dreams. Keep

on dreaming and see where it leads. Who knows, through them, you may find some things out about yourself that you never knew."

"You're right. Nothing at all to worry over, I will just see where this goes. I may go to a person who interprets dreams. It would great to see why I am dreaming what I am dreaming."

"How about we have a slice of your favorite cheesecake and a refill of your latte to celebrate that epiphany you just had?"

"Mmm, you sure know how to tempt a girl." He chuckled and raised his hand for the server to come over so he could order. After they'd ordered a slice of cheesecake and a refill for the drinks, Liliana got up, moved to his side of the booth, and cuddled close, laying her head on his shoulder.

"Samael, is there no way to lift the curse that you're under?" He was taken aback by her question, and he didn't answer her at first. So consequently, she held her peace and didn't say anything more, allowing him to have time before he spoke.

"I am working on a way, Lili. That is all I can say on it."

"Is there nothing I can do to help, Samael?"

Their talk was interrupted for a moment as the server came back, placing a thick slice of New York Cheesecake with chocolate drizzled all over it and a cherry on top in between them. She smiled over at Samael as she picked up her fork.

"Just how I like it. You're going to share with me, right?" She picked up the other fork and handed it to him.

"Of course," he said. Taking the fork from her, he slid it down and into the cheesecake, waiting for her to do the same. She sighed as she took a bit of the cheesecake and put it in her mouth. Her eyes closed in pleasure as she ate the cheesecake. He remembered her having told him the taste of her favorite dessert was like hearing a symphony as it melted on her tongue and exploded against her taste buds.

"Mmm, I swear cheesecake heals all ills." The twinkle in her eyes was endearing. He loved seeing her happy even if it was something as simple as enjoying a piece of dessert she loved with him.

He laughed. "If only." She laughed with him, but then her look turned serious as she asked once more if there was anything she could do to help with lifting the curse.

"As far as the curse goes, Lili, you help me every night when I am in your arms. In your embrace, I feel loved and safe. Other than that, there is nothing that can be done directly by you." He could not reveal more to her, even though it was on the tip of his tongue to do so. To tell all would be to risk all, and he wasn't about to risk the love they had for one another just to get one up on Eva.

"Promise me that you will continue to work on finding a way out from under the curse. I need to be with you, and that need grows day by day." The fear in her eyes made his teeth clench reflexively. His hand moved under the table, and he gave her knee a squeeze to reassure her. He smiled as her hand covered his and the fear he saw in her eyes eased.

"I promise you, baby. I will do all that I can to make sure that happens." Some promises were hard to keep, but the promise he had made Liliana several nights ago was one that he didn't plan to renege on.

Chapter Six

The dreams had intensified and left Liliana feeling that she was supposed to figure something out. Why else would she be having these dreams night after night? It was a puzzle, and she was damned if she was going to not follow through and see where it led. The dreams had Samael in them and even Eva at times. The conclusion she'd reached from that was everything was connected. They were all connected. At first, she'd chalked it up to her just worrying over the small amount of time she had with Samael, but it had to be more than that. She could sense it.

In order to remember everything, she was now journaling it. What better way to make sure she didn't forget the smallest detail? She'd always loved writing down her thoughts and dreams and had been doing so since a young age. Why not continue doing so, especially if it helped her figure out what was happening. The reason she'd stopped was vague to her now.

Settled in the bay window of her living room that looked out to a gorgeous park across the street, she held the black leather bound journal in her lap as she continued to fill the pages with last night's vision. Her pen moved swiftly across the pages as light from the sun filtered in and placed its life-giving rays along the parchment-like pages. She smiled, turning to glance out the window as she heard several of the neighborhood children run by as they played in the early afternoon heat. Turning back, she began to reread what she had written over the last few days and frowned.

The common elements in her dreams were Eva and Samael along with herself. At first she thought it was just her and Samael throughout history together. Then there was Eva having shown up in almost all of the dreams recently. No matter what name she went by in the story or how she looked, it was Eva. The universal theme with the Evas in those different lives was always that Samael was no good for her. It was seriously like a recording, playing repeatedly. The more she had the dreams, the more she knew this was past lives coming into effect. Her past life, right along with Samael's and Eva's, was in question.

What she didn't get was why she was having the dreams now and what significance they played in the present. What was she to conclude from all of this? She got the fact that it meant she and Samael were connected and had been for a long time. Subsequently, that would also mean the same thing for the relationship with Eva. It all had ties to his curse, she was sure of it.

She let out a breath, closing her eyes tightly. There was no way around it, and the more she thought about it, the more a sickening feeling filled her stomach. Her conclusion led her to believe that Eva was inexplicably involved in the curse. She wanted to consider that Eva had no clue about what was happening. In fact, she had to believe that.

The issue was that she wasn't sure if she should say anything to Eva or if she even wanted to. It felt like she would be opening up an assortment of problems, and she might find out something she didn't want to know. There was the old adage to be careful what one looked for and for some strange reason that is exactly what this felt like. If she looked further, would she find out something she didn't want to learn? The one thing she did know was that the curse had to end. She wanted Samael happy, and he wasn't as content as he could be without the curse in existence.

Her eyes opened slowly. She knew there was no way around it. She would have to find out the truth.

Good or bad, she needed to know what it all meant. Who was she? Most importantly, who had she been? She knew what she had to do; she would speak with Eva. That at least would be a starting point. She picked up her cell phone and dialed Eva's number.

"What do you mean you want me to come over right now?"

"What does it sound like I mean, Eva? Right now means right this moment." In her annoyance, she bit the inside of her cheek to hold back from showing her sister how irritated she was. That would only make Eva dig her heels in more and refuse to come over. With the cell phone between her ear and shoulder, she moved about her small home picking up this and that to straighten up. Her older sister loved to nitpick if things weren't cleaned to her specifications.

"Ugh! I am supposed to be meeting up with Clay."

"Um, the very same Clay that you said you couldn't stand?"

"Yes, the very same Clay. Don't you dare say something smartass, Liliana, or I will not come over there." Liliana had to stifle the laugh she felt bubbling up, as she didn't want to irritate her sister any more than she already sounded.

"Lili, is this truly that important? Clay is going to take me to a Puerto Rican restaurant tonight. I want to try Arroz con Pollo and a few other dishes."

"What time is he coming over to get you?"

"He's supposed to be here at seven."

"Okay, well, it's only four at the moment. That gives us about 2 hours. If you come with your clothing and have him pick you up here, we will have a bit longer. Please, E, I need to talk with you." She pleaded, trying to play on her sister's sympathies. There was silence on the other end and then she heard her sister sigh, and she knew she would agree to come over.

"Fine, Lili. I'll be over in a few. You'd better be prepared to talk while I get dressed. I don't want to be late; Clay hates it when I keep him waiting."

She grinned from ear to ear even though her sister couldn't see it. Eva really was sprung on Clay, but she wasn't willing to say anything about it. "Thank you, I promise, E. I will talk while you do what you need to do." They'd said their goodbyes and then hung up. Liliana slipped the phone into the pocket of her jeans, and with one last glance around the room, she looked to see if everything looked tidy enough for Eva's standards. Satisfied that it was as good as it was going to get, she went to freshen up before Eva arrived.

****

She'd thought long and hard about what she'd say to Eva as she readied herself. One thing she knew she couldn't do was mention anything about the curse. First, she didn't want to sound crazy, and she knew she'd sound loony if she even mentioned a curse. Next thing she wouldn't mention was the fact that Samael was a demon. It was probably going to sound crazy enough that she was talking reincarnation.

It was such a beautiful day, and she hoped that it wouldn't turn ugly with arguing and fighting when she spoke with Eva. One never knew with Eva what she would get mad at or take offense to.

She smiled as Eva announced she was there by calling out from downstairs. They both had keys to each other's homes and often just stopped by unannounced. Taking a deep breath, she tried to calm her nerves just before she went down the stairs to greet Eva in the entryway.

"Eva, thank you for coming on such short notice.

I appreciate it."

"Mhmm, if you appreciate it, you will help me take these things upstairs so I can get ready for my date while you tell me what was so important it couldn't wait." Eva held up a red makeup case, heels and garment bag that looked filled to the brim. Liliana chuckled, grabbed the garment bag, and turned to head back up the stairs to the second bedroom.

"Come on, girl. The spare bedroom awaits you." She heard Eva chuckle behind her.

The bedroom door was already open so she moved through easily and hooked the bag on the back of the adjoining bathroom door. Eva entered and placed her shoes down near the small cherry wood makeup table along with her makeup case.

Moving over to the large queen-sized bed with its golden colored comforter and brown throw pillows, she sat on it, curling her legs up under her. Eva slipped out of the jeans and t-shirt she was wearing and in only her red demi-cup bra and matching panties, settled into the chair at the dressing table and began looking through her makeup case.

"Now tell me what was so important, Lil, that you couldn't wait?"

Liliana sighed as she tried to think of what she wanted to say. She had spent all day thinking about it, but now when it came down to it, she couldn't form the words as easily. Eva looked briefly at Liliana then turned back to readying herself.

"Well, lately I've been having dreams. The dreams involve you, Samael and me."

"Okay, why's that significant? Everyone has dreams, Lili, and you're around Samael and me all the time. So you're bound to dream about us both." Eva sounded exasperated.

There was a pregnant pause as Eva, who was involved in putting lotion on her body, looked over at her. "Because the dreams feel real to me, Eva, real as in what I was dreaming happened before. They seem to be snapshots of the past." That was when she heard the laughter from Eva.

"Oh my god, you're serious? You called me over here because you feel like the dreams you're having are real. Basically, you're saying you believe in the mumbo jumbo called reincarnation?"

Liliana had to hold back the anger she was feeling because Eva was laughing at what she'd said. She had to remind herself that this was something she had expected. Most people would think she was nuts, though it hurt a bit more that it was actually her sister who was laughing in disbelief.

"Eva, I'd appreciate it if you wouldn't laugh about this."

"Well shit, you're serious." Eva looked incredulous.

"Yes, Eva. I'm as serious as a heart attack. I wouldn't joke about something like this. It's taken me a while to come to you. So please, just listen to what I have to say and don't judge me." Her eyes met Eva's in the mirror.

"Okay, I'm sorry, Lili, but do you realize how crazy that sounds? You believe that the dreams you are having are things that happened before?"

"Yes, but hear me out. It started a few weeks ago. At first, it would just be me dreaming as if I were back in time. On the other hand, in the dreams, I honestly knew that the women, even if they didn't look like me, were me. Samael never changed for the most part. I mean you and I went through various name changes, but they were always some form of Eva or Liliana. Our looks changed as well, though that never stopped me from knowing who we were. Samael has always been the same throughout."

"So what is it you want from me, Lili?" Eva had begun to put makeup on while they talked.

"I want to know if you've had dreams like this. If you ever felt you've been somewhere before. I need to know that I have your support no matter what, Eva."

"Lili, I love you. You should know that. You have to understand how crazy this sounds. You shouldn't have to ask if I support you."

"I have to ask because you seem to think I'm joking."

"I'm sorry for laughing. It isn't every day that my sister comes to me to tell me she believes she's reincarnated."

"No, it isn't." Liliana stood and began pacing back and forth.

Turning towards her, Eva put down her makeup brush. "This is really bothering you, isn't it?"

"Yes, Eva. I have always felt I knew Samael before and now with these dreams, I know I wasn't wrong. I do know him, and I feel like I have loved him forever."

"Lili, you know how I feel about him. So trying to convince me otherwise about how right he is for you isn't going to help that." Eva turned back to the mirror and began brushing her long dark locks.

Liliana stopped pacing for a moment, her eyes meeting Eva's in the mirror again. She knew she looked on the verge of tears. "I am done convincing you of that, Eva. I love him, and you can't change that. I'm trying to convince you that there's more happening here. I know we're sisters, but think about our connection. How we've always been there for one another and usually know how the other is feeling. It's almost a twin thing going on.

Where we know what the other is feeling and thinking. In the dreams, no matter what era we were in, we were still in each other's lives. I know you're going to ask if we were still sisters. The answer to that is no. We weren't always sisters, but the commonality was that we've always been in each other's lives."

Seemingly satisfied with her hair now, Eva stood and moved off towards the garment bag. Opening it, she pulled out a red sheath and began dressing. "Lili, even if I wanted to believe we were from some other time, why does it matter now?"

"I don't know about you, but I've always felt a bit empty, like something was missing in my life."

"Everyone feels empty, Lili. It doesn't mean we lived another life."

"I think I am supposed to remember something, Eva. I feel like there is something I've done or something that was done to me, and I need to solve it."

"What do that you want me to say, Lili? Or even do for that matter?" Eva had settled back down on the chair and was slipping into the red stilettos.

"I want you to help me remember. I mean, you know me better than anyone else does, besides Samael. There has to be a reason for all of this."

"All of what, Lili? I mean, you have a few dreams that you think are real and all of a sudden you don't know who you are?"

"Yes, all of this." She gave a wave of her hands then placed them on her hips. "I have to believe I am having the dreams for a reason. The dreams are in a recognizable sequence, so there has to be more to it than just because I've thought a lot about my relationship with Samael."

"I can't help you with these dreams, Lili." She glanced at the bedroom clock and then glanced back at

Liliana. "I am going to be late. The only thing I can suggest is that if these dreams bother you, you need to go and see about getting some past life regression therapy or see a psychic."

Her breath caught, and she looked at Eva with a grin, moving over quickly to hug her. "Hey! You're going to smear my makeup and mess up my hair!"

"Why didn't I think of that?" she exclaimed with a grin.

"What, that you're messing up my makeup?"

"No girl, a psychic or the regression!" Eva rolled her eyes and sighed as she began putting her makeup back into the case.

"Hrmph, well at least I could help with something," Eva said.

"Yes, you've helped. Now go ahead and go on your date with Clay. You can pick up everything later if you like."

Eva grinned over at her. "If I have my way that is exactly what's going to happen tonight."

"You look beautiful, sis. Clay is going to go nuts when he sees you."

"Well, that's the plan after all. Glad to know I succeeded."

"And see, I got you out of here earlier than you thought." She winked at Eva as they made their way down to the front door. Holding it open for her, she gave her one more hug and then pushed her out the door.

Chapter Seven

"It's working," Samael said with a satisfied smile as he looked at Remie and Clay. "Her memories have begun to weave the tale of her past together for her. Every day she wonders more and more about what's happening, and soon she will remember." The other two males nodded in unison, and Remie spoke up.

"Then I suppose the nightly visits are done, eh?" the pale angel asked as they all sat at a table at the bar having a few afternoon beers. The bar wasn't busy, which made it much easier for them to talk freely.

"I think that the nightly visits are done, yes. Even so, that doesn't mean you have to go. She has decided that she'll be going to a past life therapist."

"Ah, yes, if he or she is good enough, they can continue the work I've started. There truly isn't anything for me to stay here for, though I could use a bit of a vacation from everything else." He glanced skyward and gave them a silly grin. All three laughed in unison.

"We would welcome having you here. Besides, you might find something or someone of worth to stay around for," Clay said to Remie. Remie just smiled at that and turned to look at Samael as he spoke to Clay.

"That reminds me, I need to thank you for keeping Eva preoccupied."

"It hasn't been easy, but so worth it. Once this is over, she and I can work on us."

"Even after all this time, you still love her, don't you?" He looked over at Clay.

"Yes, even with everything she has done. I love her. Nevertheless, it'll take some time to convince her. I am prepared. I've had a lot of practice with patience." Clay chuckled.

Remie chimed in. "Others have been making bets

on whether this will be a victory or if we go back to the drawing board."

"I hope this will end well for all concerned," Samael said with a bit of hope.

"Yes, brother, you have to believe that. Otherwise, it will all be for nothing." Clay spoke up quickly as they all thanked the server for the beers she brought them. Silence settled over them as the server cleared their glasses and gave them the drinks. When the woman left, they began talking again. The one thing they didn't wish to do was have someone overhear what they were talking about. They had to blend in with the humans, as their presence, though known by a few, would cause the population as a whole to think the world was ending. It was, but not at this very moment. Secrecy was necessary and always followed at all times unless there was a reason otherwise.

"Lili told me she spoke to Eva about the visions and thoughts she's been having and that Eva has chosen not to believe her." Samael popped a few of the peanuts that were in a dish on their table into his mouth, chewing and then taking a swallow of his beer. He loved the liquid burn of the alcohol as it slid down his throat. He couldn't get drunk, but the taste was pleasurable and as a fallen, he was all about the pleasures of the flesh.

"I think it's a matter of her having gotten comfortable with Lili not remembering. Besides the added distraction I've been providing." Clay grinned and winked at the other two. "So hopefully she'll keep thinking Lili won't remember."

"You're doing a great job with that. Just keep doing what you're doing, and we won't have any issues with Eva, Clay. I owe you big time, seriously." Clay waved him off, telling him it was nothing, and took a swig of his beer as they all settled into a comfortable silence. Samael could not help but think how much of a blessing it was that Clay could keep Eva in line. He knew that without his interference this probably wouldn't be going as smoothly. When Eva got something in her head, she didn't let it go. Clay was an added distraction that tipped the scales in his and Lili's favor, and he was definitely going to use it.

****

"That's right, Liliana. I need you to relax yourself. Close your eyes and take some deep breaths. Remember the techniques that I've taught you."

The smell of frankincense and myrrh filled the room, as did music from a CD called *Zen Garden*. Liliana sighed as she let herself relax as Dr. Bhatia instructed. This was her fourth time at a past life regression session, and she was finding that she was remembering more and more of who she had been. Settled among soft pillows on the floor with her legs crossed and her hands palms up in her lap, she inhaled deeply and then exhaled slowly. Dr. Bhatia had told her that her time as a victim was over. Due to victimization in her past lives, she had fallen into the same cycle, and now was the time to put a stop to it. The karmic cycle needed mending so that she could gain a more fulfilling life and have peace.

"That's it; let the frankincense and myrrh take you to another place, another life and another you. Close your eyes and continue to unwind and breathe deeply. Let go and move into a place of mindfulness. Release any stress and any tension that you may be feeling. Push out all the negative thoughts and pull in the positive." The doctor sat across from her in a chair with his long legs crossed and his hands clasped together. He pushed his glasses up on his nose as he watched her deep breathing technique.

"Now, Liliana, repeat these words after me until

you began to see images in your mind's eye. *I'm remembering a time in the past, a time when I walked this earth as another person.* When the images stop, I want you to open your eyes slowly and practice your breathing again." Dr. Bhatia kept talking in his soft, yet authoritative voice. His words were entrancing and had such a flow to them, she found herself finding that zone that she needed to be in quite swiftly.

"I'm remembering a time in the past, a time when I walked this earth as another person." She said the words slowly and evenly, mimicking what the doctor said. She felt herself drifting, and soon, images came to her. She saw herself dressed in varying garb and having variations of her name, Liliana. What was so significant about her name? There was something to her name; she could feel it. Her name was the key to all of this. She felt so close to knowing the truth, learning who she was and who she had been. Her eyes opened, and she did as the doctor had instructed, smiling her thanks as he handed her a pad to write down the images that'd come from the session.

"So do you think that you'll be able to put into practice what you have learned these last few months?" His face held concern as if he was a mother hen looking after his chick.

"I think I've had a wonderful teacher, Dr. Bhatia. Yes. I can do this on my own." She smiled at him.

"Then I send you on your way with my blessings. Do let me know how it all turns out. I have enjoyed this passage with you. Remember, positive in and negative out." They both stood and shook hands warmly.

"Thank you, Dr. Bhatia, I have enjoyed your guidance on this journey."

The hour session had ended so quickly, and she felt much closer to knowing whom she was and what'd happened to keep her in the continual circle in which her life seemed to revolve. It was her last session with Dr. Bhatia. He'd given her the techniques she could use at home, though he allowed her to call him if she had any issues or questions. She shook the doctor's hand and then left the session, walking out into the sunshine feeling relaxed and assured that everything was falling into place.

****

"So how'd the date go with Clay?" Eva rolled her eyes and gave an unladylike snort. They were at an outdoor café drinking lattes and nibbling on pastries. It'd been a few weeks since the date, and Liliana was tired of the silence. She wanted to know what'd happened.

"Girl, please, it wasn't a date." Liliana burst out laughing only to get more eye rolling from Eva. "Well, it wasn't."

"Oh, so getting all prettied up and going out to dinner isn't a date?"

"No, it's just him taking me to eat."

"Did he pay for the meal?" Once again, Eva looked at her as if she had a second head on her shoulders.

"Of course he did." She sounded indignant.

"Then it was a date, Eva. A date, that I might add, did you some good. So answer my question. How did it go?"

"Ugh! Okay … it was a date, and it was fantastic. Don't you dare tell him, Lili. He's already as smug as hell. If his ego gets any bigger, he will need his own time zone." They both chuckled.

"There's something about him; I can't explain what it is." She sighed and smirked. "But whatever it is, I like it."

"Nice, it's about time someone caught your attention." Eva gave her a big, cheesy grin. It made her feel so good that her sister had someone else to focus on, and Clay seemed to be the real deal for Eva. Even if Eva didn't want to admit that to herself, Liliana could see it.

"I like him. I don't want to get too crazy about this. He could just be playing me. He's hard to read, and that makes me antsy." Eva picked up her drink and took a sip.

"E, it's obvious he likes you. I mean, he is a very genuine type of person. Why'd you think otherwise?" She picked up her croissant and spread some butter and honey on it, watching as the amber and yellow mixed to make delicious goo. Taking a bite of the croissant, she almost purred as the flavors hit her taste buds.

"Girl, you're enjoying that croissant like someone is going to town on your va jay jay!" They both burst out laughing, causing other patrons to briefly turn and look at them.

"You've been hanging around the young girls at the shop again, haven't you?" Liliana teased her.

"Of course I have. Where else would I learn such cool slang?" They both laughed, and then Eva turned serious. "I think like that because of my past relationships. Men seem to want me for a moment, and then someone better comes along. I am tired of being hurt like that, so it's easier to push them away before I get pushed."

"Stop having a defeatist attitude. If you want him, go for it. He seems to really, really dig you."

"I'm just going to take things slow. I haven't had sex with him yet, though we've fooled around. I make sure I tease the hell out of him, too. Let's see how long that shit lasts before he gets tired of me not putting out."

"Be careful that doesn't backfire on you," she warned Eva.

"How could it go wrong? He wants me bad, and if

he's genuine, he will be patient enough to wait for it." Eva began lavishing a croissant with the same butter and honey mixture Liliana had used.

"He could get pissed off and think you're playing games. Perhaps think that you're too much of an issue to want anything serious." Something flickered in Eva's eyes. Liliana wasn't quite sure what it was, but the expression passed quickly before she could remark on it. Eva made a tsk-tsk sound and gave one of her signature *whatever* looks before popping the pastry in her mouth and chewing.

"If he gets angry and thinks I'm playing games, then who needs him?"

"E, you're playing games, though. Teasing him like that without following through. That's one of the worst games you can play. Speaking of need, it would seem you at least want him, and who knows, that may turn to need."

"This has nothing at all to do with need. It's lust pure and simple. Perhaps he will prove me wrong, but I doubt it. Lili, I think I know what I am doing. Thank you for caring, but I will be okay. We will be fine if there is anything happening in the relationship department. Now let's finish our drinks and croissants and go to the movies, as we've planned."

"You're as stubborn as hell, girl, but all right. I promised you some girl time, and I am going to make good on that promise." The conversation soon turned to other things, and they spent the rest of the day enjoying one another's company as sisters often do. In the back of her mind though, she tried to stem the thoughts every time they came. She worried that the curse was never going to end and she'd lose Samael. She also couldn't help but think that Eva was treading on thin ice with Clay. It seemed that the Jackson sisters had men issues and would never find happiness.

Chapter Eight

A few weeks later, she pressed against Samael in her bed as a light breeze filtered in from the open window in the bedroom causing the curtain to flutter occasionally with its power. It had been a hot day, and the evening didn't seem to be cooling off either. On the small cherry wood nightstand next to her bed was a large glass of ice cubes with only a minimal amount of water. Condensation on the clear glass dripped down to pool onto the doily beneath it. She was stroking her fingers lightly over his muscled chest, her head lying on his shoulder. It had been a quiet night for them, one spent in bed talking over what the therapist had taught her and how she felt it was beneficial.

"Do you think you are close to a breakthrough?" he asked, trailing his fingers along her spine as she cuddled her naked body up close to his. His breath caught as her hand moved to stroke along his lower stomach, dangerously close to his hardening cock. His cock twitched against his stomach, and she giggled.

"Yes, I think it won't be too long before I remember the past and why it seems I am doomed to repeat it. I know that once I figure out my issue, we will be able to figure yours out. We are too tightly bound together for there not to be a resolution for you, too." She dragged her nails across his stomach once more, watching as his cock jerked. A shiver traveled through her body as his hand cupped her ass and then he trailed his finger down the crack of her ass.

"You're playing with fire, Lili."

"No more than you are, Samael. Not my fault you decide to ask twenty questions while we are naked in bed together." Moving down his body, she placed her hand at the base of his cock, tightening her grip as she stroked him. His pubic area was shaved just as hers was, which made it nice when giving him head. No hair to worry about when playing. Using her free hand, she reached over and took a drink from the glass, letting a small cube of ice pop into her mouth. His eyes met hers over the rim of the glass, and he gave her an exceptionally wicked smile. He knew what she was up to, and it thrilled her. They were both exceedingly kinky and fed off one another. She set the glass back down and returned to her task.

Looking into his eyes, she grinned as she leaned forward to tease her very cold tongue along the head. She heard him hiss and felt him arch up. Loving the response he gave to her teasing, his reaction spurned her on. She swirled her tongue around the opening of his cock, purring as she tasted the salty sweet liquid that pooled there. He uttered a groan, once more arching into her.

"Cup my balls, Lili, and suck me."

She needed no further urging from him. She wanted him as undone as she always was when they fucked. She moved the hand that was cupping his cock to make sure his balls pushed into the palm of that hand then moved to her knees. Kneeling over him, her mouth wrapped around the head of his cock. He grunted as she applied harder sucking pressure to the head of his penis and then popped him out of her mouth, only to run her tongue down the vein on the underside as his fingers tangled in her hair.

"Shit, you're a tease, Lili."

She giggled and continued to lick along the vein until her tongue stroked where her hand still gripped him at the base of his shaft. Easing that hand slowly up, she let go of his balls so that she could lick and suckle there. Popping one into her mouth, sucking gently, and then giving its twin the same treatment, she loved how he squirmed. She felt him lift his hips off the bed and arch into her so she knew she was hitting all the right spots. She felt him moving and then his hand was between his thighs, and he was cupping his own balls. She recognized what he wanted as he moved them up, revealing his perineum to her. She smiled because she knew he was so sensitive there. He loved having the area between his balls and anus licked, and she loved how much it drove him nuts when she did it.

"More licking baby, please, give me more licking right there." He took over stroking his length, holding it flush against his body, as he was apt to do, with nice long strokes. He fisted himself at the head as his other hand hugged his balls. Her tongue licked at the skin he had exposed to her, and she heard him groan. "Fuck, your tongue is so hot and wet." She giggled as she heard him gasp when she gently nipped him there. Kneeling between his legs, she looked at him with a smile as his hand slowly moved up and down on his shaft.

"Gonna share?" she said to him. He smirked and stopped his stroking, bending his cock slightly towards her with his hand at the base as if to say it was all hers.

"Mmm, now that is what I am talking about, Samael."

She moved closer, dipping her head down, taking him into her mouth as much as she could until he was hitting the back of her throat. Once again, his fingers tangled in her hair, and she felt him thrusting into her mouth. Wet sucking noises filled the room along with groans from him. She could tell he was close from the way his fingers tightened in her hair. Looking up, her eyes connected with his, the look from him intense. She hummed around his shaft, letting the vibrations add to the sensations she was giving him. The only way to describe how he felt in her mouth was velvet covered steel.

Samael tugged at her head. He wanted her to look up at him. Her eyes met his, with her lips still wrapped deliciously around his cock. "Enough. I want to be inside of you. No, let me rephrase that. I *need* to be inside of you. But not before I have a bit of fun."

He growled and tightened his fingers in her hair as she continued sucking on him a few moments longer before letting him slip from her mouth, as if she hadn't heard his *enough*. Eagerly, she moved to lie flat on her back on the bed watching as he reached for the glass and picked out an ice cube, holding it up and winking at her.

Her breathing sped up as he trailed the ice down between her breasts. She felt goose bumps rise on her skin as the water from the ice ran down her body. Raising the fast melting cube he stroked it in a circle around her nipples, watching as the skin tightened around them, making them hard buttons of flesh. He leaned forward, his eyes still on hers, as he flicked his tongue over one and then the other. She cried out and vaulted up into his mouth. The cold from the ice and the heat from his tongue added different sensations to her body and set her on edge.

Then he made a path down the center over her chest to her belly, letting the ice drip into her belly button for a few seconds, and then he dipped his tongue into it. He sat up, reaching for another piece of ice, winking at her as he began a trail down from her belly button, and she knew exactly where he was heading.

"Damn, and you call me a tease."

He smiled but didn't speak. Pressing on, he brought the piece of ice to her clit. When that piece of ice hit her clit, she almost shot off the bed as she bucked. Her clit began to throb and tingle almost painfully, the feeling she received from it powerful. Putting the ice into his mouth, he pressed it to her clit, licking at her with the added sensation of the cold from the ice cube.

"Oh!" Her stomach sunk in as she drew in a deep breath. She felt like she was burning up. The feeling of a heated mouth with the coolness of the ice enveloping her clit made her screech in pleasure. His hands moved to hold her legs still, his tongue curling around her clit over and over, which set her legs to trembling. He had her teetering on the edge of orgasm, and she almost came, but then he pulled his mouth away.

She saw him reach for what she suspected was another ice cube, and then she heard the telltale clink of ice on the glass. He moved back into position, and she gasped as she felt him slide a piece of ice inside of her. She bucked on the bed and groaned. She frowned and looked down at him, but the look on his face made her beam. He was hurting to come just as much as she was, if not more. His next words had her scrambling to do as he wished.

"Lie on your side, baby, facing away from me."

Smiling, she turned to her side, facing away from him, knowing that whatever he did to her next would be what she wanted and needed. Her smile widening as he moved to lie behind her in spoon fashion. A soft sigh escaped her lips as his fingers stroked over her side, brushing fleetingly over the side of her breast and then down to her hip where he grabbed that leg and brought it over his own, cuddling her close. "Are you nice and wet for me, Lili?"

She groaned. "Yes, I am very wet for you, Samael."

"Show me, Lili. I want you to put your fingers in your pussy and then pull them out and let me see them." His words turned her on even more, and she felt her cream gushing from her. Her breathing ragged, she eagerly did what he asked. Slipping her hand between her thighs and dipping them into herself, she moaned as finger tips stroked over sensitive folds and then inside.

"Ohhh." Her breath caught as he nipped her where her shoulder and neck met just as her fingers dipped into her channel. Her hips bucked with her need, and she pulled her fingers out quickly so she would not orgasm. She held her fingers up for him to show him how wet she was.

"That's beautiful, Lili. Your fingers are soaked. Lick them clean." Smiling, she took her fingers and placed them in her mouth, licking them clean of her juices. She felt him moving behind and then he was thrusting inside of her. She let out a long gasp, arching back against him. He thrust in until he was in as deep as he could go and then held himself still. She felt his lips at her ear, his teeth tugging at the lobe.

"I love taking you from behind like this. I can touch every part of you." His breath tickled her ear as he whispered softly into it. She shuddered as he nipped the lobe again. He was right. This was one of the best positions to be in with him. His thrusts seemed deeper and his hands touched her body so reverently that even if she wanted to she couldn't speak. Her head fell back against his shoulder, and she moaned.

"Move with me, baby." His goatee tickled the side of her neck, and she shivered with pleasure.

No more urging needed from him. She moved into his rhythm, her hand moving to cup the back of his head, tangling into his long tresses. Whoever said you had to be in the missionary position for it to be making love didn't know what they were talking about, she thought. Samael was inventive, and she adored that about him.

His cock seemed thicker, harder and even longer

in this position, and it hit just the right place, her g-spot. Slowly, he loved her, their panting filling the room as they neared completion. Both of their bodies bore a light sheen of perspiration, which made his hands slide over her as he moved from her breasts to cup her lower belly. Liliana cupped her breasts once they were bereft of his touch, tugging and pulling at her hard and sensitive nipples.

She moved her leg from his, laying it on top of her other one, placing pressure around her opening on his cock. He groaned and nipped her shoulder. She felt the beginning vibrations running through her body as her inner muscles contracted around his cock.

"Ohhhh, Samaellll!" She wailed and pushed back hard against him. His hands moved to tighten at her hips, holding her to him, and then he climaxed with a shout, pulling her deeper into her own orgasm. Her eyes closed and behind her eyelids swirls of different colored lights filtered through until she lay against him spent. He stroked within her a few more times as her body's contractions pulled at his pulsing cock and emptied it of his cream. They lay in a heap together, panting, neither one daring to speak.

All through the night, they reached for one another and made love. The connection between them filled with an urgency to join not only sexually but also mentally. There truly were no words to describe how she felt about him or he about her. All they could do was whisper words of love as they made contact with one another frequently throughout the long night.

Chapter Nine

Liliana sat up in bed with a start, tears streaming down her face. Her chest heaved, and her heart beat erratically. It felt just like she had run a marathon. She placed her hand on her heart as if that would stop it from beating so fitfully, her glance moving to the clock on her dresser. Its neon green color informed her it was five in the morning. She didn't have to look to know Samael was gone. It was the price of the curse, right?

Her dreams had finally revealed to her the truth. This last dream showed her a camp by the Tigris River that she'd called home with Samael. From that very vision, she'd learned who she'd been. She also had to acknowledge that her flesh and blood sister, Eva, through the ages, had lied to her continually. She should feel relieved that she knew the truth, but all she could feel was sick to her stomach with worry, hurt and anger.

She was Lilith, and had been Adam's first wife, the Adam she now recognized as Clay Quinones. He'd also been the young Adam who'd come to her when she was a child, her friend and her protector. No wonder she'd latched on to him again as an adult. Her dreams had revealed to her that even Eva didn't know everything. It was ironic that the one person Eva had wanted had always been within her grasp, but she'd not been able to see it because of her envy. Envy was such an ugly thing.

Eva didn't want her with Samael because Eva had wanted her to be as unhappy as she was. This was because Eva had been a jealous bitch thinking that Adam wanted her and not Eva. She'd be a victim no more. Confronting Eva would be facing the truth and ending a curse that should never have existed. Karma was going to be a bitch named Liliana Jackson.

The next thought was, now that she knew what'd

happened, would she still love Samael the way she did before knowing the full extent of his curse? Was she in love with him because her subconscious thought that was what she was supposed to do? So many factors made this an all too scary proposition. What if in finding out what she had caused, the cycle not only broke, but their love for one another also dried up? Too many what ifs out there needed answers. Samael knew about the curse and all that it entailed. Was she angry with him because of that? No. Part of his curse was to know and not be able to inform her about it. She would not direct the anger she felt at Samael; no, it all would belong to Eva.

Her mind made up, she turned over, reaching for her cell phone and dialing Eva's number. She didn't care it was five in the morning: she wanted answers, and she deserved them. She listened to the ringing on the other end. *Come on, Eva, pick up the damn phone.*

"Lili? Is something wrong? Why are you calling me so early?"

"Oh yes, there is loads wrong, Eve." She placed emphasis on the name Eve. "How about you come over and straighten this out?"

"Eve?" She sounded ready to protest.

"Yes, Eve. I know who you are." As Eva tried to protest, Liliana cut her off. "Don't bother trying to explain over the phone. Get your ass over here and explain it to me in person." Liliana hung up the phone. Standing, she went to her dresser and pulled out a comfortable pair of shorts and a t-shirt to throw on for when Eva got there; she also brushed her hair and teeth. Cleaning up and making herself presentable made her feel like she would be on an even keel with Eva. Those actions also made it possible for her to calm and center herself. No more tears. She needed to be strong, letting her anger fuel her.

She found that the anger hadn't lessened. She remembered when Eve had cursed them by the Tigris. Eve had had no sympathy and would not listen to reason. It hurt, and it angered her. In all these years, Eve could have surely put a stop to it. Leaving her bedroom, she made her way downstairs and stopped dead in her tracks when she went in the living room to wait and Eva was already there. She recovered quickly and watched as Eva stood.

"So, sister dear, when were you going to tell me that you're a demon as well?" Liliana's arms crossed her chest as she prepared for battle.

"When did you remember?"

"Does that really matter? I've remembered everything."

"You've remembered everything? Well, then that means you know what I want."

"Just answer me one thing. In all the years we have known one another through time, but most especially this present time that you've been my sister, you never once thought this was all a mistake? I didn't want Adam. The one I wanted I left the Garden for and that was Samael. You were too blind in your jealousy to see that!"

"Yes, I'd thought about it at one point."

Liliana frowned at her answer. She knew her face had to show the disbelief she was feeling and cocked her head to the side. "Oh? And when the hell would that have been?"

"When we had our talk about the date I had with Clay."

"I'm angry. Eva, I'm angrier than I've ever been with you. So many years have gone by." Tears filled her eyes and threatened to spill over; she blinked, trying hard to stop them from falling. She knew if she allowed them to fall, she'd have a hard time stopping. "So many years lost between Samael and me. Hell, so much time lost with you. There are so many times throughout our histories together that we were real sisters. If you'd had one ounce of sympathy or even the love you say you feel for me, you would've stopped this nonsense. This wasn't about me. It never was. It's always been about you and your selfishness."

"You're right. I've been selfish. I'm sorry, Lili, so very sorry."

"No, you're not getting off that easy. I know what I have to do now. I have to free Samael and myself from this curse by speaking my true name."

"I have taken care of you, Lili!" Eva huffed in frustration and moved farther into the room.

"You only took care of me when it suited your needs, Eva. Or should I call you Eve?"

"Lili, please—"

Lili raised her hand to stop her from talking. "Please what, Eva? Why should I allow you any thought when you didn't give a damn about how I felt? Because you've changed? Is that what you want me to believe?"

"I have cha—"

Lili cut her off. "Don't even try it. How is it possible that you have changed that quickly? Tell me how a demon can change."

"Things have changed, Lili. I promise you."

"You have a long way to go to prove that to me, Eva. There have been too many lies from you. The funny thing is, I can't hate you. I am one who believes that things happen for a reason. I don't think this was because I needed to learn a lesson." Eva's brow raised, and she crossed her arms.

"Are you trying to say I need to learn a lesson?"

Liliana laughed. "And you think you don't need to

learn one? Think about it this way. As much as you have been trying to keep me from Samael, you've never once gotten what you've wanted or needed, have you? You haven't had a decent relationship through any of this. So with you thinking you don't need to learn anything that just tells me you aren't ready to admit you're wrong."

"Lili I..."

"I am Lilith." Liliana shook her head, and looking directly at Eva, she spoke the three words that would forever change how things stood between them. It was like the breaking of chains that held her down as she said those words. She no longer felt heavy. Hearing a sound, she turned and looked behind her towards the door and in the early morning light, there stood Samael, her demon and lover. Tentatively, she took a step forward, smiling as he held his arms open. She ran into them with a sob. The dam that held the tears back broke, and she sobbed uncontrollably. He was actually there with her, and she was holding him in the daylight.

"My Lilith." His lips touched her forehead lightly as he kissed her.

"You're really here, Samael. You're standing here in front of me and not a hallucination but a wonderful reality."

"You remembered as I hoped you would."

Eva spoke up, and both of them turned to look at her.

"Samael, what did you do? The rules were that you could not tell her anything! She had to remember on her own!"

"You're right, Eva. The rules of the curse were that I couldn't tell her anything, and I didn't." He grinned. "There was nothing that said someone else couldn't remind her." Both Liliana and Eva gazed at him, waiting for him to finish.

Samael turned to gaze at Liliana. His hand moved to cup her cheek and stroked gently over her lips, then moved to cup the back of her neck. "I knew I couldn't tell you anything. Then I got to thinking about the angel, Remiel."

"Remiel? Why does that name sound so familiar?" Liliana had forgotten about Eva being in the room, until she heard her speak and answer the question for Samael.

"Remiel is the Angel of Visions. Let me guess. You used him to enter Lili's dreams."

"Ah, she catches on so well. Yes, that's exactly what I did. I couldn't trust that you'd do what was right, and time was running out. All I needed was for you to be distracted." Liliana saw the beginnings of a smile on Samael's face.

"Distracted? Who'd you use?" Before he could answer, Eva's eyes widened, and her mouth hung open like a fish gasping for air. "Clay. You used Clay. Why'd he do it? Is that why he has been spending time with me? I knew it couldn't be because he wanted me. He had a fucking ulterior motive!" Eva looked furious.

"No, he didn't, other than to put right what you destroyed all those years ago."

Liliana looked at Samael. "She doesn't know, does she?" she said softly.

"No, baby. Her trap, as clever as she was with it, also trapped the both of them, just as it did us."

"What do you mean it trapped them? Who the hell are you talking about?"

"I am talking about you and Clay, my dear Eva," Samael said to Eva.

Liliana watched the moment of clarity wash over Eve's face, making it apparent she realized whom the 'he' was.

"He's Adam, isn't he?" Just as Samael appeared when Liliana spoke her true name, Clay appeared standing just behind the other couple. He held his hand out to Eva, but she refused to take it.

"No, I won't go. You lied to me. I'm a mere distraction, right?" she growled out furiously. She turned frantic eyes to Liliana. "Lili, please, I'm sorry."

"No, I've had enough of your bullshit. Go please, and I'll let you know if and when I want to deal with you again."

"What about our business?" Eva was sputtering, no longer as cool and collected as she always was, which proved to Liliana that she wasn't a hard ass like she pretended to be, demon or not.

"The business will be fine. I didn't say I wouldn't be working. I just have nothing to say to you, and right now, I am not sure I ever will." She turned back to Samael and wrapped her arms around him, holding tightly to him, burying her face into the side of his neck with a whispery sigh.

Clay moved around Samael and Liliana and stood towering over Eva. This time he took her hand without asking for it. The look he gave Eva seemed to silence her and keep her in place. "I think it's time we left, Eva. We are finished here and unless Liliana invites you back or initiates contact, you will not bother them. It is done." Eva gawked at Clay, yet no words passed through her lips. With a smile, Clay nodded to Liliana and Samael.

"We'll take our leave now." Then they were gone.

"I'm not sure I'll ever get used to that." She chuckled.

"The disappearing act that we demons are fond of?" Taking her hand, he tugged at it, sitting on the large, black leather sofa and pulling her onto his lap.

"Yeah, that's very unnerving. I was used to it with

you when I thought I had only one demon in my life, and now I find myself surrounded."

"I thought you were used to that from me?" She leaned up, kissing him, teasing her lips over his and gently tasting him. His tongue ran across the seam of her lips begging for entrance. Her eyes closed, and her head fell back into the crook of his arm as they indulged in each other. Tongues swirled together, hands moved over each other's bodies and before long, the room filled with heavy breathing. Parting her lips from his, she looked at him, still not quite believing he was before her.

"Is it really over, Samael? I mean, you won't be taken from me again?"

"It is, and it isn't." His fingers stroked over her frown to smooth her forehead.

"Remembering who you are is only the beginning to our story, not an ending." He grinned at her as she playfully hit his shoulder.

"You know you scared the shit out of me, right?"

"I will be here for the rest of your days, and mine, taking care of you. It has been designed so that our lifelines always intersect. Never fear that we are over, for even when we are no longer as we are now, we will be together again."

"Doesn't it stand to reason that the same can be said for Eva and Clay?"

He nodded in agreement. "Yes, it stands to reason that'd be the path for Eva and Clay. Alternatively, Eva would have to be sensible about everything that's happened. She can still go against the natural progression of how things were meant to be. They have a long road ahead of them. She's got a lot of jealousy and anger issues to deal with that concern him."

"I don't know why I care."

"You care, my love, because it is who you have

always been. Caring and sweet, and she's been a huge part of your life. She's your sister and has been throughout time. Give it a bit. Perhaps you'll forgive her."

"Perhaps." She shrugged her shoulders, not wanting to think of that, at least not yet. "I must thank Clay and Remiel properly."

"You will, but they'll understand if we don't leave this house for a few days." She giggled, shaking her finger at him.

"I have other things to do besides lay about and be your sex slave." He leaned forward and nipped her finger, causing her to shriek. She laughed, and he leaned forward, kissing the tip of her finger.

"So tell me about these other things you have in mind to do besides being my sex slave."

"Um, you got me there. Do you have any ideas?" She grinned.

"Well, if you can't be my sex slave, how about I be yours?"

"Mmm, now that's very promising, my Samael. I love you so much. The one thing I could not bear was to be without you in the light so I gladly kept you in the dark. Just so I could have a piece of happiness with you."

"As Clay said, it is done. I love you, too, Liliana. I'd give up my wings again if it came down to it. You're worth that and so much more. Now we have forever."

"That we do, my demon, that we do. So how about we be each other's sex slaves?" Giggling and leaning forward, she kissed him soundly, cutting off his chuckle as they began to revel in their forever together.

BOOK TWO

DEDICATION

I dedicate this book to my family who let me write like mad during NaNoWrimo. I confess to being a wild woman during this time and for your love and patience I am forever grateful. I would also like to thank Em Petrova and Marie Medina for your wonderful insight. To my readers who have been dying to hear Eva's side, this is for you.

KARMIC LUST

DEMON TEMPTED

Karmic Lust, 2

Nikki Prince

Copyright © 2013

Chapter One

Eva Jackson stared at the back of Clay Quinones' head and frowned. How was it possible that she hadn't known who he was? She followed the lines of his strong back up the hill that overlooked the city. He stood just at the edge looking out. Swallowing hard, she dared herself to speak to him, the quintessential Adam to her Eve, and to act as if everything was okay. His name had more than hinted at who he was, but she'd been so wrapped up in what she was doing she hadn't even recognized that fact.

"So you're not just a deliveryman for C&C Incorporated, are you?" She tried to inject a little humor, but even that fell flat, so she asked what was really on her mind. "Why have you brought me here?"

He turned to her, and she was taken aback by the look in his eyes. She stumbled backwards, not out of fear but out of the need to hide. His countenance shamed her.

"Do you honestly have to ask me that, Eva? No, I'm not just a delivery man—I'm part owner, and you know exactly why I brought you here." Oh hell, why did he look even more striking now? At that moment she saw how truly powerful he'd become. The anger radiating off of him was tinged with some other emotion she didn't want to place.

"Clay, if you've brought me here to treat me like shit, you can go to hell." Sheer bravado, something she didn't truly feel, but damn if she wouldn't make up for it in spunk. He burst out laughing at her, and she knew the look that came over her face was one of incredulity. He laughed for full minute before he spoke.

"That's a good one, Eva. How about the hell you put everyone through with your jealousies and lies all these years?"

She purposefully didn't answer his question and asked one of her own. "How long have you known who I was?"

His ghost of a smile chilled her, and she had to look away. After seeing that look on his face, she wasn't sure she even wanted an answer to that. She moved away from him to stand at the edge of the hill so that she could observe the city.

She'd always felt so in charge around him, but now? No, she didn't. He'd allowed her to feel that way, but it wasn't the truth. Clay had always been the one in charge.

"I need to go back to Lili and explain." She searched for a way to leave, but his words stopped her.

"What's to explain? That you purposefully went after the one she loves and at every turn tried to stop her from remembering who she was? Where would that get you? Besides the fact she doesn't want to speak to you right now."

"I need to explain to her how wrong I was."

"Now is not the time, Eva. You need to leave Lili

and Samael alone for now. Lili told you she didn't want any contact with you. I think you should honor that wish. Let them heal and recover from your misdeeds."

"If I'm so bad, why the hell are you even bothering with me? Also, do tell me why this feels like revenge?"

"That is a question you need to answer on your own, Eva."

"What are we waiting for? Why did you bring me?" She turned to stare at him, and the rest of the words died in her mouth as she saw the angel with black wings that now stood next to Clay.

Clay turned to the angel and gave a nod of respect, as if he knew that he'd be coming. She had her answer; this was her time for judgment. Clay had brought her there to face the consequences.

"Kamuel." Her gaze went from the angel to Clay and then back to the angel—the very seraph that had expelled Adam and Eve from the Garden of Eden. His presence didn't bode well for her.

"Hello, Clay and Eva." The pale-skinned angel with long red hair and piercing green eyes held her gaze, and she gulped hard.

"Hello, brother," Clay said as Eva tried to recover her voice. Kamuel nodded at Clay then advanced to stand directly in front of Eva.

"Do you know why I'm here, Eva? This isn't like the last time we met." His gaze pierced into her, making her catch her breath.

"No ... no..." She repeated the word as if it was going to save her from her fate. He was right; this wasn't like the last time they'd met. That time had been when he'd expelled them from the garden. She'd held out the hope that she'd never come face to face with him over another botched deal.

She'd said no, yet that wasn't entirely true, as she had some idea. She just didn't want to voice it. Eva accepted who Kamuel was and what he represented. Kamuel gave a small laugh that held no humor and leaned in close.

"Eva Jackson, also known as Eve, the time has come for you to receive the consequences for your past transgressions. Are you ready to hear your penalties?"

Eva had known this day would come. You didn't do what she'd done and get away with it. She'd known she was being watched, and nothing escaped this angel's notice. Nothing. She'd fooled herself into complacency. She looked one last time at Clay and then back at Kamuel. Clay's face didn't betray anything, so she couldn't tell what he was thinking.

"Yes, Kamuel, I am." She was resigned to the fact that she'd had this coming, and who could dodge Karma forever? No one could, and from the look on Kam's face she was going to get a big kick in the ass, from Kismet. Destiny always came around to bite you in the ass, and now it was time for her ass to get bitten.

"We've watched you through the years, Eva, and have been disappointed in the road you've taken. A road, I might add, you could have paved differently."

She was about to speak but Kamuel held up his hand, keeping her in silence.

"We all have been given choices. What choice we make can mean our glory or our ruin. You're being given this time to sort everything out. But also to see if you can be what you truly should've been from the beginning."

What I should have been from the beginning? What is he talking about?

Kamuel paused and moved away to look at the city below as he clasped his hands behind his back, apparently in thought. Eva shifted, waiting for him to deliver her fate. She didn't have long to wait. Kamuel turned to her, his eyes showing the only betrayal of the trouble he felt in handing down this sentence. They seemed to shimmer with a fiery heat, searing her to her very core.

One would think as a demon she'd be stronger than she felt at the moment. She chewed nervously on her bottom lip, rubbing her hands together, the other sign that she was uncomfortable.

"Eva Jackson, you have been found guilty of casting a generational curse and for that you will pay with the loss of your powers, until a time when you've shown us that you can be deemed worthy enough to have them back. You'll also be placed under Clay Quinones' watch." She felt something alter within her as soon as his words left his mouth, and she gasped softly.

"I'll be under Clay's watch?" Her humiliation was complete.

She peered at Clay over the angel's shoulder. Clay's face looked impassive. She wanted to reach out to him, needed him to do the same. She wanted him to tell her that everything was going to be okay, even if it wasn't. However, that wasn't to be at the moment and with good reason. Kamuel.

"Yes, it's how we wish it to be. You're too much of a liability to yourself and anyone else. You'll remain under Clay's guidance until there comes a time when *we* feel you have learned your lesson." Kamuel paused once more, and she knew it was for effect, before he spoke again. "Clay has a way with you. There is no better guardian for this than Clay. Now come here and stand before me. It's time."

Swallowing hard, Eva moved forward, not daring to look back at Clay. The shame she'd felt earlier was now twofold. She stood in front of Kamuel, her eyes downcast. She found she couldn't look at him—it hurt too much. Eva recognized it was the weight of her wrongdoing pressing her down and making her contrite.

"Too many times you have listened to the wrong voice in your head. How many times must you falter, listening to the snake?"

She knew the question was rhetorical and not meant to be answered, so she didn't. When he didn't say anything else she did take the chance to speak.

"Kamuel, will I lose who I am?" She couldn't help but ask that question.

"You mean the fact that you're a demon, Eva?"

She nodded.

"It is with great sadness that I say this to you, as you were meant for better things. Your powers, if you wish to call them that, will cease."

Tears filled her eyes. Not because she believed she didn't deserve what was happening, but because being a demon was all she knew.

"Will that make me—?" She couldn't say the words.

"Human, Eva? In a sense, yes, that would make you human."

The tears fell then, hot against her cheeks, and she turned away, not willing to share that part of her with Clay or Kamuel. It had been so long since she was human, how would she even know how to do this? Her choices over time had turned her into the demon she'd become, the demon she'd loved being.

Clay spoke up then. "Eva, you were human once before. You started as human. This isn't something that is entirely new to you."

Eva glanced at him over her shoulder. "I know it's what I was in the beginning. That was so long ago."

"Eva, it's the punishment that most befits your

crimes. Liliana is a mere human that you toyed with for a very long time. Now you will basically get to fill her shoes."

"Will I ever be a demon again?"

"Perhaps, perhaps not. You may wish to stay human."

Never! I would never wish to stay human. I don't want to be that weak ever again.

Kamuel placed his large hand on her shoulder as he stood in front of her. She was about to ask him what he was doing, when she felt a searing tug in her chest. All she could do was gasp and grip his hand, which still clutched her shoulder. Glancing at her shoulder, she saw his hand held a bluish glow and from it radiated heat.

Her demon-hood was slipping away from her, and she couldn't do a thing about it. The pain continued, and Kamuel's hand glowed brightly.

"Kamuel." Eva moaned out in pain, the urge to struggle high.

"Don't fight it, Eva. If you fight this, it will be beyond painful," he warned.

Eva immediately stood still. If the pain she was feeling was any proof that what he was talking about would be worse, she didn't want any part of it. She didn't realize she'd closed her eyes until she felt another hand touch her opposite shoulder from behind.

Clay—she could tell his touch anywhere. She knew he was giving his support against the pain in the only way he could.

"You are now for all intents and purposes the human Eva Jackson. The only thing left of your demon-hood is that you can and will be able to feel Clay's presence." Kamuel's words seemed to echo in her ears. Nothing would be as it had been or as it should have been. Only she could change her future.

There was one last tugging sensation and a feeling of something slamming into her chest full force. Then Kamuel was moving away from her, and she collapsed. Luckily Clay was there to catch her. Darkness settled behind her eyes, and she discerned no more.

****

Clay watched Eva's chest rise up and down gently, showing that she was okay and just in a deep sleep after her ordeal with Kamuel. She'd been out for a while, but it was only a matter of time before she came to and wondered where he'd taken her.

They were in the house where he'd taken residence ever since he'd been drawn to the place where Eva raised literal hell. Besides, he needed some place to bring her after their dates so as not to arouse suspicion.

He'd finally gotten 'his' Eve back. Though they weren't out of the woods yet by any means. Much more would have to be conquered for that to happen. Eva would try to fight. She was unable to do anything but that. Anger would come first. The anger would stem from having her demon-hood taken away from her. With the change Eva was no longer able to use her demon abilities. She was unable to speak into others' minds. Nor was she able to just appear out of thin air. Now she was for all intents and purposes human.

Out of the corner of his eye, he saw her shift on the bed where he'd laid her, and he acknowledged that she was awake. He didn't step forward; he'd wait for her to speak.

"Clay, what happened? The last thing I remember was talking to Kam and then the pain."

"Yes, the pain was from Kamuel taking your power as a supernatural and rendering you into the Eve of old."

"Did you know this was going to happen?" There

was accusation in her voice, as if she was screaming that he was the reason for what had happened to her. She still needed to learn she was the reason for what had transpired.

He answered in a roundabout way. "You had to have known something just like this would happen once Lili realized what you'd been up to."

Her chocolate brown gaze bored into his, and he was once more caught up in the pull he always felt toward her.

"You didn't answer my question." He'd be lying if he said she didn't know him.

"Yes, I knew there was going to be some kind of retribution for what you did. It was a long time coming, Eva, and you had plenty of time to turn back, but you never did. Was there a reason for that?"

She got out of bed. He moved to help her, but she raised her hand to ward him off. She made her way, if a bit wobbly, over to settle in the recliner that faced the balcony of his two-story home. For the moment he'd let her feel she was in charge when it came to touching her, but that wouldn't last long.

He liked how she looked in his long-sleeved shirt that he'd changed her into when he'd brought her home. He wanted her as he always had.

"Why did you undress me?"

That response was typical of Eva, always changing the subject instead of answering a question given to her. It was like a defense mechanism, automatic and reliable. It was something he'd have to get her to realize and then perhaps they could move on.

"Because you'd passed out, I thought you'd be more comfortable in that. You act as if I left you completely naked."

"You might as well have. Where are my bra and

panties?"

He chuckled. "There's no way in hades that you're shy, Eva."

"Not shy, no. But I like to be the one to decide it's time to take off my clothes."

"Don't worry. I didn't take advantage of you. When we do get together and fuck, I want you conscious for that." Eva gasped, and she turned those beautiful eyes on him, fury within them.

"Who says I will let you touch me?"

"Who says you won't, Eva? You enjoyed my touch before. No, we haven't gone all the way since the garden. Just some fun petting and kissing, but I could have more from you and you know it."

"You're a bit too full of yourself, Clay Quinones."

"You're right, but I don't believe in playing games. We want what we want, and I want you and have never strayed from that."

"You've never strayed in wanting me? I beg to differ; when it came to Lilith, she was always your first choice." She said it so low that he almost didn't hear her. He wondered if she could see the regret he felt in his eyes.

"That was all in your head. Now would you like to rest some more or eat?"

"What I want to do is leave here, Clay."

"You know that isn't possible. You're under my guidance. We won't be leaving here until I am ready to do so."

"This isn't going to work."

He moved from his place by the bed and stood next to the chair. Neither of them looked at each other. Silence filled the room for a long time until he heard her sigh in what could possibly be frustration.

"I'm going to go and get you something to eat. As a human, you need to fuel your body and often. We can have more conversations like this another time. In fact I am sure we will have a lot of conversations like this." He turned on his heels and made for the door, calling over his shoulder.

"Oh and you'd better hope this works. This is your last chance for redemption."

He opened the bedroom door and then closed it softly behind him, leaving her to mull over his last words.

Chapter Two

She watched as he exited the bedroom, and she had to wonder what else he hadn't told her. She knew he was a demon as she'd been, so there had to be some secrets he held.

How could he have gotten so close otherwise? Liliana hadn't known much about him beyond the fact he'd been the deliveryman for C&C. At least that was what she'd told Eva when she'd introduced them at Diego's. She was sure though Samael had been privy to who he was.

He'd had all his faculties about him; he'd just not been able to tell Lili who he was. Everything else hadn't been off limits for him to be familiar with. She didn't need him to remind her that this was her last chance. She felt that it was with every bone in her body. Now what to do so that she could change her course and get everything all figured out? When the door finally closed behind Clay, Eva allowed herself to breathe. Just his mere presence was enough to make her feel giddy and needy all at once. So much so it was hard to focus at times when he was around. It almost made her question why Kamuel paired her with Clay.

The angel had to sense the desire she had for Clay. How would that serve their purpose? The desire she had for him was strong, but she didn't want to let him see it. However, that seemed to be something he just discerned if the heated looks he was constantly sending her way were any indication.

Eva couldn't let him touch her. If she did, she'd be lost. This was about getting through this and … and then what? It was the "and then what" she had no clue about. Okay, so then she'd find a way to get through this. She didn't have a plan, but that would be part of the lesson, she was sure of it.

She was tired. She'd been playing this game forever and if she were honest, she'd admit to him that she was tired of the games. As far as she was concerned, that wasn't going to happen. She'd be admitting defeat. Drawing her legs up close, she wrapped her hands around her legs and laid her head on her knees as stared out the window. She felt trapped in this human form. It made her feel strange, being human again. Shaking her head she tried to make sense of her punishment.

She wished she could go to Liliana and apologize. Though how one apologized for what she'd done, she wasn't sure. The last moment with Lili still played in her mind.

The phone had rung, which in itself was odd, as she usually was the one who called Lili early in the morning. She'd picked it up, thinking something had happened to Liliana.

"Lili? Is something wrong? Why are you calling me so early?"

"Oh yes, there is loads wrong, Eve." That particular way she'd said "Eve" had made it obvious Liliana was pissed. *"How about you come over and straighten this out?"*

"Eve?" She'd swallowed hard, trying to act as if she didn't know what Liliana was talking about.

"Yes, Eve. I know who you are." Liliana had cut her off before she could get even one word out. *"Don't bother trying to explain over the phone. Get your ass over here and explain it to me in person."* True panic had filled her then as she hung up the phone and quickly made her way to Liliana's home. She didn't fake being human—she used her powers. She was instantly at Lili's and sitting on her couch when she'd come down the stairs. Liliana had stopped short when she'd seen her, and

Eva had stood.

"So, sister dear, when were you going to tell me that you're a demon as well?" Liliana crossed her arms over her chest as if she was preparing for battle.

"When did you remember?"

"Does that really matter? I've remembered everything."

"You've remembered everything? Well, then that means you know what I want."

"Just answer me one thing. In all the years we have known one another through time, but most especially this present time that you've been my sister, you never once thought this was all a mistake? I didn't want Adam. The one I wanted I left the Garden for, and that was Samael. You were too blind in your jealousy to see that!"

"Yes, I'd thought about it at one point." That was the wrong choice of words, judging by the look that Liliana had given her. She'd watched as Liliana's head went to the side and the look of 'You must be fucking crazy' came over her face.

"Oh? And when the hell would that have been?"

"When we had our talk about the date I had with Clay."

"I'm angry. Eva, I'm angrier than I've ever been with you. So many years have gone by. So many years lost between Samael and me. Hell, so much time lost with you. There are so many times throughout our histories together that we were real sisters. If you'd had one ounce of sympathy or even the love you say you feel for me, you would've stopped this nonsense. This wasn't about me. It never was. It's always been about you and your selfishness."

"You're right. I've been selfish. I'm sorry, Lili, so very sorry."

"No, you're not getting off that easy. I know what I have to do now. I have to free Samael and myself from this curse by speaking my true name."

"I have taken care of you, Lili!" Her words had been futile and out of place, but all she'd thought about was defending herself and trying to get Lili to understand how sorry she was.

"You only took care of me when it suited your needs, Eva. Or should I call you Eve?"

"Lili, please—"

The other woman put her hand up to stop her from talking. *"Please what, Eva? Why should I allow you any thought when you didn't give a damn about how I felt? Because you've changed? Is that what you want me to believe?"*

"I have cha—"

Liliana had cut her off from saying any more. *"Don't even try it. How is it possible that you have changed that quickly? Tell me how a demon can change."*

"Things have changed, Lili. I promise you."

"You have a long way to go to prove that to me, Eva. There have been too many lies from you. The funny thing is, I can't hate you. I am one who believes that things happen for a reason. I don't think this was because I needed to learn a lesson." Eva had crossed her arms over her chest.

"Are you trying to say I need to learn a lesson?"

Liliana had laughed at her. *"And you think you don't need to learn one? Think about it this way. As much as you have been trying to keep me from Samael, you've never once gotten what you've wanted or needed, have you? You haven't had a decent relationship through any of this. So with you thinking you don't need to learn anything, that just tells me you aren't ready to admit you're wrong."*

"Lili, I..."

"*I am Lilith.*" Liliana's gaze never left Eva's, and then she spoke those three words that would change the dynamics of their relationship. They'd both turned toward the door as they heard a sound behind them. Samael stood there dark and proud. All Eva could do was watch as Liliana took a step forward and then ran into Samael's open arms.

"*My Lilith.*" Samael had kissed Liliana softly after he said her name of old.

"*You're really here, Samael. You're standing here in front of me and not a hallucination but a wonderful reality,*" Liliana said.

"*You remembered as I hoped you would.*"

The words they spoke seemed to be only for them, but being who Eva was, she'd had to know how he'd done it, so she did the only thing she could do and that was ask.

"*Samael, what did you do? The rules were that you could not tell her anything. She had to remember on her own!*" Again she knew this wasn't her brightest hour, but she wanted to know.

"*You're right, Eva. The rules of the curse were that I couldn't tell her anything, and I didn't.*" He'd had the audacity to grin at her. "*There was nothing that said someone else couldn't remind her.*" Both women had kept watching him, waiting for him to finish. Samael had turned to Liliana. Apparently unable to stop touching her as he spoke, "*I knew I couldn't tell you anything. Then I got to thinking about the angel, Remiel.*"

"*Remiel? Why does that name sound so familiar?*" It was Liliana who'd broken the silence over that bit of news.

"*Remiel is the angel of Visions. Let me guess.*

You used him to enter Lili's dreams."

"Ah, she catches on so well. Yes, that's exactly what I did. I couldn't trust that you'd do what was right, and time was running out. All I needed was for you to be distracted." Eva saw the curl of Samael's lips as he began to smile. *"Distracted? Who'd you use?"* Clarity slapped her in the face before he could answer. She stood there dumbfounded. *"Clay. You used Clay. Why'd he do it? Is that why he has been spending time with me? I knew it couldn't be because he wanted me. He had a fucking ulterior motive!"* Anger built up like a hurricane within her.

"No, he didn't, other than to put right what you destroyed all those years ago."

"She doesn't know, does she?" Liliana had asked softly.

"No, baby. Her trap, as clever as she was with it, also trapped the both of them, just as it did us."

"What do you mean it trapped them? Who the hell are you talking about?" Her intended target had been Liliana and Samael only.

"I am talking about you and Clay, my dear Eva," Samael said.

Her mind had been racing as she tried to wrap it around what Samael had said.

"He's Adam, isn't he?" Just as Samael appeared when Liliana spoke her true name, Clay appeared and stood just behind the other couple. He'd held his hand out to her, but she'd refused to take it.

"No, I won't go. You lied to me. Your only desire was to distract me, right?" she'd said to Clay. Then turning to Lili, she tried to plead with her.

"Please, I'm sorry."

"No, I've had enough of your bullshit. Go and I'll let you know if and when I want to deal with you again."

"What about our business?" Eva was sputtering, no longer as cool and collected as she always was, which she hoped proved to Liliana that she wasn't a hard ass like she pretended to be, demon or not.

"The business will be fine. I didn't say I wouldn't be working. I just have nothing to say to you, and right now, I am not sure I ever will." Then Liliana had turned from her and effectively dismissed her. Liliana had hugged Samael to herself.

Before she could say anything more, Clay had walked from behind Samael and Liliana and taken her hand without even bothering to ask. The look that he'd given her spoke volumes. She'd better keep silent.

"I think it's time we left, Eva. We are finished here and unless Liliana invites you back or initiates contact, you will not bother them. It is done." Once again words wouldn't come to mind, and she stood there just staring at him as if he'd grown another head. Clay had smiled at Liliana and Samael, and then they were gone. He'd brought them to the hill, and she hadn't been sure why, until now.

There was a clearing of a throat and a touch on her shoulder. Eva turned her head, and her eyes held Clay's.

"How long have you been standing there?" He held a plate of food as he stood at her side.

"I didn't mean to scare you. I've been here for a little bit. Luckily what I've brought can be eaten cold."

He nodded to the sandwich and chips he'd placed on her plate. He held the plate out to her, and she stared at it for a moment. As the silence grew, she knew he would be stubborn, so she finally took it from him and gave a mumbled thanks. Setting the plate in her lap, she looked down at the food, hungry yet not.

"So what's next?"

"Meaning?" He appeared to be waiting for her to have an epiphany, and whatever that was it eluded her at that instant.

"Shit, Clay, I never thought of you as being coy." She huffed. "So what's next? You make me pay for all my ills and then what?"

"Well, I expect that all depends on how you deal with what's happened. Everything happens for a reason. You've been reduced to a human so that you might learn some humility for what happened."

"I've already apologized."

"Yes, I know you have. But are you truly sorry? Obviously Kamuel and the others don't think you are."

She opened her mouth to speak, and then just as quickly closed it. What good would it do to argue the point? They all had to see a change in her, most especially Liliana. If she was ever going to receive forgiveness, it had to come from them seeing the changes in her. She picked up the sandwich and began to eat it, once more letting her silence fill the void.

Chapter Three

"Don't go home." His eyes darkened with passion.

"Until these chains that hold me are gone, I'm better off here with you."

His gaze sparked with something she didn't want to understand, but he said, "The chains are of your own making." So he gave her the spare bedroom, though they both wanted her firmly implanted in his bed. She felt as helpless as a fly because of course she couldn't refute what he'd said. It was the plain truth that she'd made this hole for herself and no one else.

He didn't try to make a move, which confused her, since her appearance was the same. She just wasn't a demon anymore. So she couldn't comprehend why he seemed disinterested. It made her happy and pissed her off all at the same time. She fluctuated between relief and wondering what the hell was wrong with her now? His actions seemed to tell her that he didn't want her because she was human, which was how it had been when she was Eve. Did he not want her since she was basically human? He hadn't when she was Eve, right?

She was getting antsy. He hadn't allowed her to leave the house, and she'd been there with him for a week. He'd left her from time to time with the warning that she'd better not leave the house. What could she possibly do being the frail human that she was? Nothing, not a thing, zilch was what she could do. It sucked.

Standing in front of the bathroom mirror, she wiped the condensation that had arisen from the steamy shower she'd just taken. It had felt so good to relax under the jets of water and to close her eyes and pretend she was somewhere else. She let the towel drop from her body and turned quickly as she heard the door open. Clay stood there.

Her gaze traveled down his body, taking in his chest and his cock, hard and straining against the fly of his pants. Right before her was proof what she'd been thinking was wrong. He did want the new Eva.

She felt her nipples peak as his heated gaze moved over her body. When he locked eyes with her, he had the most devilish grin. He didn't look at all apologetic, and his words testified to that fact.

"I heard the shower stop, so I figured you were done."

She thrust her chin up and squared her shoulders, ready to do battle. "Clay, I am sure ogling me isn't part of the deal. You didn't even give me time to get out of here and dress."

"Looks like a great perk to me."

She rolled her eyes as he smirked, his gaze on her full breasts and her painfully hard nipples.

"Really, you're resorting to bad puns?" She let the sarcasm drip heavily from her words.

"Mhmm, really, you know me. I can't resist a bad pun." He moved closer, and there was nowhere she could go. She was pinned between the sink and him. She'd forgotten how tall he was and how he made her feel so dainty.

He gripped her naked hips and tugged her forward, and then she brought her hands up and pressed against his chest so she wouldn't fall on him. Though she was sure he'd have caught her easily. God, she could feel every muscle through the t-shirt he was wearing, and the jeans molded ever so nicely to his ass.

"Let me go, Clay." She had to hold out, even though she was getting extremely wet between her thighs and feeling the urge to let him fulfill the ache she could never get away from when he was present.

"Why? You've wanted me just as much as I've wanted you from the very beginning."

"Because I want you to. In fact I need you to let me go." Her voice hitched as he pulled her even closer.

"No, you don't and I can prove it." Slowly she watched his head dip and then his firm, warm lips were covering hers. And God help her, she melted against him with a quiet mewl of pleasure. She curled her fingers into the softness of his t-shirt and groaned as one of his legs slipped between hers and pressed against her bare pussy.

Clay ran his tongue along the seam of her lips, seeking entrance just as he pushed his leg a bit higher to rub against her throbbing clit. As she moaned, his tongue filled her mouth, hot and insistent, swirling deep.

Suckling his tongue, she felt rather than heard the soft growl that emitted from him, and then he pulled his lips from hers. Panting softly, he placed his fingers under her chin and looked into her eyes.

"Tell me again you don't want me."

His leg was still between hers, and the painful ache continued to build in her clit. She needed release. She began sliding herself against his leg, her gaze locked with his.

"I can't tell you that. It'd be a lie, right? So yes, I want you. But don't get this shit twisted. I want you to fuck me in every way known to man. But that's all I want. This need we've had for each other for a long time is just that—need."

"Damn you, Eva."

"That's already happened, Clay. I've been damned."

He picked her up by the waist and settled her on the counter. She looked at him warily. What was he up to?

"You want just sex. I'll give you just sex."

He sounded angry, and she couldn't fathom why, but she'd take what he was willing to give her in this moment. She'd missed his touch, though she wasn't going to admit that to him.

He bent his head and placed his mouth on her mound, licking her slit. She cried out in pleasure. His tongue was as wet as it was hot, and as horny as she was it wouldn't be long before she came.

She rocked into his mouth, unable to grip his head as she wanted since she needed to brace her hands on the counter to keep from toppling off.

Damn girl, I'd forgotten how good you taste.

Eva whimpered when his words sounded in her head. She'd forgotten about that little demon trick.

"Stop talking and make me come." Keep this light, keep it real. She couldn't afford to give him her heart ever again. She yelped as he nipped the inside of her thigh with his teeth, in retaliation for her words, she was sure of it. Clay loved being in charge.

You'll come when I say you can come, and not before.

"You're always so dominant." She gave a deep, crooning sound when he wrapped his lips around her clit and suckled hard.

No coming, not until I say you can.

Her hands went to the back of his head, and she rocked into his mouth, her head falling back as she closed her eyes.

"You're not my husband anymore. Hell, you're not even my boyfriend. Stop telling me what to do."

Eva, my dear, you're going to awaken the sleeping dragon. Keep talking.

She cried out as Clay slid two fingers inside her aching pussy and pressed against her g-spot. Rocking into his fingers, she was so close to doing what he'd warned her not to do.

"All I want from you is a fuck. Get that through your thick skull."

In the next moment his face was inches from hers, though he kept his fingers buried inside her. "You're not a demon anymore, Eva dearest. Which also brings me to the point that you're not in control right now, I am. In fact I always have been."

"But—"

"No buts are wanted. Though if it's your ass we are talking about, I am willing to negotiate." His words inflamed her. She gushed around his fingers as fresh cream was produced, and he chuckled. His eyes held the knowledge that he knew she needed him.

"You love it when I take charge of you. You always have, and you always will."

Clay was right. She'd always wanted to please him, had been willing to do whatever it took to make him happy. He'd made her happy by taking care of her and loving her. At least she had been happy until she thought he'd wanted Lilith. That had been so long ago. What kind of cruel joke was being played now that she had to continue to be with him? She was contrite, but that wasn't what they wanted.

"You're right. You're in charge. I love it when you're in charge. I adore it when you take what you want. Let me come, please, I need to come so badly." She whimpered as her inner muscles began to tighten up. Yes, she had stooped to pleading with him, so urgent was her need to get off and fast. Her legs were starting to tremble and if he didn't say she could come, she'd do it anyway.

Leaning forward, Clay pressed his lips to her ear and whispered, "Ah, such beautiful words from your lips." She felt compression on her g-spot as he curled his fingers. "Now come."

She needed no further urging. Her legs trembled and shook. She came hard, crying out his name as she bucked over and over again. His mouth muffled the rest of her cries. Damn, she'd missed his taste, which was now flavored with her essence. His fingers were still inside of her raising havoc with her senses and causing her orgasm to stretch out in what she considered to be beautiful torture.

When he lifted his lips from hers, she opened her eyes. His brimmed with passion, lust and something else she wasn't sure she could define even if she wanted to. It scared and thrilled her.

"So much time wasted, Eva."

"Don't. Not now, not with your fingers inside of me and me just coming off the best fucking orgasm ever. Please, just let it rest for now?"

"We need to talk. But you're right—not in this moment. Not when the smell and the taste of you has me so hard that I am close to coming in my pants."

"Why didn't you just take me?"

"I have plenty time to fill you, but I wanted to savor you." He pulled her closer, his hands at her waist as he nuzzled her neck, breathing her in. Eva couldn't help the sigh of contentment that passed her lips. He pulled her tightly to him, and she squeaked. She was brought flush against him, and she felt the imprint of his cock. He was so close to her aching center. It didn't matter that she'd just come hard from the ministrations of his magnificent mouth.

"Clay…"

"Eva … I thought you didn't want any talking?" She couldn't stop the giggle that passed her lips. She grasped his shirt and pulled it up and off of him. True, she'd been that bold and said that to him.

"Touché."

She tossed the shirt to the floor and began working on the snaps of his jeans. She tugged them down his waist right along with his boxers and let them fall around his ankles.

Eva fixed her gaze on his body and could not help but admire him. What a fine specimen of a male he was, so virile and hers for the moment. Something she'd wanted since time began. He'd been hers for such a small span of time, and she had to wonder if Kamuel was right. Everything had happened because of her choices.

She caressed her way up his chest then cupped the back of his neck as she wrapped her legs around his waist. Kissing him hard, she nipped at his full bottom lip, caressing the back of his head.

His cock slid along her sodden sheath. She rose against him, wanting to help guide him within her. When he slid in fully, they both let out a shout. She gripped him tighter with her legs. His strong, capable hands gripped her ass and ground her into his thrusting.

Her breath caught. He encircled the rosebud of her ass with his fingers. She shuddered and uttered a sob. He slid his tongue across her earlobe and his hot breath caressed her there.

"I am going to fuck you here, too."

She knew it wasn't just talk but a promise. A promise she wanted him to complete. She offered no protest, just nodded. He kept his fingers there, torturing her with the slow swirl as he thrust his cock into her so deeply he hit the mouth of her womb.

"No argument, Eva?" he goaded.

"No, I told you I want this." She shook her head and then in the next moment arched her body into him as he hit her sweet spot.

Clay was giving grunts and groans of his own,

letting her know that he was enjoying this just as much as she was. If she'd ever had any doubts about him wanting her, they were dispelled right then and there.

"Oh damn, damn, damn … fuck!" She couldn't help the stuttering words as fireworks spread through her body. The whirlwind orgasm ripped through her, leaving her a shuddering mass of nerve endings.

He kept thrusting even through her quaking and as sensitized as her body was, it sent her into another orgasm. His hiss tickled her ear and was her indication that he was coming. Soon she was flooded with his juices that mingled with her own, spilling between her thighs wetting them both.

When her world had stopped spinning, she realized that he was pulling from her. She was about to get up when he told her to stay put. The command in his voice made her purr and yet set her on edge all at the same time. He chuckled as he ran some water on the cloth he'd chosen to clean her.

"When are you going to learn, sweets, that I am the Alpha in this relationship?"

She glared at him sharply. "Is that what this is all about? You showing you have a big dick and can tell the little woman what to do and how to do it?" The audacity of the man always astounded her. The little voice in her head whispered to her that she loved every minute of it.

"It's how it was supposed to be, Eva. You came from my rib, not the other way around."

The brush of the towel between her thighs made her tense, as she was still very sensitive there. He cleaned her somewhat gingerly but efficiently and once he was done, he set about cleaning himself. She took that opportunity to jump down from the counter. Grabbing her towel that she'd dropped earlier, she wrapped it around herself. She gave a parting shot over her shoulder.

"Should have thought about that when I picked up that apple."

His laugh could be heard behind the closed door of the bathroom, and she knew she hadn't fazed him one bit—she'd only encouraged him.

Chapter Four

"Get up, Eva." Clay was nudging her shoulder gently.

Eva pulled the covers over her head and growled out a petulant *no*. She was too warm and snuggly to get up. Why was he waking her up so early in the first place? At least it seemed early. She peeked out from under the comforter and hid her face again quickly. Yes, it was early.

"Why do I have to get up? Let me sleep."

"You need to get up, so that you can get to the store."

She sat up and smiled at the thought of being able to go out, but she was also going to possibly see Liliana. They needed to get things hashed out and the sooner the better, though it didn't make her feel warm and fluffy inside.

"Lili isn't expected to be there today."

That bitof news deflated her. She sighed and got up.

"You could have warned me that you were going to get me up at the butt ass crack of dawn. I stayed up so fricking late last night."

"Part of being human is that you have responsibilities you didn't truly have as a demon. Meaning if you need sleep, as your human body indeed does, then you take your ass to bed on time."

"Ugh, you're fucking insufferable." She glared at him as she got out of the bed and proceeded to the bathroom to shower. "How long do I have before we need to leave?" she called over her shoulder as she entered the restroom.

"You have an hour, but remember if you're hungry, that time is cut short. To help you out, tell me what you'd like and I'll have it ready for you."

"How about some Revoltillo de Pollo, please. That is, if you have time." Her stomach growled.

Basically she was asking him for scrambled eggs with chicken. He'd made it for her before. One thing that she was finding out was things tasted different than they had before her change. She liked that fact a lot, and damned if Clay wasn't spoiling her with doing all the cooking.

"It's good to see you've been learning some Puerto Rican words. How can I deny you anything when the lady says please so prettily?"

In answer to his remark, she closed the door on him. Smug ass, she couldn't help but chuckle.

Through the door she heard him. "I heard that laugh."

"Oi! Stop bothering me if you expect me to be ready on time." The closing of the door was her answer from him, and she sauntered toward the shower and got in. Man, she hoped it wasn't going to be a long day, but as tired as she was, it probably would be.

****

A few hours later, she was safely ensconced in the back office and going over inventory that had just come in. It honestly felt good to be back and doing something, though she missed Liliana being there. She was definitely missing Lili after a few hours of having to look at the books and matching everything that came in. This was Lili's forte, not hers. As far as she could tell, everything was in order so the only thing left to do was to price items and get them put out so customers could buy them.

She moved around the large desk to one of the open boxes and grabbed the first one on top. She grinned as she saw what they were. Cock Rings. But not just any cock rings. These actually vibrated, which was supposed to give the male more pleasure right along with his female partner. It was ribbed to vibrate against her clit. It was also wireless and remote controlled to a distance of ten to twelve feet.

It also had a ten-speed function for the vibration and still managed to be compact and light enough and made of a stretchy silicone material. *Mmm, delicious.* What fun it would be to use on Clay. Would he ever give her that much power over his pleasure? Hell, if she thought about it, she had an arsenal of items to use on Clay.

If she could treat their relationship like a friend with benefits situation then she could get through this. She couldn't allow him to have her heart ever again. It had hurt too much before. There was no denying that she wanted him or that they were good in bed together. Fuck, they were good out of the bed together too. Wherever they wound up, it was like instant combustive need. It threatened to consume her if she didn't watch out.

She wouldn't let it this time. She'd learn her lesson, be turned back into a demon and go about her business.

"That's all I need, to be in love with Clay Quinones all over again."

She said it out loud. She needed to hear it. Knowing what she was up against was her best defense. She glanced back down at the box of cock rings and began to price them. She was buying one today. Nothing like having a little fun with the demon. It would be interesting to see what happened and if he'd let her play. She just hoped poking the monster wouldn't get her hurt in the process.

Heck, he seriously couldn't think that she wouldn't bring work home to test out. He'd be her test subject, and they'd both draw pleasure from it. She giggled as she thought of him being helpless and unable to stop her from having her fun. That brought to mind scarves and cuffs, something that would keep him incapacitated enough the experience would be all about the pleasure he was receiving. Now that was enough to make her wet and needy. She hadn't gotten off in a day or two, so perhaps a morning delight would make things a bit smoother.

She was constantly on edge, but then that was her fault, as she'd not let him touch her since the incident in the bathroom. She'd been of a mind that she could take care of her needs herself; she didn't need to complicate anything.

Locking the door so she wouldn't get any surprise visitors she slipped out of one leg of her dress pants and sat behind the desk. The panties she wore had easy access and were soaked through. Most of that came from thinking about using the cock ring on Clay. The rest came from what she was about to do.

She leaned her head against the back of the chair and closed her eyes. Clearing her mind of all other thoughts, she focused on Clay and how much she'd always wanted his touch. It was his fingers sliding against her clit, teasing at her entrance and making her gush her cream. It was his fingers that pressed down hard, making her legs shake.

"Clay…" She heard herself whimper in a voice that was purportedly porn-like.

"Hola precioso."

She gasped and opened her eyes. There, leaning against the desk with his arms over his broad chest, was Clay. She should have expected it. He was a demon— why wouldn't he just show up whenever and wherever he wanted to?

She continued to stroke her fingers over her clit. He'd already caught her, so why should she stop because he was there? He seemed to like watching her so she'd give him a show. Standing, she removed her pants and panties completely then relaxed back into her chair. She reclined back farther in the chair and propped her feet on the desk, spreading her legs wide, giving him a grand view of her pussy.

"Is this what you want to see, Clay?"

His response was to continue to smile at her and give her a nod of what she could assume was a go right ahead. Her gaze holding his, she shivered as once again she let her fingers play with her clit. Though he got to his feet and walked around the desk toward her, she didn't stop for one minute. This was her show, and she held the cards. She'd come when she wanted to come and not before.

He positioned himself behind her and leaned in close, his face pressed to her ear. "Any time you call my name." He nipped her earlobe. His words seemed incomplete to her, and she had to ask.

"Any time I call your name what?"

"It will bring me to you. We still have that connection."

As he spoke, he'd placed his hands on the front buttons of her white shirt. Slowly he freed each one from its buttonhole until he spread her shirt wide. She was on display for him, and it thrilled her. Strong, capable hands undid the front clasp of her bra, and he pulled the cups away from her breasts.

Clay was right—there was a connection. There always had been, but she was determined to break it. To have him relinquish his hold on her one way or the other was her goal. But first … first she needed his touch.

The wet heat of his tongue made her whimper as

he licked across her earlobe and then down to his neck. He grasped her breasts and tugged at the nipples in unison.

"Don't stop the show, Eva." His command ran through her head.

"You need to stop telling me what to do, Clay."

Though she said this, she couldn't stop even to prove him wrong. Her thighs were already coated in her juices, and more of it was spilling out in copious amounts as she thrust in two fingers and began to finger fuck herself.

"You have a full store out there, Eva. So are you going to be able to stop yourself from coming so hard that they hear every little sound you make?"

She sobbed and bit her lip. His words affected her in a way that she was sure he wanted. The thought of being the center of attention while coming was thrilling to her. He knew her every little secret.

"I want that, Clay, but not here…" she stuttered out, and swallowing, she tried to sound a bit more convincing, "not here."

"Then I suggest when you start coming, you press your mouth to my arm and muffle the sound." He kissed her hard and then nipped her bottom lip. "Now back to making yourself come for me."

"This wasn't for you," she gasped out as the sensations originating from her hand radiated throughout her body. Liar, her body seemed to say.

"That's my Eva, strong-willed and always ready for a fight even in the midst of a highly erotic situation." He smacked his fingers against her clit, and she groaned. "Let me let you in on a little secret. This is always for me."

She was too far gone to argue that point with him, and his smack just sent her into a hard orgasm. With a moan she pressed her mouth to his arm to try to stifle the sound of her coming. When her body finally stopped shaking, she shuddered and opened her eyes. Clay was still looking down at her with a smirk. She watched in awe as he brought his hand up from her pussy and licked his fingers clean.

"I've always adored how you taste, Eva."

She tried to not let his words bring up the jealousies that she'd been holding on to forever. It was time to let those go, right? But the old adage of habits dying hard and all that jazz seriously did apply. She wanted to ask him why he had always seemed to be following after Lili if he adored and wanted her.

Jealousy. It had to stop, but how?

"Shut up and kiss me, Clay."

He smirked more and leaned back in, kissing her deeply. He thrust his tongue into her mouth, letting her taste her juices as their tongues dueled. Sometimes it was better to not talk. She knew that now.

Chapter Five

They'd settled into a nice routine over the last few weeks, and Eva began to wonder if she'd ever see Liliana again. She went to work as she had before, and she hadn't seen any sign of her 'earthly' sister. Clay had told her that Liliana was with Samael and had given no further information. She could only assume it was because Liliana still didn't want any contact with her.

She'd been seeing a lot of Jess and Remiel, but no Lili and Samael. Remie she knew was hanging around because he had the hots for Jess. Their relationship was developing slowly, but it was beautiful to watch young love. It made her yearn for something she didn't want to begin to think about. *Focus, Eva.*

She had her back to the door when she heard it open and close. Guessing it was Jess coming in to tell her something, she turned with a smile of greeting.

Her heart started pounding when she saw who it was—Liliana. *Damn, did that old saying 'speak of the devil' fit in this moment.*

She looked beautiful as always, though the scowl on her face didn't bode well for Eva.

"You're looking well, Eva."

It sounded as if Lili thought Eva had been tarred and feathered. Eva wanted to say something smartass, but considering the circumstances, she figured she'd better not.

"Thank you, Lili. So do you. I was just doing some pricing. If you need the office, I can go out with Jess." She didn't know what to say to her sister. Right now she sounded like a babbling idiot.

"Have a seat, Eva. We're going to have a talk. Sort of your 'come to Jesus' kinda talk."

Eva wasn't going to get away that easily. This

was expected, and she also recognized that it was needed. For the last few weeks she'd been waiting for this to happen. It was way past time, so she didn't put up a fight.

Eva nodded and settled in the chair behind the desk, as it was the closest to her, and waited for Liliana to sit as well. Liliana didn't sit; she went to the small fridge in the room and pulled out a bottled water. She opened the bottle, took a drink and then turned, holding herself erect.

She looked so proud, so hauntingly beautiful, and all Eva wanted to do was beg for forgiveness. She was finding it hard to look at her, but she forced herself to do so. She owed Lili that at least.

"I've been avoiding you for a lot of reasons."

"I know ... and I've deserved it. I'm so sorry, Lili." She wanted to defend herself, but more than an apology was due.

Lili raised her hand, effectively cutting off anything else that Eva wanted to say.

"No, please no more apologies right now. I want you to hear what I have to say." Liliana took another sip of water and then turned to look into Eva's eyes.

Eva stopped trying to speak. She needed to just listen to what Liliana wanted to say to her. She watched the emotions flowing over Lili's face. There was pain, anger, and even love. All things she recognized, but all things that had the power to pull Lili even further away from her. She stopped analyzing what the possible outcome would be as Lili spoke up again.

"For as long as I can remember I've looked up to you and loved you. When the memories came back and I realized that you'd made it impossible for me and Samael to have anything outside of our nightly visits, I wanted to hate you. In fact for a few moments I thought I did." Lili choked up again and took another sip of the water. Pain filled her eyes. She blinked several times as if to fight back the tears.

Liliana turned away from her and moved off to stand near the door. She had one hand on the knob. Eva could tell she was about to leave. She jumped to her feet and propelled herself over to Lili and then placed a hand lightly on her sister's shoulder. She could feel Lili's muscles tense. She took her hand away and backed off.

"Lili … please don't leave. Yell at me. I deserve it. But please don't walk away."

If she didn't keep her in that room, they'd probably never talk this out. Eva thought Lili was going to disregard what she said and still leave, before she saw her shoulders slump. She turned back. She didn't move all the way back into the room, nor did she walk out. That at least was something.

"You're fucking right you deserve it. You were my sister, Eva. Yet you let so long go by without telling me the truth. You could have freed me from the curse. You chose not to. Why?" Eva noted that Liliana managed to keep her voice lowered so they weren't heard.

"I was selfish and angry. I wanted to punish you and Samael."

"Did it ever occur to you that I didn't want Adam and in fact I still don't want him? I left. I made the choice to walk away. That should have counted for something."

"No, I was blinded by jealousy and rage," Eva admitted.

"I have to ask. The love that I had for you—still have for you. Did you ever have that for me? Do you even know what love is?"

She'd known Liliana was going to ask that sooner or later. Eva ran her hand through her hair and chose her words very carefully so as not to wake the lioness within Liliana. She had to make sure she didn't piss her off with what she said. She wiped tears from her eyes, squared her shoulders and jumped in feet first.

"I thought I knew what it was, when I met Adam all those years ago. I'd tried to please him, yet it always felt as if you were the one he wanted. I accepted that I could never compete or add up to what he wanted in a wife. So I went after the object of his affection."

"Me, or who in your delusional state thought was the object of his affection. Once I left with Samael, I had nothing to do with him. I didn't want him then, and I don't want him now. Samael is the one that I love and will always love."

"I know that now. I couldn't have been more wrong. You have always shown me love, and I treated you horribly. All I can do is prove to you that I am sorry and I do love you."

"You still haven't answered me on that subject. Do you even know what love is? You say it so easily and if I didn't know what you'd done, I'd believe you." That meant there was some hope for things to change. She had to keep trying.

"I know what it is. I also know I have to prove to you I know what it is and I can feel it. Please, all I'm asking for is a chance."

Liliana was shaking her head, her beautiful curls making a soft swishing sound on her shoulders. It was an odd thing to focus on, but Eva wasn't sure she could look in Lili's eyes and see the disdain there anymore. Fuck, being human sucked. Liliana's words made her look into her eyes again.

"You're damned right you're going to have to prove that shit to me. I'd thought about buying you out."

Eva knew she meant buying out their joint

business. "Why didn't you?" she dared to ask.

"One reason is because I wasn't sure if I was going to come in here and kick your motherfucking ass. But the one thing you taught me and I remembered was that we aren't like that." One of Liliana's hands had made it to her hip, and she peered at her beneath long lashes. "One last time, Eva. That is all you get. You fuck this up, and we're through. You get me?"

"Yes, I got you, and I totally understand." Eva wiped the tears from her cheeks and sniffed. She grabbed some tissue and dabbed at her nose.

"I do want to say thank you for taking care of our business while I was gone. I found myself needing some time away."

"That's understandable." She was about to say more when Liliana spoke up and effectively ended the conversation. With the circumstances being as they were, she figured it would be better to let it go and figure out everything else later.

"We have a lot to get together. Our east coast client Sharon Dare has requested several cases of those specialty condoms along with the glow in the dark vibrators. It's for the fetish party that she's having. I want to see if we can sell something else to go along with that."

This was pure Liliana Jackson; she rolled with the punches, said her piece and then went straight to work. Eva loved that about her. She was going to prove to her sister that she could transform herself into the sibling she should have been. She missed the friendship she had with Lili most of all, and that was where she was going to start.

"We have what she asked for before, and I am sure we can get our suppliers to give us more." Liliana nodded her head and finished off her water.

"We need to get them out by the end of the week and then our focus will have to be on pushing out the inventory we have before the end of the year," Lili said.

"This will be a piece of cake. We've been doing so well the last few years. I don't see that changing anytime soon. Do you?" Eva put her head to one side as she fixed her gaze on Lili.

"No, I agree, but it's better to be on top of things. One never knows when they will be blindsided by something." Lili cast a glance at her.

"I will get in touch with C&C, or do you want to do that?"

Eva took a deep breath. She'd let what Lili said pass because she was sure she deserved more than just snide remarks. Truth be told though, she wasn't sure how long before she couldn't take it anymore. Once again, being human sucked. As a demon she could have done more than just simply nod and agree. Yet at the same time Kamuel had put her in her place to learn a lesson. But damned if that meant she had to take abuse.

"I'll do it. You've done a lot while I was gone. So I will take care of that for us. Oh, I did want to ask, as I've not seen him. How is Clay?"

"He's fine if a bit insufferable." Eva sniffed dismissively.

"I'm told that they took away your powers as a demon. Is that true?"

"Yes, I am for all intents and purposes fully human and definitely fallible."

Liliana grimaced, but if she was going to say anything, it was cut short by a knock at the door. Liliana opened the door wide, and they both watched Jess saunter in. She had the biggest grin on her face and was as bubbly as all get out. She held a big sheaf of papers in her hands.

"My two most favorite bosses together again in the same room at last. I'd begun to wonder if we'd ever be one happy family again."

Both Liliana and Eva laughed as did Jess. Eva wasn't sure if she knew what had happened between Liliana and her, but she did know she most likely had felt some of the residual tension popping off both women.

"Are you smiling because a certain platinum-haired male has been snooping around here?" Liliana asked Jess.

Jess rolled her eyes and laughed. "Yeah, he seems like someone used to getting what he wants all the time. I've decided to let him stew a bit. I haven't agreed to a date yet."

"Remie is a great guy, Jess, seriously," Eva said.

Jess grinned at them. "Okay, being set up by your bosses is kind of a weird situation."

"Jess, you're like family."

"I know, Eva, and I appreciate everything you and Lili have done for me, truly I do. I've just had horrible luck in the men department, and I am not sure if getting into another relationship would be beneficial for me."

"We just want you happy and besides he took a liking to you on his own. Nothing to do with anything we said," Lili chimed in.

"Again, I thank you two, but I am going to take this slow. Every time I rush, something comes in to mess it up."

Eva was the first to ask about the papers Jess still held. "So you going to tell us what those are?"

Jess blushed and giggled. "Oh yeah, these just came in. It's the flyers you ordered Eva to hand out and hang up around town for the big anniversary sale." She moved over to the desk and set the flyers down. She handed one to Eva and then to Lili. They both thanked her and looked over the flyers.

"I like them. Thank you for ordering them, Eva," Lili said. "This is grand advertisement for our anniversary month. I appreciate you taking care of this while I was gone."

"It's both of our responsibilities to take care of the store." Exasperated, Eva couldn't help the bite that flowed through those words. Shit, she may have been a sorry excuse for a sister, but she fucking knew how to run *Two Sisters Sinful Delights*. She watched as Lili arched her eyebrow as if to say she was going to let that one slide. Sweet Jess was clueless as she babbled on incessantly about the upcoming anniversary and what a good thing it would be for the business. Crisis averted for now. Thank the Lord—saved by the Jess.

The rest of the workday went well once she and Liliana got back into the groove of how they'd worked together before. It was actually quite nice to be working with her sister again. One could hope it was a sign of good things to come.

Chapter Six

Liliana paced back and forth in the master bedroom, only stopping when she heard Samael clear his throat.

"Wearing a hole in the carpet isn't going to help the situation, Lili."

"I know, Samael, but pacing is better than blowing up, isn't it?" She studied him beneath her lashes, still so amazed that he was hers.

"There isn't anything wrong with being angry. It becomes a problem when you hold on to it."

"I'm not trying to hold on to anything. I want us to be able to move on. It's been a month."

"We are moving on, Lili. We still have each other and forever."

"But until this situation with Eva is resolved, I don't feel like I can move on. I feel stuck, in stasis. I wonder if we'll ever have a relationship again."

"Clay is working on it, Lili. This didn't happen overnight, so we can't expect that it will be done just as quickly."

She observed him with a pout on her lips as he strolled over to her and pulled her close, gripping her below the black t-shirt of his that she was wearing. She fixed her gaze on him and nodded in agreement.

"You're right this was a long time coming, and it won't be something that we can fix right off." She wrapped her arms up around his neck as she peered into his eyes. "It just makes me sad that Eva and I don't have the relationship that we used to have. I miss having a sister. Though she wasn't just that—she was a friend too."

"See now that's the key. You said, don't—not can't. If you'd said can't I fear you'd be right. Who knows? If everything turns out the way it should, you may have your friend and sister back." He leaned in and kissed her softly, caressing her ass in fluid motion that had her aching for more. If anything the lust she felt for her dark demon was building, not dwindling.

"You're right. That's enough talk about this right now. I need you." She lifted her head up and kissed him, all the hunger and desire that she felt for him in that kiss. She'd get through this. She had Samael, and it would all work out. Hopefully, just hopefully, Eva and Clay would go along for the ride and be okay in the process as well.

****

Eva found herself seated at her favorite table at Diego's trying to wait patiently for Clay, who by the time on her watch was about ten minutes late. The place was hopping with the usual crowd and close to being wall to wall on a Thursday night. She could have her pick of the men there, but she wanted Clay. Damn him. He'd promised her drinks and dancing since she'd gone a whole month without, as he put it, *causing any issues*. It was like he expected her to blow shit up.

The existence they'd settled into was one with sexual benefits and nothing more. She wouldn't allow there to be anymore. When the situation seemed to get too heavy she either left or she put things back into prospective by turning the circumstances sexual again. It was going to be the only way she could save herself, especially when he decided to walk away from her.

Nursing her lemon martini she glanced around the room, and her eyes met for what seemed to be the hundredth time eyes of the deepest green she'd ever seen. She found herself looking away from him quickly just as she had the last few times. Something about his gaze made her feel a bit disconcerted. She wasn't sure why that would be.

He was handsome, of course, with pitch-colored hair that curled at his shoulders and a tanned body and damn if that body didn't fill out that suit well. So why did she feel as if something wasn't right? She was being silly. That had to be it, a long day in a human body made for an overactive imagination from this girl. She had the strangest feeling that she knew him.

"May I have this seat?" How the heck did he get over to her so fast? She looked up into those deep green eyes and swallowed. Fuck, Mr. Slick had made it to her table. He was trouble. She could sense it just by looking at his swagger. He was worry that she could ill afford.

"I'm waiting for someone," she said hastily.

"Well then he won't mind if I keep the pretty little lady company." He settled in the chair next to her, and she frowned.

"Little lady?"

"Oh I'm sorry, darlin'. I'm old school."

"Apparently you are. Women don't like to be called little lady anymore."

"Do forgive me. Would you accept another drink from me in apology?"

She held up her glass showing she still had a bit left from her first drink. "I'm nursing my lemon drop martini."

"How about I get you an apple martini instead of boring old lemon, hmm?"

He raised his hand anyway and ushered over the waitress who happened to be at the next table. He ordered the other martini for her, and the waitress was off to the bar. Before she could protest the waitress had come over and set another drink before her.

"You seriously didn't have to do that."

She looked toward the door to see if Clay had arrived and by the time she turned around, Mr. Slick was even closer than he had been before. So close she could see his eyes dilating and for some reason she found that she couldn't look away. Hell, she didn't want to look away.

"Oh but seriously, I wanted to do it. Take the drink. I don't bite unless asked."

The more she looked in his eyes, the more she forgot what she was looking for and why she was there. She shivered, raised her glass to her lips and drank a bit of courage.

"My date will be here soon."

"So you said and the time keeps ticking by. My name is Oz, and you are?" Why did it feel like he already knew the answer to that question?

"My name is Eva."

"Eva … what a beautiful name you have. I am a lover of names myself, and I know what your name means."

"Oh, do tell." She'd play dumb. She knew exactly what her name meant, but she wanted to see if he was all talk or if he really did know.

"It means giver of life."

He'd hit the bull's eye. So he wasn't all talk, but he was a player who played the game well.

"You're right. Wow, and here I thought you were just trying to come on to me."

"Who says I'm not?" he countered.

His voice was as smooth as butter melting on toast, and she found she was drawn to him. Though always in the back of her mind she thought of Clay and what he would think about the whole situation. Just as she was about to say something, she felt a touch on her shoulder and turned to see the object of her thoughts standing there.

"Hey baby, sorry I'm late. Mind introducing me

to your friend?" Clay sat on her opposite side, so she was sitting between two very virile males. She looked at one and then the other.

Oz leaned back with a lazy grin on his lips. "Yes, please introduce us."

"Clay, this is Oz. I just met Oz sitting here waiting for you. He was kind enough to give me another drink and keep me company." There was so much testosterone at the table one could cut it with a knife. She placed her hand on Clay's thigh under the table, giving it a gentle squeeze. That seemed to calm him if but for a moment.

Oz was the first to move, and he reached over and held his hand out. Eva waited with bated breath to see if Clay would take his hand. She let that breath go when Clay shook the other man's hand. The handshake seemed to go on longer than it should with Oz yet again making the first move of letting go of Clay's hand and lounging back in his seat. *Shit! Is he really just going to continue to sit here?*

Clay stood and held his hand out for Eva. "Pardon us, Oz. I'm going to dance with my woman. Come on, Hermosa, I promised you a dance."

She took his hand and moved away from the table. She and Clay looked back to see Oz smirking and raising his glass in salute.

"Okay, Clay, what was that bit of cock holding going on over there?"

He'd pulled her onto the dance floor, bringing her close for the slow music that played. He didn't say anything for a moment, so she laid her head on his shoulder as she let the melody take over.

"Just making sure he knows you're my woman."

She pulled back to gawk at him. "Your woman? I didn't think you were into such caveman antics, Clay."

"So tell me, what's the difference between me holding the jealous card and not you? I didn't think you had a monopoly on that."

Those words effectively put her in her place, and she laid her head back on his shoulder. Clay was jealous. It sort of gave her that warm and fuzzy feeling inside, but she wasn't sure she liked that one bit. Though to turn the tables on him and let him be the simpering fool? That had merit. She gave a soft snicker.

"That laugh doesn't bode well for me. Do tell me what you're laughing about."

"Now what fun would that be?"

"Your friend has finally left our table." She peeked over Clay's shoulder and saw that Oz was indeed gone. The sigh she gave was one of relief.

She turned back around and nuzzled his neck, breathing in the scent that was purely Clay. He always smelled so earthy and masculine.

"What was the holdup?"

"Holdup?" Clay asked.

"Don't play dumb. You know exactly what I'm talking about. I'm referring to the fact that you were late at least thirty minutes by my calculations, and that's not like you."

"You're right, Eva. I'm sorry. There was something I had to deal with."

"You couldn't have called me? You have my cell number; even a text would have been fine. Hell, you can even talk to my mind. You're a fricking demon, for hell's sake."

"True enough on both accounts, especially me being a demon and ostensibly an inconsiderate one. Forgive this demon's ill manners." He pressed his lips to her ear. "Now my dear, let's enjoy this dance." His words made her smile, and she couldn't stay mad.

Besides this was the first time in a long time she'd been dancing, and she needed to enjoy it.

Luckily for them the next song was another slow song. "Another slow song, eh, Clay? Got the DJ in your pocket as well?"

"Yep, I thought you knew?"

His rich baritone made her quiver, and the nip he gave to her neck made her wet with anticipation for the promise that the night held.

"I don't doubt that at all."

As they moved around the dance floor, she couldn't help but feel someone was still watching. That someone, if she had to guess, was the mysterious Oz. Oz seemed to be temptation on two legs. She'd be dead if she didn't find him attractive.

She was glad that Clay had come when he had because she sure as hell wasn't sure if she could have resisted much longer. Why on earth was he even bothering with her? There were plenty of beautiful and available women in the bar. She had to hope that he would go about his business and leave her alone.

****

From his table Oz kept his gaze on Eva and the one called Clay. He had such grand plans for the two of them. Tonight was just for scoping out the competition, and he'd effectively done that. Eva was enraptured with Clay and vice versa, so now the trick was to get close enough to make them falter.

He took a drink of his brandy and grimaced at the slow burn derived from the liquid heat. He watched as the couple continued their slow gyrating on the dance floor—a precursor to sex. Eva's head fell back, and she laughed at something Clay had said, having forgotten him already. This was just where he wanted them, nice and comfortable and thinking that everything was going to be all right.

"Have your fun now, kiddies, because ol' Oz has some fun planned, and you're not going to like it one bit." Oz was a planner. He never did anything halfcocked. He'd be doing the same for this one, planning everything down to the last detail.

Chapter Seven

It was almost time to close, and there were a few other stragglers milling about in the large store. Jess had called in sick, something she rarely did. There had been no one else to work, so Eva had volunteered herself, and Lili had been fine with it

She hadn't been sleeping well at all for the last two weeks. At the sound of the door chime, Eva looked up from the cash register. The smile froze on her face as she saw who was standing there.

"Oz." How the heck did he find her?

"Yes, it's me. Don't look so happy," he teased.

The male in question gave her a predatory grin and moved to stand across the counter from her. When she just stood there looking at him, he said hello, bringing her out of her contemplation.

"Well, hello there. You're a hard person to track down."

"Oh yes, forgive me. Hello, and why pray tell would you be trying to track me down, Oz?"

"I was charmed by you and wanted to get to know you. Seeing as our meeting was interrupted."

"Oz, I'm with someone." She didn't even know if that was what she could really call what was happening with Clay. She had to try to cock block somehow.

"Are you married to Clay?" he quizzed.

"No, not exactly. It's complicated." How would she even begin to explain her situation with Clay? She couldn't really. It wasn't something that needed to be shared, besides the fact that most wouldn't believe it.

"When you give an answer like that, it tells me you're single. That means I have a chance."

"My God, do you ever give up?" She regarded him incredulously.

"Not with something I want, no."

"All I know is your first name, but I don't know anything else about you."

"That can be arranged, Eva. My name is Oz O'Dea." He held out his hand for her to shake. She eyed his hand as if it were a serpent ready to pounce and then shook her head at her silliness. She took his hand, and her breath caught at his strong grip.

"Well Mr. O'Dea, you're holding my hand a lot longer than you should."

He gave her a small smile, stroking his fingers over the inside of her palm. Her breath caught, and she identified a look of lust in his eyes and something more. But just as quickly, that look was gone, and she was left to wonder if she'd imagined it.

"Ah, but it's never a bad thing to hold on to such a beautiful lady." He released her hand but not before kissing the back of her knuckles. Her eyes widened, and she couldn't help snatching her hand back.

"Has anyone ever told you that you take too many liberties?"

"Yes, but you have to admit you liked it."

Before she could answer, there was a clearing of a throat. A customer came up holding several items. She hadn't even noticed the customer. She felt her cheeks heat up.

"I'm sorry, ma'am. Let me ring you out." From the corner of her eye, she saw Oz move to the side to look at some merchandise. She rang the woman out and bagged her items then handed them to her. She'd finished with the first customer and then lost sight of Oz while she'd taken care of the other patrons.

The door chimed again, and the cleanup crew walked in holding their various cleaning tools. They waved at her.

"Hey Jeff and Brian, good to see the both of you again. It's been a while."

"We'll walk you out when you're done."

Both men waved back at her and went about their business to clean. She made one last check of the store. Satisfied that only the cleaning crew was left, she locked the door. Eva grabbed the cash drawer and went back to the office to close out the drawer.

"I do hope you'll let me escort you out."

Gasping, her eyes wide, she covered her mouth with a hand and held back the urge to scream. Leaning against the office wall was Oz O'Dea.

"You shouldn't still be here!" she squealed out when she finally found her voice.

"I'm sorry. I'd wandered off through the store and got stuck looking at all the delightfully sinful items you have on display." He pointed through the open door out to the store.

He'd said he was sorry, but he didn't look it one bit. He had a smirk on his lips and a twinkle in his eyes. Her gaze moved to his fingers as they stroked deftly over his goatee. He wasn't like Clay at all. He held a different kind of beauty. He seemed darker, more ominous and wonderfully treacherous.

She recognized these were attributes that she'd possessed at one time. Perhaps that was the draw. Oz moved slowly forward. She stood and backed up. All she had to do was call out and Brian and Jeff would be right there. But she didn't do it. He backed her up against the wall, bringing out his hand slowly.

She flinched. "What are you doing?"

"You think I would damage you?" He stroked his fingers over her cheek.

What an odd choice of words, she thought. "No, not really, I just wasn't sure what you were going to do."

He continued to stroke her cheek, and her heart started to race.

"Stop, Clay will be here soon."

"No, he won't. I heard the guy that you have cleaning say they would walk you out. Why would you need them to do that if Clay was going to be here?"

He brought his other hand up to stroke along her throat, holding it where the pulse beat rapidly. Her breathing deepened.

"Besides, Eva, you seem to like my touch. Your heart is racing."

"No, you need to stop." She felt trapped.

She was rooted to the spot. She moaned when he placed his hand on one of her breasts and cupped it through the blouse.

"And my dear, your nipples are hard as little stones."

"That doesn't mean that you have the right to touch me."

Oz scowled and removed his hands from her body. He backed up with his hands in the air so she could see them. The scowl didn't last long as he seemed to quickly overcome her rejection. "You're right, Eva. I'm sorry. I was just taken in by your beauty. Forgive me?"

Should she? Forgive him? Her mouth was fixed to say no, but then she found herself saying the opposite.

"Sure, this time. But don't let it happen again. I really need to finish here. Please, perhaps we can talk another time." *Shit. Why did she say that?* The smile that went on Oz's face made her quiver—a wide grin showing all of his teeth like the Cheshire cat. Eva had a feeling she was the proverbial canary. She remembered all too well those times of baiting someone to do as she wanted them to do when she was a demon. The irony of it all hit her full force. Before she could retract her offer,

Oz O'Dea was all over it with acceptance.

"Sounds grand. How about I take you to dinner tomorrow?"

"Um…" She hesitated, and it was unmistakable.

"I promise to be a good boy."

She rolled her eyes. "Do you even know what good is?" *God, why the hell am I always agreeing with Oz?*

"Oh yes, I know. I just don't always practice it," he teased her.

When he was acting like this, it was easier to agree to do whatever he wanted. He made everything seem a bit more tempting.

"I don't know, Oz. I will have to see. Clay may have something planned."

"Then I will come and take you to lunch. I won't take no for an answer."

A noise caught her attention, and she saw Clay standing in the doorway, his arms over his chest, his mouth in a set line.

"Clay, how long have you been there?" She knew the answer to that. He'd been there from the beginning. He was a demon after all, and she'd summoned him by saying his name.

"Long enough," he said gruffly.

"And the plot thickens," Oz whispered, looking over his shoulder at Clay.

"Coincidence that you found Eva again, Oz?"

"No. Just great deduction and asking the owner of Diego's where to find this lovely little miss. She was just going to agree to have lunch with me. Before you interrupted, that is."

Clay turned his dark gaze on her and smirked. "Is that so, Eva?"

"I didn't know that you had monopoly on all of

my time." It angered her that he was jumping to conclusions and not going to allow her to make her own decisions. "So yes, I have decided to go to lunch with him tomorrow."

"I see." It was all Clay said, but it seriously was enough for her to know he wasn't going to be in a good mood when they went home. "Time to finish up what you were doing, Eva, so we can go home. Brian and Jeff have already left since they know I'm here to make sure you get out safely."

"Ah, I expect it's time for me to go then," Oz said.

"Yes, I expect it is," Clay growled out.

"Clay, stop being so rude," Eva said.

"It's okay, Eva. I'd be doing the same thing if I were in Clay's position. See you tomorrow. I'll call here to see when you'd like to go to lunch."

Oz grinned, gave a nod to them both and sauntered out. Clay followed after him, and Eva could only assume he was making sure that Oz left completely. She flopped down into the desk chair with a huff and closed her eyes.

"What the fuck was that about, Eva?" He was back and of course he was pissed off to the nth degree.

"Ugh!" She kept her eyes closed for a few moments before addressing him. "What's wrong with going out for a friendly lunch? As far as I remember, they said you're my watcher, but they didn't say you were my keeper."

"I made me your keeper! You're mine."

"Wow, Clay. It's the year 2013. The caveman act has got to stop. You act as if I am a toy that you get to do with what you want then put back on the shelf when you're tired of it."

She'd been wrong. Clay was beautifully dark—

even more so when she had him riled up.

He advanced on her, and grabbing her wrist, he pulled her up until she was pressed fully against him. His lips inches from hers, he growled out, "You will not go with him. It isn't just the fact that you're mine. There is something wrong with him." That got her angry.

"You think something's wrong with him? Or do you really mean something is wrong with me?" she exclaimed.

"What the fuck are you talking about?"

"I've never been what you wanted. It was always Lilith. Now that someone does want me, something's wrong with him?"

Clay's eyes seemed to darken even more as he snarled and pressed her against the wall. If she didn't know him, she would have been afraid. He grabbed her other arm and had her successfully pinned to the wall.

"I've always wanted you. When will you get that through your fucking head?"

"You only want me when it's convenient to want me." Her chest was rising and falling quickly as she pushed against him with her hands on his chest.

"Let me go."

"No."

She gasped as invisible hands seem to pull her skirt and panties down her body. Clay was using his abilities to undress her. He slanted his lips over hers, the kiss heated and probing. The skirt and the panties pooled at her feet.

How's this for wanting you? He thrust his tongue into her mouth and swirled it around. She moaned as his touch and taste flooded her senses. She had no defense against him, and he knew it.

After tugging at her bottom lip, he drew back, panting hard. "Well?"

"All it shows is that you wish to fuck me. Well, go ahead. Fuck me, Clay." Once more he proved that he could turn her into a human puddle of goo with just a mere kiss. It didn't take much in truth, which either meant she was easy or that she was hard up. She didn't know which was worse.

"Oh I'm definitely going to fuck you, baby. It will be nice and hard until we are both screaming our pleasure."

Her hair had fallen out of the French roll she'd retained it in that morning and was around her shoulders. With her gasps filling the room and her blessing for him to fuck her, he went back to the task.

He let her hands go, and she arched into him, cupping the back of his head. Smoothing her hands down his arms, she undid his slacks and shoved her hands inside to cup his ass. She rubbed her hands over the strong flesh of his ass and purred as he helped her get him out of his pants by pushing them the rest of the way down.

He made quick work of her blouse, tossing it to the office floor. A wicked grin came over his face as he unsnapped the bra, leaving it for her to shrug out of it. He spun her away from him, smacking his hand against her ass. She uttered a low cry as the sting sent pleasure straight to her clit.

"Mmm, what a sexy ass you have, baby."

"Clay! We don't have any lube."

He chuckled and then his hot breath was at her ear. "Lover, you own a sex shop. Write some off."

She couldn't help but laugh at that herself. "You always make my brain scramble."

He nipped her ear harder. "Don't move. You stay right there, and I'm going to go get that lube." She heard him shuffling around and shot him a look. But she stayed pinned to the wall as he'd requested. The noise she'd heard was him kicking off his shoes and pants and then tossing his shirt to the floor. He was now gloriously naked. She squeezed her thighs together, trying to stem some of the throbbing there, but that only made it worse. She moaned.

"Hurry, Clay! Hell, you're a demon, move faster." She gasped as she felt him up against her back again.

"That fast enough?" She heard the sound of what she assumed to be the lube being placed on the desk.

"Yes, so much better. I think you're keeping me waiting on purpose." She mewled as he bit her shoulder then licked over it. At the same time he delivered a bite to her ass, and she bucked against him. Once more he was using his skills to thrill her.

"You're probably right, darling girl."

"Clay, I've never done this before."

"I know, baby, and I'm going to be gentle. But you need to relax for me."

He pulled her away from the wall and put her over the arm of the chair facing away from him so her ass was in the air. She squealed as he placed another smack on her ass. Each slap was in the very same place as the first, and the burn sent tingles through her body. She loved it when he did that.

She felt him spreading her ass cheeks and then he was tonguing her pussy from behind. Pleasure shot through her whole body. She reared back, wanting more of his tongue within her hot recesses. She rocked back and forth in the large desk chair. She was going to come hard. The thrust of fingers filling her made her cry out as he curved them toward her g-spot.

"I'm going to come soon. I can't hold back."

"I don't want you to hold back. I want you to take

what you need from me."

She wailed when he took his fingers from inside of her. Then she hummed with happiness as she felt the strong slide of his cock deep into her heated core and his hands moving to grip her ass.

"As wet as you are, Eva, I don't really need the lube, but I will use it just the same."

He was right. She was leaking all down her thighs. As an afterthought she knew they would have to clean the chair. Then all thoughts of cleaning were swept from her mind as the friction from him rocking back and forth into her and the rubbing of her clit on the chair brought her even closer to climaxing.

"That's it, baby, come for me. Come for your demon lover."

Needing no further urging, she came in a rush, her inner walls tightening convulsively on his cock and milking him for his cream. His shout followed, and soon he was filling her full of his cum.

Chapter Eight

She lay there against the chair with him still inside her. They were both still panting heavily from their mutual orgasm. When he stirred, she groaned in protest. His kiss to her shoulder calmed her. He placed something in her hand and when she glanced to see what it was, she had to smile.

In her hand was a small pink vibrator that was effectively called the 'life saver'. She'd been told by customers who'd purchased the little toy that Life Saver was an accurate name.

"Use that on yourself when I'm getting close. I want you to come with me. This isn't just about me getting off; this is about the both of us finding pleasure together. Ready for round two?" His voice was deep and heavy with a sensuality that made her toes curl and her pussy cream.

She sensed him leaning back and then felt the coolness of lube being spread over her rosebud. His touch was gentle and soothing, and she relaxed.

"Yes, I'm ready." She grunted as he eased a finger into her asshole and wiggled it around.

"Relax," he whispered.

She dipped her head to show him she understood. Then she took a large breath and exhaled, making sure she wasn't tensing up.

After the first finger, he soon thrust in another one and wiggled both within her.

"Is this better or worse, Eva?"

"It's a bit odd feeling, but it actually feels really good."

He played with her ass for some moments, letting her adjust to being stretched and preparing her to be able to take all of his cock. The soothing coolness of the lube was squirted once more against her ass as he slipped his fingers from her hole. He pulled from her pussy gently, and she moaned. The bottle made a squirting sound as he squeezed more lube from it and when she glanced back, she saw him stroking the liquid over his cock, his eyes on her as he did so.

"Damn, you're beautiful." The strokes he gave to his cock were long, slow and very deliberate. Just watching him do that to himself made her mouth water, and she could not pull her eyes away from the sight.

She couldn't help but laugh even through the nervousness. She'd been a demon, but now as a human all the feelings and emotions were different. "Hmm, and you say that as you're looking at my ass."

"Every part of you is a sight to behold. No one has ever been as beautiful to me as you."

His words affected her deeply, and she couldn't speak. She just gazed at him in acknowledgement.

"Now I'm going to enter you. Relax. I don't want to hurt you."

"I'm ready, Clay. Do it, please." Was that really her voice, sounding sultry and chock-full of need?

He forged ahead. The tip of his cock breached her anal ring, and she grasped the arm of the chair to hold herself steady for his invasion. There was a little bit of discomfort at first, but because he'd primed her for what he was going to do, it lasted but seconds. She was amazed at how good it felt, but she knew it would feel better if he was fully within her, so she pushed back against him with a shudder.

He cried out as his cock penetrated her completely, and he was balls deep within her ass. It was a different sensation from him being inside her pussy but no less pleasurable. He was so thick and long that it added pressure to her g-spot. Eva now understood why some women could get off from this.

"Fuck, Eva!"

"I thought that's what we were doing? No more talking—fuck me and claim my ass for your own."

He let out a ragged chuckle, kissing her shoulder first before he began to move slowly within her. It was astonishing how her body adjusted to accommodate him there.

"You're so tight and feel so fucking amazing."

"I thought I told you to fuck me?"

No more words were said as he continued to fuck her. The sound of their heavy breathing filled the office and bounced off the walls. It was time to use the vibe. She turned it on, and then slipping her hand under her body, she placed the toy on her clit. She cried out as white-hot need spread through her body quickly. Pleasure radiated from her clit and through her whole body. Shivering, she made small mewling noises.

"Fuck, I'm going to come."

His thrusts sped up until he was taking her fast and furiously. She ground herself against the vibrator and bucked back against him. He roared as he came inside her ass, filling her with his cum once more. In response she came hard as well, calling out his name. The convulsions seemed to go on forever.

Moments went by. Her breathing returned to normal, and the pleasant weight of his body on top of hers made her realize how truly small she was compared to him. She suspected that he'd come to that realization himself as he kissed her shoulder and then rose from her, pulling out gently.

"Stay there, baby. Going to go get something to clean you up."

"Okay, you do that. I swear my legs are jelly right now. I couldn't move even if I wanted to." She'd have to thank Lili for purchasing such a comfortable chair for the office. Who knew it had such great uses other than sitting in it?

She drifted while he was gone, her eyes fluttering open when she felt a cool cloth cleaning her. She sighed. It truly was wonderful to be catered to by him. She wasn't going to tell him that though. He already had a big head because he could make her melt with his touch.

"Looks like I've tired you out."

"Yeah, you have. This human body tires more easily than a demon's, Clay. But then I am sure you already know that." He helped her rise, and that's when she noticed that he was already redressed.

"It's only been a while. You'll get the hang of things soon."

His words brought to light that this was indeed a punishment that might never end. Just as she'd made it impossible for change between Samael and Liliana, it was what was happening to her. Did she deserve it? Of course she did or why would Kamuel have been sent to complete such a task? She was getting her just desserts.

He brought her face up to his with a light touch of his fingers under her chin. He kissed the tip of her nose then nudged her toward her clothing.

"I didn't mean to make you sad. Get dressed. I'll clean up in here, and then I'll take you home."

If she hadn't been so drained, she would have taken offense at him ordering her about, but she would let it slide. Her mouth quirked in a wry smile as she leaned down to pick up her clothing and began to dress as he'd commanded. Clay was busy wiping down the seat where they'd played.

"You do know if I wasn't so tired, I'd give you an earful."

He snickered. It was a sound that she wanted to

hear every second of the day if she could. Compelled to move forward, she stopped just in front of him. When he looked up, she pressed a soft kiss to his lips. The smile that spread across his face let her see inside the demon to the man that he used to be and in fact still was. Adam. She blinked and then the moment was gone.

Turning back to the chair, he began cleaning it again. In that moment her feelings were much deeper than she let on. How to hide it? She had to hide it. She couldn't be hurt by him again because it would destroy her this time.

"I think the chair is clean," she joked.

"Yeah, I'm sure you're right. Let's go. I've put the vibrator and the lube in your purse so we can use those at home."

"Speaking of toys, there's one I've been meaning to get for you."

"Oh?"

"Yep, it's one actually for the both of us. When I saw it, I knew it would be something we could have some fun with." It was no use trying to hold back all the excitement she was feeling at the thought of using it on him.

"Do tell. Especially with that shit-eating grin you have on your face, I can tell you have been plotting this for a while."

"It's a cock ring with a clit stimulator and a wireless remote control." She chattered on incessantly, telling him all the details of the cock ring, the good reviews it had received and what it should do for the both of them.

While she talked, he'd grabbed her hand and started locking up. He paused for just a moment and then with a shake of his head he kept moving until they were at the front door. He opened it, stood just outside as she set the alarm code and then followed him out, locking the door behind them. Gazing out into the parking lot, she noted that his car was right beside hers.

"So you're not interested in the cock ring, I take it?" She glanced in his direction.

"Why do you say that?"

"You shook your head and got silent on me. So that makes me think you won't try it."

"Hmm … yeah, that's because I'm thinking about it." He put his hand at the small of her back and walked her to the vehicles.

"Oh, so that's what it means." She unlocked the car and got settled inside. He indicated he wanted to talk to her, so she rolled down the window. He leaned in with his arms resting against the car.

"Means, I'll think about. I will see you at home. I have one more stop to make."

"Sounds good. I need to take a long soak in the tub anyway."

He gave her a peck on her lips and then moved away. She started the car and drove off. She was losing herself to him, heart and soul. How on earth would she keep her needs separate from her heart?

****

Clay watched her drive away, waiting till her headlights were mere specks on the horizon. Satisfied she was gone, he rotated toward the angel that stood at the edge of the parking lot. He headed in that direction. Once he reached him, they both blended seamlessly into the darkness.

The stood in the in between, the realm between the earth and the heaven—the crossover point at the Nether. It was a place where they were neither in darkness nor light. It was a place where everything was in a holding pattern and time stood still. Silence carried them for a few moments then Clay took it upon himself to speak.

"Kamuel, to what do I owe the pleasure of your visit?"

"If I said checking on your progress that would mean I was lying. As you know we are always aware of what's going on."

"Yes, which is why I wondered what brought you here."

"I'm here to give you a bit of warning, though I can't tell you exactly what's happening."

"A warning? What kind of warning?"

"There's an old enemy about. An enemy who's thirsty for blood and won't stop until it's received."

"Understood, Kam. An old enemy meaning someone I've had to deal with before. But seeing as I'm still here and so is my enemy, this must be a vengeance issue."

"I've always rooted for you. If prophecy had mandated that I could help, I would have, as would many of the others."

Clay clasped the other male's shoulder.

"I know and appreciate that fact. The ramifications for changing the written law and rules can be a tricky thing to be sure. No hard feelings, Kam, even if this doesn't turn out the way I hope it does. Eva still has a will of her own, and she is guiding our path more than I am."

"Just watch your back, as well as Eva's. Oh and Samael and Liliana, they are to be figured into the equation and protected as well. The enemy will use them as well he can."

"Will do, Kam, and thank you again." The use of 'he' didn't mean much to Clay. A supernatural adversary could take any form. The danger could come in male or female form. He'd speak with Samael about keeping vigilant.

"Be well, my friend." With a great flutter of wings, Kamuel was gone just as quickly as he'd appeared.

Back at his vehicle, Clay just sat with his hands on the wheel, thinking. It was remarkable how used to human things he'd become after all these years playing at being one. He could have left the car there and been back at home quickly, but leaving the car would raise questions he didn't wish to answer. In this world he had to play at being human in most instances or risk violating the natural order of things. Even demons had rules.

He started the car and drove toward home. He would heed Kamuel's warning. It wasn't given lightly. Knowing that someone was coming for them made him even more watchful. It also made him a bit more suspicious of the new male suddenly in Eva's life. She was going to give him hell and most likely rebel if he told her to watch out for Oz. So he would have to do the surveillance himself. History showed him as weak for always listening to what she'd said. It hadn't been weakness though, unless love was a weakness. This time he'd be the one to make sure they were on the right path.

Chapter Nine

She woke up in a cold sweat, Clay's white dress shirt clinging to her skin, as she clung to the covers, a scream having left her lips. She tried to calm herself, taking in slow, deep breaths. Clay burst open through the bedroom door, looking around as if he expected someone to be there. The small lamp on the nightstand by her bed cast his shadow on the far wall. She must've fallen asleep waiting for him after her bath.

"Eva, what's wrong?"

He moved quickly to her side and pulled her up against his body. He was in a pair of sweatpants but otherwise bare. He cupped the back of her head with his hand, stroking her hair gently.

"I'm sorry. I just had the most god awful dream."

"Do you want to tell me about it?" His voice sounded so strange. She wasn't sure why.

"I suppose I could, but it wouldn't do any good."

"Let me be the judge of that," he whispered.

Clay sat on the bed and pulled her naked form into his lap, still running his fingers through her hair. She snuggled close, pressing her face to his neck and closing her eyes. She took in a deep breath then let it all out.

"The serpent from the garden was in my dreams."

Eva didn't elaborate on the identity of the serpent. She saw the recognition of who she was talking about on his face, but he didn't say anything so she continued speaking. "He was tempting me, and I couldn't stop him. I wanted his temptation even though I knew it wasn't for my good."

"It was just a dream, Eva. You're here with me. I'll always take care of you."

He rocked her gently, pressing a kiss to the top of her head. His voice was soothing and hypnotic. She nodded and wrapped her arms snugly around him.

She inhaled, and her breath caught. Something was squeezing the breath from her chest, making it hard to breathe. The tightening got worse. Just as she was going to ask him to stop squeezing so hard, she arched back in horror.

Eva was in the grasp of a large, ebony-scaled snake and not Clay. The largest snake she'd ever seen. Struggling only made the snake's coils tighten. Once it held her immobile, its huge face moved inches from her own.

"You're mine, Eva." After every word, a hissing sound followed along with a long flick of its tongue.

"No! I don't belong to you! Let me go!" She used her hands to push at the snake's body and just when she'd get leeway from one coil, another would wrap about her body. She had to face facts—she was trapped.

This was no ordinary snake. Serpents didn't talk. This was a manifestation of a demon. Perhaps she could reason with a demon. She had to hope and pray that she could and that there was something the demon wanted from her and that that something was not her life.

"Now why would I do that? Trust me, you will want this. In fact you need this."

"I'll stop struggling. Tell me what you want. Why do you think I need this? Who are you?" The snake pressed its large head against her cheek and rubbed, shivered. She could smell death and the pit of hell on its breath as the tongue flicked out against her lips. The sound of a raspy chuckle would echo through her head. The serpent looked at her and stated, "Damn right you will stop struggling, lest you wish to die."

"I don't want to die. No, just tell me what you want." *Where was Clay?* She needed Clay. Her ribs were starting to feel bruised from the rough handling by the demon.

"You need this, my dear, because you always have wanted what you shouldn't have. You've always wanted knowledge, the man who wasn't yours and everyone else be damned, right?"

"That was in the past," she protested.

"Not so far in the past, Eva Jackson, celebrated in the past as Eve."

"If I need you, then show me who you are, who you really are."

"Not going to happen yet. First I'm going to have some fun with you."

This demon knew all her secrets, but the problem was what was he going to do with that information? Perhaps if she kept him talking, she could find out what he wanted.

"What did I do to you?"

The serpent laughed yet again. "Do? You did nothing to me, personally. I'm a demon. I choose my fun."

"Then why are you here? Or most importantly why did you choose me for your fun?"

"Lust and greed, my dear, is what brought me about, something you have plenty of." The serpent's head turned toward the door and cocked to the side. Then his green eyes took her in once more.

"Till we meet again, my dear." His coils wrapped about her body one more time.

She was getting dizzy from the pressure, and it wouldn't be long before she succumbed and passed out. She looked into the serpent's eyes. Startling deep green. Where had she seen such eyes? His eyes changed to a yellow, and she thought perhaps she'd been seeing things. She heard her bedroom door open. The light from the hallway shone in, and Clay stepped into the room.

The demon was gone. It was like it truly had been a dream, but her ribs were hurting—proof that it hadn't been.

"Clay." She jumped up and ran into his arms, pressing her face into his chest. He held her close and kissed her forehead.

"Hmm, what brought this on? Miss me that much?"

"Nothing, I just had a bad dream is all."

She wasn't going to tell him. She'd take care of this herself. She wasn't sure how, but she wouldn't bring him into this. She'd have to do this on her own. She'd spent too many years letting others be pulled into her own personal hell. She wasn't going to do that again. She'd figure this out. She had to. She held on to him for a few moments longer.

"Are you sure?" He peered into her eyes, concern appearing in his own. She nodded.

"Yes, I'm sure. It was a bad dream, but you're here now. Everything will be fine. I'm okay."

"If you're sure you're all right?"

"Clay, I'm fine. I promise, now come and hold me. I want to go back to sleep. This darn human body of mine needs sleep."

She took his hand and led him back to the bed. Tossing the covers aside, she climbed back in and patted the side next to her. He held up a finger to indicate one minute and quickly divested himself of his clothing. He tossed it to the chair.

"Sure I will, since you ask so sweetly, dearest Eva."

He teased her by sliding into the bed next to her. He pulled her close and tucked her head under his chin so that she was lying on his chest. She exhaled and tried not to think of the pain twinging her ribs. She would not think about it. She'd ignore it, and it would go away. Yes, that's what she had to do.

Besides, Clay was here. There was no way that the demon would come back with Clay being right here with her. For Clay to not sense that another demon had been around had to mean the serpent was cloaking himself. It was hiding from Clay, which told her it wanted her and her alone. Yes, she could take care of this—she had to.

She moved against him, trying to get comfortable finally. She found the perfect spot and stopped moving. He slid his hand down her body and cupped her lower back. She bit her lip to stop the cry of pain before it escaped.

"You finally settled?"

"Mhmm, you smell good." Distraction, she needed to distract him.

He kissed the top of her head, then reached over and turned off the lamp.

"Now I know you must be tired, if you're giving me compliments. Get some rest," he kidded.

Her giggle turned into a huge yawn. His body shook as he snickered. One more graze of his lips on the top of her head and then he lay back on the pillows, tugging her close into the spoon position.

"Good night, Eva. I will wake you in the morning."

"I'm sure you will have to. I think I will sleep like the dead tonight."

"Enough with the talking woman. Rest. 'Cause if you don't, I will be doing more than just holding you." At first, in her sleep-hazed state, she wasn't sure what he was talking about. Then she felt the insistent poke of his cock. Her breath caught but as tired as she was there was no way she was going to do anything.

"Sleep first. I will take a rain check on the other."

She nodded and closed her eyes. Letting out a huff as her body calmed, soon she slept.

****

Asmoday, otherwise known to the human as Oz, looked on from the twisting nether of perdition as the demon of old held the newly made human. His anger built each passing moment he was thwarted and taken off task by a lesser demon such as Clay. He had to be careful or his plan would be found out before it could come to fruition.

"Soon they will understand the true meaning of despair. Tonight was only a taste, Eva and Clay. Just a small flavoring of my disdain and power. Soon the Eve of the Garden will once again present herself, and I will be there waiting in the wings."

Another demon strode up to stand beside Asmoday. He screeched manically as he looked down at Clay and Eva through the looking glass that could show any point in time a demon wished to see.

"Damn, don't you think you should stop messing with those two? They seriously fucked you up the last time."

"Fuck off, Vestis. If I need your commentary, I will fucking ask for it." Asmoday didn't even turn his head to look at the other demon; he knew who it was just by the laugh and smell of him. The red-eyed demon was as shadowy as pitch with snow white hair. Down in the Nether the demons were in various forms: some in human, some in their demon form and some in their bestial forms.

Vestis cackled once more. "Come, come now, you may have need of me. I am corruption, remember?"

"Yes, I recall that it's what you do best. I may have good use of you with this one. I want this to break them."

"Oh, break them? Sign me up for that shit. Thinking about that gives me a fucking hard on." Vestis cupped his cock and held it. Asmoday shook his head.

"Vestis, just saying your own name gives you a fucking hard on."

"You got me there," Vestis agreed. "Nevertheless, I want to be there if you have need of me."

"I'll think about it. Now get the fuck out of here. You're messing with my fucking erection." Asmoday scrutinized the couple in the bed.

Vestis chuckled and was about to turn down into the annals of the labyrinth but stopped short to state in a wicked voice, "You do know that I can help you with that, Asmo."

"Trying to tempt the tempter?" Asmoday said sardonically.

"Fuck, yes. I've wanted you a long time." Vestis gave a vicious shake of his head, practically drooling.

"You'd better understand one thing, Vee. I am the top. I don't ever fucking bottom." Vestis moved forward to stand next to Asmoday, and then knelt before him, his hands roaming up Asmoday's naked thighs. Vestis licked his lips as he stared at Asmoday's cock.

"Agreed, Asmo. Now fucking shut up and put your cock in my mouth."

Asmoday tangled his fingers in Vestis's hair, pulling at it hard. As Vestis opened his mouth, Asmoday gripped his cock and shoved it between his lips. He hissed in pleasure as the demon's mouth wrapped about his cock and he sucked hard, drawing him in fully till his balls slapped against his chin.

"Oh fuck, Vee! Suck me hard, drain me." Asmoday moved his hips faster and faster, making sure that each thrust pushed his cock down Vestis's throat. Vestis eagerly licked, sucked and lapped at the cock being shoved unceremoniously down his throat, while squeezing Asmoday's thighs. He didn't care that he was shoving his cock down Vestis's throat, and as it turned out neither did Vestis. He seemed eager for it. So Asmoday gave it to him and then some.

While he was getting sucked off, Asmoday continued to stare at the couple in the bed, his lust and anger growing with each thrust into the other demon.

"Ahh, what a perfect bottom bitch you make, Vee." He tugged at Vee, continuing to wrap his hair tight in his hands.

Vee growled around the thick cock in his mouth. He dug into Asmoday's flesh, his clawed fingers only making him grumble in pleasure. Unable to help it, he progressed to pounding into Vestis's mouth then without warning, he flooded the other demon's mouth with his cum. Through that glorious orgasm, he still continued to fuck Vestis's mouth.

Asmoday watched as Vestis drank every bit of his cream, even going so far as to suck until he was completely drained and nothing was left. He groaned with pleasure as Vestis milked him dry.

Satisfied, he pulled his cock from the other demon's mouth and then leaned down as if he were going to kiss him and said, "What a glorious cock sucker you are. Now be a good bitch and take your leave. I'm done with you, at least for now."

Vestis whined, and Asmoday looked him dead in the face, baring his fangs. "Go before I lose patience." Vestis scurried away with one last mien and then he was gone. Even the demons would learn he was in charge.

Chapter Ten

Eva was tired, extremely so. It seemed to be the running pattern as of late. The dreams seemed to be intensifying. She had hoped what had happened was just a fluke. But that hadn't been the case. Every night she was having dreams. Lately they'd been of the erotic nature, making her wake up anxious, needy and worn out.

So far when Clay asked, she'd been able to blame it on being human again. Which if one thought about it really wasn't that far from the truth anyways, being human made her fallible now. She was weaker now than she'd ever been as a demon. Part of her identified with the fact that she should be telling Clay what was going on, but the other part of her wanted to be able to take care of the issue on her own. She knew she was being plagued by a demon. She just didn't know why.

It wouldn't do to have two males upset. She'd had to tell Oz a few days ago that she couldn't make it to their lunch, and that hadn't gone too well. Disappointment had rung loud in clear in his voice. In the vein to keep him happy, she'd told him she'd set up another time to meet him. He of course said that he'd just call her in a few days.

"God, that man was serious when he said he doesn't take no for an answer." She'd thought she was alone in the storage area when Liliana spoke up.

"What man?" Lili peeked her head around the corner.

"Shit, sis, I didn't know anyone else was in here. I was working on finding something for an order we have."

"Yeah, I just happened to come in here a few minutes ago. You startled me as well. So who are you saying doesn't take no for an answer? I thought you and Clay were doing okay?"

Since when did she confide anything in her sister since their fallout? Never, but it could be a good way to work on their relationship. Perhaps a way of letting Lili see that she could trust her to be honest and that she truly was changing. Sitting down in a chair she waited a moment to try to find the right words.

"No, it's not Clay really. He and I are..." She hesitated. "Well, I don't know what he and I are. The male in question is a guy I met at Diego's while I was waiting for Clay. I find myself intrigued by him, but at the same time I want to run in the other direction."

"Well, that's most likely your subconscious telling you to do just that. Run in the other direction, Eva, and don't mess with this guy. Besides, if you do mess with this other guy, it could mess up you and Clay."

"But it's just a friendly lunch. It can't hurt anything. As for me and Clay? Not sure if there is a me and Clay, as I said, and a lunch with a friend shouldn't be a problem even with him."

Lili grabbed a box off the shelf and shrugged as she headed for the open doorway. "You could be right. Good luck."

Eva stared after her and shook her head. That was a great conversation compared to what they'd had of late. She'd take it. For the first time in weeks, she felt like things could possibly turn around for her and Lili.

After exiting the storage room, she was about to head back out on to the floor when the office phone rang. She answered.

"Two Sisters, can I help you?"

"Ah, just the woman I wanted to talk to," Oz said. Eva rolled her eyes at the ceiling. It seemed the man was all knowing and could tell when he was being talked about.

"Damn, man, are you psychic?"

He chuckled. "Why do you say that?"

"I was just thinking about you." She shouldn't have said that.

"Wonderful, then you won't mind coming out with me in about an hour for lunch?"

He hadn't ordered her so that alone gave him a brownie point.

"Sure. I promised you we'd go. Why don't you meet me at Dennison's Grill in an hour?"

"Sounds great, I'll be there. Goodbye, beautiful." She shouldn't see him. This was a train wreck waiting to happen. But she couldn't help herself.

Before she could reply Oz had hung up. She didn't want to think about what Clay would say. She already guessed he'd be upset. He'd all but forbidden her to see Oz. It was a social lunch. What could it hurt? Plus, as she'd said to Lili, they weren't a couple.

An hour later she sat across from Oz at the quaint bar and grill chatting over a spinach and chicken salad about anything and everything. Oz wasn't so bad when you sat down and just talked to him. She didn't understand why she'd been ready to write him off.

"See, I'm not such awful company," he said.

"No, you're not. Why does it always seem like you're reading my mind?"

His mouth quirked in a grin, and he countered with another question. "Why do you say that?"

"Well, I was just thinking that you're not such a horrible guy after all. And then what do you ask me? Basically the same thing I was thinking."

"That was just a coincidence. What fun that could be to know another's mind."

She took a sip from her tea, setting the glass

down and then picking her fork back up.

"I'd hope so. It would be a bit disconcerting if you could read my mind, let alone anyone else's." He took a big bite of his hamburger and chewed slowly. Eva couldn't help but see the alpha within that male. She'd have to tread lightly with him. There was nothing wrong with having a good time. She'd been working hard at the store, so a little downtime was warranted, and she sure as hell was going to take it.

"So since I don't read minds, you want to tell me what you're thinking?" He leaned forward and batted his lashes at her. She laughed.

"I was just thinking I'm having such a great time."

"Well then, you wouldn't mind doing this again, would you?"

He gave a whooping sound, causing all the other patrons and staff to turn and look over at them.

"Shhh, Oz. There isn't cause for all that."

"But of course there is. A beautiful woman such as yourself has admitted to wanting to spend more time with me."

"I'm sure you've tempted plenty of women."

"I've had my fair share." He shrugged his broad shoulders.

"Now I still believe that you're being modest. But that's okay. I don't need to hear about all your conquests."

"So they're conquests now? You make me sound like a playboy of the worse order."

"Naw, Oz, just a man who likes women and plenty of them."

"I guess I can't dispute that. Now enough of that. How about we finish having this wonderful lunch, and then I'll get you back to the store?"

"Thank you. I really needed this. I was feeling so drained. But being here right now, I feel better than I have in a while." She started eating again.

"Well that's a good thing then."

It was the truth. For some reason when she'd met up with him at the restaurant she'd instantly felt perky and not at all like dragging about. It was odd, but she wasn't about to complain about that small blessing.

****

Clay stood outside of Dennison's, barely controlling the anger that had built in him as soon as he called the store and been told that Eva had gone to lunch with Oz. Didn't she realize that she was his and he'd made it perfectly clear that he didn't want her to go out with Oz again?

He was about to storm into the restaurant but was tugged back by Samael who'd come with him. Samael had been with him when he'd talked to Lili to see about taking Eva to lunch.

"Let go, Samael."

"No, bro. What are you going to do?"

"I'm just going to talk to them."

"Not with that mood that I can feel you're in. You don't want to talk; you want to kick some ass, am I right?"

"Samael, she's in there with that fucking ass. I need to get her away from him."

"Clay, listen to how you sound. I'm telling you, man, if you go in the half-cocked, all it's going to do is piss her off and push her away even more."

Clay shrugged out of Samael's grip, though he didn't go into the restaurant like he wanted to. He rubbed his hand over his head and stood there watching through the window as Eva laughed with Oz.

"I want to fucking bash his face in."

"He keeps this up you may get the chance. But until then, bro, you need to back off this. You're to watch her and guide her, but you're not her custodian, as far as this goes."

"I see her making a mistake. I have to stop her."

"You sure you're not guided by lust?"

"Fuck yes, this is lust. On the other hand, there's something in my gut that says this man isn't who he seems to be."

Samael moved closer to the glass and looked at the laughing couple at the table as well. He cocked his head to the side then turned to face Clay.

"Then we will watch him close. Dog his steps and see what we find out. We can always get Sal and Remie on his scent."

Clay dipped his head in agreement. "Ah yes, Salathiel is a good choice. He helped me and Eva before when we needed to escape from the garden. Remie is always a great choice as he's been hanging around a bit more. He's already said he's willing to help with anything we need."

"That's why I thought of him. We can contact him at the usual spot." The usual spot was the hill overlooking the city. It was a haunt that had become a refuge at times when Clay needed to get away and think about how things were going. Talking it out with Samael had calmed him down.

"Thank you, bro. Let's get out of here before they come out," Clay said, with one last glance at Eva.

"Anytime, now let's go to Diego's. Drinks are on me."

"That's going to be a lot of drinks, my friend." They headed toward the parking lot and the waiting C&C work truck they'd come in. Samael clasped him on the back.

"We'll have the boys meet us there and find a solution to getting rid of Eva's new suitor."

"Sounds like a great idea, man. 'Cause if we don't get rid of his ass soon, I think I'm going to lose it." Clay peered over the roof of the vehicle at Samael.

Samael grinned. "Eva wants you, and you and I both know that." He unlocked the doors with the electronic key, and both men got in.

"Yeah, Eva wants me, but I'm unsure of what else she wants. I think her being human again has made it impossible at this point to fully get what's going on with her."

"One step at a time, bro. There's been a lot of damage done by Eva. Perhaps this is the way it's supposed to be played out."

"You could be right. But this really fucking sucks."

"No one ever said the female species was easy."

"You got that right."

Clay backed the car out and headed towards Diego's. Eva was tying him in knots. That much was certain.

Chapter Eleven

The silence across the table as she sat down to dinner with Clay later that evening puzzled her. She'd been trying to talk to him all night. Trying to get him to talk to her was near impossible today. The most he'd said was a yes or a no with several grunts. He was being a child, and it was thoroughly irritating. Damn it, he was a demon not a kid. Why the hell was he acting so childish? She tossed down her napkin and stood. Grabbing her plate and moving away from the table, she stormed out towards the kitchen. She placed her plate in the sink and leaned on it for a moment as she gathered her thoughts.

Clay's mood swings the last few weeks added to the puzzle. One moment he was taking her tenderly and in the next he was silent and sullen. Her needs were on a whole different level now, being human. She required interaction, and she needed words and not silence.

She'd be damned if she was going to put up with his juvenile behavior, and she didn't know what she'd done to cause it. Of late her breathing even annoyed him. She'd been making it a habit to have lunch with Oz every day when she was at work since then. The lunches with Oz had been just that, lunch and friendship. There was only so much she could take. As a demon, silence was welcome, but as a human female she was finding that she needed that kind of contact.

She needed to know what was wrong with Clay. All of which meant she'd have to go back in there and confront him to figure out what had pissed off the demon and put him in a state of silence. A noise behind her caused her to turn; Clay stood in the doorway, his arms over his chest.

Eva leaned against the sink and waited for a few minutes to see if he'd speak first. It wasn't long before he obliged her.

"I've been waiting for days for you to confess that you went to lunch with Oz. In fact you've gone to lunch with him every day for the last two weeks. But still you haven't spoken of it."

There it was—the reason for his anger and silence. The fact that she'd dared to not listen to him and have lunch with another man.

"Clay, I told you that I was going to have lunch with him."

"And I told you I didn't want you to do it."

"We will never agree on this. You don't own me. You're my guardian, not my keeper, nor my husband. You don't have a really good reason for me not to go to lunch with him."

"There is something wrong with that man. I've said it before, and I'll say it again. He gives off something that I don't like." Clay growled, and the oddest light came into his beautiful eyes. He took one step towards her, stopped then turned on his heels and left the kitchen. The slamming of the door let her know he was gone. When her hands started hurting she realized she was white-knuckling the sink.

She'd been right before—this wasn't going to work. They were too volatile around each other. Both of them wanted dominance. One alpha too many, and they'd wind up tearing each other apart.

The sound of her cell phone ringing took her out of her reverie. She pulled it from her pants pocket and glanced at the number. Oz. Did she really want to take the call? It rang insistently again. *I need to take my mind off that moody demon.* Oz was pure distraction and harmless. She was going for it.

"Hey Oz, what's up?"

"Just calling to see if you'd like to go have a

drink?" *Why not?* A little voice in her head whispered to her: *Because Clay wouldn't like it.* That made her all the more determined to do it anyway.

"Sure. Where would you like me to meet you?"

"There's always Diego's, or would you like to go somewhere else?"

Eva thought about it and decided that she wasn't going to let Clay limit what she could do and where she could go.

"Diego's is fine. We can even dance if you like."

They talked a little bit longer while she washed the dishes and cleaned up then she was hanging up the phone and heading towards Diego's against Clay's wishes. Against that small voice in her head too.

****

"What are you going to do, Clay?" Salathiel asked, his voice a deep timber that was befitting such a large brute of an angel. He was all brawn, with chestnut-colored hair closely cropped and with light gray eyes that in different lighting shone blue.

There was obvious concern in the angel's gaze as they both watched Eva drive off.

"The only thing we can do at this point—keep watching and protect her if we need to. Follow her, Salathiel. Keep close watch. Don't let her know you're there."

"I won't. I'll be vigilant and let you know what's going on, if anything." Salathiel nodded, spread his wings, and he was off to watch after Eva.

****

"I really don't understand why he thinks he owns me." Eva picked up her apple martini and took a sip. Oz always insisted that be what she ordered since it was what he'd brought her the first time they'd met. They'd already danced a few songs and now were sitting comfortably at a corner table just talking.

Oz looked at her as if she had a second head.

"You really have to ask that? Damn, every male in here wants to own you."

Heat filled her cheeks, and she took another quick sip of her drink. To be wanted above all other women, loved and desired? What would she do for those things? That wasn't even the question really. It was more like: What hadn't she done for those things before?

"There's always someone more desirable than myself, Oz."

He took her hand in his and patted it gently. Eva glanced at his hand holding hers. "Baby, you are desired."

At his words, her gaze shot up to his.

"Oz…" She couldn't get her hand out of his; he would not let her hand go. It wasn't the type of hold that hurt, but it was firm.

"No, no let me finish. If you were mine, I'd give you everything you could possibly ever want. We would be powerful together."

She shook her head and *blink*, all of a sudden she felt so lightheaded. She wanted to be desired, but there was more to it than that. Something elusive was hiding from her, and she couldn't put her finger on it. When her head cleared, she took a sip of her drink and focused on a spot just above Oz's shoulder.

"You know of course I'd love to have a man who'd give me all of that. But what I really need right now is my sister to forgive me. So that I can get back what I lost."

"My dear, what is it you could have possibly done to your sister that you need forgiveness?"

"It's a long, long story, Oz. I don't think we have time to go over it. Let's just say I was a fool and now I have to figure out how to make it right."

"Why should you have to make it right? She should be the one to grovel and to make things better." Something in his voice made her look up at him, and she frowned.

"What do you mean?"

"Well, it seems to me from our conversations that being the older sister, you've always taken care of Lili."

"Yes and no." She couldn't tell him about the times she'd been looking out for herself and trying to keep Liliana from finding out the truth. He wouldn't think her so wonderful if she told him all of that, now would he?

"You're not telling me something. We're friends, aren't we?"

"Yes, we are," she agreed fervently. God, what was it about him that made her want to agree to anything and everything he said?

"Then you can tell me anything."

He pushed the apple martini closer to her hand again, urging her to take a sip. She drained the glass. The liquid burned a nice, heated path down her throat and warmed her insides. She raised her glass to show the staff she needed a refill, then set it down again.

"Some things can change one's opinion about the other person though, Oz."

"My opinion won't change. In fact I will most likely think even more highly of you." He gave her a charming smile, and she could not help but smile back.

They both grew quiet again when the waiter brought her drink to her. Once he'd moved away she turned her attention back to Oz.

"I don't know…" She hesitated.

"I can give you anything you'd like."

"That's a very big promise." Now where had she

heard that before?

"Trust me … you're deepest, darkest desire can be yours or even just something as simple as your sister forgiving you."

She cocked her head to the side and leaned back in the chair with her arms crossed over her ample chest. "Anything I desire? Who are you that you can promise such a thing?"

"Does that really matter if you get what you want?"

She was starting to feel a bit uneasy so she picked up her drink and drank it quickly as she glanced at her watch. "I really should be going."

"What's the rush?"

"I'm just tired." She gave a fake yawn to try to emphasize her newly acquired weariness.

"My dear girl, do forgive me," Oz said smoothly.

"There's nothing to forgive. Thank you for letting me unwind." She stood. He got up with her, but she waved him back down. "It's okay. I can walk myself out. You still have a full beer. We can talk tomorrow." She waved and moved off toward the exit, where she turned back and gave one last wave.

Once outside the bar she shook her head to clear it, breathing in the clean, fresh night air. Her head cleared, and she once again had her faculties. The fog that seemed to have occupied her brain lately lifted.

Chapter Twelve

The house was pitch black when she arrived, and she could only assume Clay was resting. She opened the front door quietly and tried to close it without making a sound. It took a moment for her eyes to adjust. Once they had she progressed slowly through the hallway. Satisfied that she'd done just that, she crept past the living room, ready to head upstairs to her bedroom. Just as her foot hit the bottom stair, she heard Clay's voice.

"Where have you been, Eva?"

She could hear the censure in his voice and didn't want to deal with that tonight. She kept her back to him. "Not tonight, Clay. I haven't been sleeping that well, and I don't need this. So please, just drop it for tonight." She didn't hear him come up behind her, so she gasped when he wrapped his arms around her waist and pulled her flush against him.

He pressed his lips to the side of her neck from behind, kissing her softly, his hold at her waist tightening a bit.

"No talking. I will let our bodies do the talking for us."

"If we're going to do this, then it's my turn to be in charge," she insisted.

"Get upstairs now and undress. Then I will decide whether or not you're in charge."

He let her go, and she hurried up the stairs. Behind her, the rustle of his clothing was apparent. Eva couldn't wait to be in her room to undress—she did so as she made her way up the stairs, dropping her clothes as she went. They were both naked by the time they stepped into her bedroom, and she flipped on the light switch.

He turned her quickly, kissing her right there in the doorway. He brought his hands to her body, moving up her to cup both breasts, pulling at her hard nipples. His touch thrilled her and shot pleasure all the way to her clit. She uttered a cry of unadulterated pleasure, her hands covering his.

"No ... stop." She groaned. If he continued to touch her like this, she wouldn't be able to do what she wanted to do with him.

"We're not going through that again, Eva. I'm not going to stop touching you."

"It's only for a moment," she tried to assure him. "Go lie back on the bed. I want to try out that cock ring on you."

"Eva, I never agreed to that."

"But you're a big demon, you'll love it. I promise. Besides I want to see how it feels against my clit." He finally looked as if he would relent, and she breathed a sigh of relief when he finally did.

Clay strolled toward the bed and stretched on his back, his cock jutting straight out from his body.

"Come on before I change my mind. I'm fucking hard as a rock." She nibbled on her lip to stop the grin that spread across her face and could tell she'd failed miserably.

Damn, the man was perfection, his abs nicely sculpted and his cock thick and long. She looked at him a bit longer then made her way to the nightstand to retrieve the toy. She'd already put the batteries in the little wireless controller in anticipation of this happening.

When she made it back to the bed, she straddled his thighs, setting the toy next to his body on the bed as she leaned forward and kissed him hungrily. The feeling of his hard cock brushing her lower belly filled her with excitement. She groaned as he nibbled at her bottom lip and cupped her ass, kneading the flesh.

Resting back on his thighs, she cupped his cock,

gripping him tightly at the base in the way she knew he loved. He grunted and arched into her snug grip as she started stroking him.

"I'm more than ready for you." He nodded toward his cock and gave her a wink.

"I know you are, Clay, but I love to touch you."

"I can feel and smell how ready you are for me. You're wetting my thighs. Going to let you play for a while, but don't be surprised if I flip your ass over and just fuck you."

Clay was right— she was sopping wet and getting even wetter by the minute. She wanted time to play with him, and she was going to make sure he gave it to her.

"Just give the toy a chance before you have your way with me."

Leaning down, she licked her tongue over the head of his cock, tasting his pre-cum. The little drop of liquid was salty and sweet, his own unique taste. She loved the way his thighs clenched together as if he was anticipating what was next. He hissed in pleasure, and she couldn't help but take it a step further by teasing her tongue in a circle around the head of his cock. She cupped his balls and gingerly licked the crest of his prick as she gripped him securely.

Grasping him tightly, she took as much of him into her mouth as she could. She sucked and squeezed, hearing him moan with what sounded like appreciation. She observed his face as she gave him head, loving the taste of him in her mouth. Even as she sucked him, she was grinding herself shamelessly against his thighs. The chemistry between the two of them had always been powerful, and this moment was no different.

He growled, "Enough teasing. I want you so badly right now you're going to make me spill." He thrust his hands into her hair and pulled her away from his cock. She started to protest, but the expression on his face told her that he wasn't going to take no for an answer.

Continuing to straddle him, she picked up the cock ring and slipped it on him slowly. His eyes darkened. She smiled as he raised her by the waist until she was dangling precariously over him. She braced her hands on his chest then pushed back with a soft groan as she impaled herself on his shaft. She pushed all the way back until he was seated fully within her.

"Now you can flip me to my back and fuck the living daylights out of me like you want to." A ripple of pleasure shot through her at the lust in his eyes.

She held the wireless controller in her hand and turned it to the middle setting. A light buzzing sound filled the room. She was riveted to the spot, loving the expression that came over his face. He groaned and shut his eyes briefly then did as she requested and flipped her to her back. The action pushed him deeper into her. Locking her legs around him, she gasped as the stimulator rubbed deliciously against her clit.

Clay pressed his face to her breasts, licking and sucking at the nipples. A small cry left her as he tugged at one of her nipples with his teeth. He teased that breast for a moment then gave the other breast the same treatment. His touch always gave her the utmost pleasure, and tonight was certainly no different.

Holding on to the back of his head, she rolled her hips, keeping pace with him as his thrusts began to build.

"Oh that feels so good, Eva…"

"Mhmm, like the toy, do ya?" She was trying to tease him, but as his thrusts became savage, she welcomed the wildness and held on tight.

"Fuck yes, I love it."

He was a handsome specimen, but when he was

in the throes of passion he was beyond gorgeous. She loved how he filled her so completely, so thick that he was snug against her inner walls. Soon she couldn't think straight. The pleasure was too great, small mewling noises building within her and then escaping through her parted lips.

"Oh god, Clay, baby." Unable to stop herself she kissed his shoulder, then cried out as he hit her g-spot.

"You're close, Eva. You're so fucking tight and wet around my cock."

"Harder, give it to me harder," she urged.

"I'll give you anything, Eva." His words sounded like a promise. But hell, anything would sound like a promise in this moment. He was balls deep inside of her—who was to say he wasn't just caught up in the moment? She wouldn't hold on to his words being true. Because if he were lying to her and she believed it, it would kill her.

She was screaming within moments of him fucking her hard and fast, the controller falling from her hand to the bed as she clutched at his shoulders, holding on to him so he wouldn't get dislodged. Her orgasm flowed over her, and each wave she crested brought her to the next level. It was a crescendo of sensations that seemed never-ending. Vaguely she heard him call out and then she was flooded with his warm cream.

When she thought she couldn't take it anymore, Clay shut off the cock ring. She shuddered with thankfulness.

Then he was sagging against her, holding her to himself as they calmed. He pulled from her and fell beside her, his arm over his eyes. He too appeared at a loss for words. That was fine with her. She didn't think she could form a coherent thought at that moment anyway. She closed her eyes, telling herself she'd only rest for a moment.

She awoke with a start and found something cold and wet between her thighs. When her eyes adjusted she realized she'd fallen asleep for a few moments and that Clay had gotten up to return with a towel to cleanse her.

"Thank you," she whispered, glancing down as he cleaned her with the cool cloth.

"We need to talk," he stated just as softly. He was intent on cleaning her. Even the act of him washing her was sensual, and she bit her bottom lip to stop herself from mewling like a kitten.

"I know, but not right now. Please, Clay. Let's have one night where we aren't fussing and fighting."

"We can't keep skirting around this." She could hear the seriousness in his tone, and she was of a mind to believe that he'd be pursuing this again. There was no way around it. Eva knew it was something that had to be done as well.

"You're right, and we'll talk soon. I promise."

He finished cleaning her and left for a few minutes. Upon returning, he picked her up and carried her from the room.

"Where are you taking me?" She wrapped her arms around his neck.

"To my bed. You're mine. My first mistake was letting you sleep in that room instead of in my own. I am rectifying that problem right now."

His words yanked at her heart, and it was all she could do to not make a fool of herself. She didn't say anything, just buried her face against his neck, breathing in the scent that was uniquely him, and let him carry her to his bed.

Once in his room he placed her on his cool sheets, as the covers were already pulled back. He got in beside her and drew her near, covering them both with the cover and reaching over to turn off the lamp. Silence filled the room, with the exception of their breathing. This was pure comfort. Something she hadn't had in such a long time. The last time she remembered having anything even close to this was in the garden.

She lifted her head to place it on his chest and stroked his chest lightly. He wrapped his arms around her. It was amazing how right all of it was beginning to appear to her. Her mind drifted to days gone by, and soon she was dreaming about when they'd been in the garden and the trouble had started. When her discontent had driven a wedge between them and destroyed their happiness, a wedge that still seemed to exist today.

Chapter Thirteen

Paradise

Glancing over at Adam, she smiled and waved as she watched him fishing in the Tigris. They had everything they could ever want or need in the garden. She never wanted to leave. It was a perfect place to raise children if they were to be blessed with them as well.

Adam moved farther down the river until he was just a speck on the horizon. She decided it was time to go and gather some fruit for them to eat. As she walked through the tall grass she jumped back when she heard a small hiss. She'd almost stepped on a serpent. Bending she picked it up so that she could remove it from the path, not at all afraid that it would hurt her.

She almost dropped it when it spoke.

"You know there are other things in this garden to do. Things that you will find to be much more fun than just sitting around waiting for something to happen."

"How is it that you can speak?"

"A miracle. Miracles do happen, you know," the snake stated. Well, that is correct, Eve thought.

"True enough," she said to the snake.

"Why are you content to have as little as you do? You're told to do this and that. Aren't you smart enough to make your own decisions? You could have so much more yet you settle for so little."

"I make decisions," she retorted as she held the snake.

"Like what? Name one thing, first woman. Made of man and made to follow man."

The snake was right. She didn't make any such decisions. Adam did it all, and she followed. But she was content with that, wasn't she? It was how it was supposed to be.

"Well," hissed the snake, if a bit impatiently.

"How is this even your business?"

"I'm only thinking of your best interest."

The serpent gave a raspy laugh and brought its wide head up so that it was staring into her eyes. As she was about to declare that she did more than just listen to what she was told, she heard Adam calling her from the thicket. She placed the snake back down and spun on her heels to make her way back to Adam.

"That's right, run back to the one who rules your steps." She faltered for a moment, examining the snake as it sat there on the rock, coiled perfectly in the sun. "When you're ready to listen to reason, remember I'm a true friend and always around."

The parting words of the snake stayed with her as Adam walked up to her and held her hands.

"Where'd you run off to?"

"Nowhere in particular—was just walking about the garden. I was planning on gathering some fruit, but I got a bit distracted."

Adam began leading her back to the Tigris. "Lilith used to like to walk around the garden too."

She looked at him sharply. *How dare he mention his first wife? Why would he do that?* She didn't say anything, just nodded and continued following him to the Tigris.

****

Present time Clay's bed

Eva woke with a start, still in the room with Clay holding her. There was light flooding the room at the bottom of the curtains. She could tell it was daytime, what time of day she wasn't sure, but morning just the same. The dreams were becoming more and more frequent.

Maybe she should talk to Clay about the dream.

Or perhaps she should talk to Liliana. She'd had dreams as well, albeit dreams that had been induced by Remiel. But maybe Liliana could put some light on what was happening to her. She was grasping at straws, but she wanted to figure this out and she wanted to do it without having to bring Clay into it. She couldn't shake the feeling that something was wrong somewhere.

"I can feel you thinking," Clay said.

"Sorry, am I moving too much?"

He chuckled. "Wasn't thinking of feeling you think literally. I'm a demon. I don't need much sleep if any."

"Well that's true." She stayed where she was, with her head on his chest.

"So tell me what has you so antsy?" He tangled his fingers in the back of her hair, stroking gently.

"There's just a lot going on, Clay. You know that. Shit, you're a big part of what's going on."

"True, now tell me what's wrong anyway."

She sighed. "Something just feels off. I can't put my fingers on it. But something is wrong."

Her cell rang, the ringtone alerting her to the caller being Liliana. She lifted herself away from Clay and grabbed the cell.

He sat up against the headboard as she settled next to him on the large bed so she could take the call.

"Hello, Lili?"

"No, it's Samael. I didn't want to just come over there without asking. I can't find Liliana. She said she had to do something at the store before it opened, but that was hours ago. I went to the store to see if she was there and she wasn't. I was told that they hadn't even seen her. The store was still locked when they arrived, and nothing was out of place."

"Samael, that would mean she never made it to

the store." That was so unlike the Liliana she knew. She was always responsible and if she said she was going to do something, she was going to do just that.

"I've gone to every likely spot she could possibly be, and I can't find her. I was hoping she was there with you and Clay." Eva could hear the worry in his voice, and her heart skipped a beat.

"No, Samael, I haven't seen her since the other day." She frowned and looked at Clay. "Um, Samael, you should be able to find her. You're a demon." She was stating the obvious.

"Yes, which is why I'm worried. I should be able to find her wherever she is, and that's not happening. Hence me making the call to you."

"We're wasting time. Get off the phone and get over here. Clay is with me. We can figure something out." She hung up the phone and looked directly at Clay. He spoke before she could even say anything.

"Liliana's missing." She nodded, and tears filled her eyes. He pulled her close and kissed the top of her head.

"Samael can't find her." Being what he was, Clay would know what was said and wasn't said. She was happy that he didn't state that fact. She didn't need to hear that from him.

"Which means a demon or demons have her, right?" It was scary, but it was the only possible explanation for her disappearance.

He got out of bed, picked up his clothing and dressed hastily. He didn't answer her at first, which in itself made her even more nervous. She followed his lead and tried not to think of what could have happened to Liliana. Lili was still a human. Which meant that Lili could be in grave danger, especially if a demon had her.

"Clay, you have to find her."

"We will find Lili. I promise you that."

As they made their way downstairs, Clay took ahold of her hand and squeezed it gently. She kept her hand in his, needing his strength. If anyone could find Liliana it would be Clay and Samael.

At the foot of the stairs was Samael. He looked as intimidating as ever, perhaps even more so now that she was a human.

She let go of Clay's hand and rushed the rest of the way down the stairs and pressed her hands to Samael's chest.

"Samael, this isn't Lili. She wouldn't just walk away." She knew how much Lili loved Samael. Eva had spent most of her existence trying to mess up what they had. So she knew that Lili would never just walk away, at least not by choice.

"I know and I will, Eva. I just needed to make sure she wasn't here and being shielded from me for some reason. It's the main reason I'm finding it so hard to locate her."

Eva turned to look at Clay. "The two of you should be able to find her, right? I mean, if you put your heads together? Besides we also have Remie and others we can call on, can't we?"

Clay took her hand once more and strode past Samael. Taking her to the couch he sat her down and then took a seat next to her. Samael stayed where he was at the foot of the stairs. His face was an unreadable dark mask.

"We're going to do everything we can to find her." Clay placed a hand on her knee and stroked gently.

"Then you guys need to go now. Don't sit here with me. Get out there and find Lili, please," she urged him.

"Eva, you have to promise me that you won't go

off and do anything crazy. Leave this to us. Promise me that before I leave here."

"I won't go anywhere except here and work."

"You know that if you call my name I will come, right?"

"Yes, I know. Now please go find Lili. I'll be okay, just keep me informed of what's happening." They both stood, and Clay leaned down and took her lips in a deep kiss. When he pulled away she stroked her fingers over his cheek softly.

"Go." Nothing more was said, and Clay and Samael disappeared as demons often did, leaving Eva alone. She sank back down on the couch, hugging herself, and tried to think good thoughts about her sister.

"God, please help Lili wherever she is. I have so much to make up for."

She was just going to put that out there to the universe. She knew she wasn't in good favor with the One who could perform such a miracle, but it never hurt to ask for help when one required it.

Chapter Fourteen

"I did what you asked me to do, Asmo." Vestis stated as if he were waiting for some form of approval.

"Yes, you did quite well, Vee. You did quite well indeed."

Asmoday threw a glance at Vestis who stood just off to the right of him in the nether and was wringing his hands together, obviously proud of himself. It was dark and dank where they were. Deeper in the belly of the nether where the cross over from the human plane began to blur, becoming nonexistent, and more and more demons were present.

"Then what are you going to give me for completing the task for you?"

Asmoday regarded Vestis sharply. "Who are you to ask what I'm going to give you? Remember that I told you I am the top? That would be in all things, Vestis, and you best remember that."

Vestis shrank back, and Asmoday placed his gaze on the spot where angels and demons crossed from one plane of existence to the next. He was looking for a certain demon to cross through. He couldn't have made it more obvious that a demon had taken Liliana Jackson. So the issue of Clay taking so long was a mystery to him.

"As, what do you wish me to do with the woman?"

"There's nothing you need do with her. You have her shackled here in the nether as I requested? Then she can't get away. Your job is done, Vee."

Vestis didn't move, and Asmoday knew he was still waiting for some kind of handout or reward for following Asmoday's orders.

"Yes, I have her fettered here in the nether where you asked. She is unconscious. She doesn't know where she is."

"She wouldn't know. She's human and pretty much clueless, as they always are." He paused for a moment, seeing movement at the crossover point. It wasn't Clay. Nor was it the other demon Samael who seemed to always show up around Clay. They were fucking tied at the hip. But then their history was common knowledge, though one would have thought that Samael and Liliana would go their own way.

Holding Liliana captive he would be a fool to think that Samael wouldn't try to find her. It would all work out; this was part of his plan. Samael would come, and the others would follow. Destroy one and he'd destroy them all.

"Asmoday, why do you hate them so much?" There was caution in Vestis's voice as he asked that question.

"Why do we demons do what we do?" He posed the question back at the other demon.

"It's because we can?" There was still hesitation in the other demon's voice.

"Bingo. We do what we do because it's what we do best and since we can't do anything but that."

"So there isn't any revenge that you're seeking?"

"No, it's nothing as hardcore as revenge, just plain and simple wanting to do evil for the sake of evil. No big epiphany. It is what we do and what we do best. What better kind of evil to do against one that didn't see it coming?"

"I suppose you're right," Vestis said.

"You suppose I'm right?"

Asmoday hated to be contradicted and to have this little maggot of a demon do it infuriated him. He fixed his gaze on Vestis and as Vestis cowered from him a wicked grin curled at his lips. As he walked forward

Vestis backed up until he was pinned against the sharp wall of the nether. Asmoday hooked a sharp claw under Vestis's chin and glowered. Vestis tried to make himself as small as possible against the jagged rocks.

"You'd better think before you speak from now on, Vestis. As easily as I give you pleasure I can give you pain."

Vestis shook his head vehemently and held his hands up as if to ward off Asmoday. "I'm sorry. I didn't mean to overstep my bounds. I got too comfortable. Forgive me."

It was pathetic when a demon pleaded, thought Asmoday. It lessened the other demon in his eyes. Though he ascertained that he needed to keep this particular coward around in case there was some cleanup that needed to be done once he had everyone where he wanted them.

"Damn right you did. Now as for a gift, I will give you the girl once I'm done with her."

Asmoday saw the light of interest that entered Vestis's beady eyes. He was such spineless vermin, but Asmoday would keep him around to get things he wanted done.

"Asmo, that would be a perfect present, I accept. I promise to break her."

Asmoday jeered and shook his head. "Oh I know you'll break her. You can't seem to keep your toys in working order."

"I can't help it that they're so fucking squishy."

"Now it's time to play a little game with the soft human."

Perhaps Samael and Clay weren't as smart as he thought they were. They should have been looking for the female so he'd just modify his plan—he was versatile like that. He was smarter this time, and he'd make sure that they all knew it.

"Now, Vestis, I want you to watch the portal. If you see Clay or Samael come through, you tell me that very instant. You got it?"

"Yes, I got it. But it will cost you extra."

Asmo watched him tense as if he were waiting for him to blow up. He didn't give him the pleasure; he was surer now that Vestis would love to be hurt by him. He'd give him pain on his own time and not before. After all he was the one in charge of everything, not the other way around.

"Cost me extra, Vee?" He leered wickedly.

"Yes, I want more of you plus the girl."

"You'll get more of me when this is done and done to my satisfaction and not before. Now watch the portal. No one is to come or go without me knowing. Got that?"

"Yes, yes I got it. Watch the portal and let you know who comes and goes."

"Good boy, I may just fuck your ass yet."

He left Vestis in search of his other prey with the sound of the other demon's moans of want in his ears.

****

Eva had decided that she couldn't stay home. She needed to be busy doing something while Samael and Clay looked for Liliana. So doing the only thing she could, she went to work at the store. At the moment she was knee deep in products and pricing them and setting them up on the display table. She was hard at work in the back of the store setting up a display when she heard someone come up behind her.

Hands slid over her eyes and she struggled, using her elbow to hit whomever it was. She heard a male grunt, but the arms didn't loosen. She revved up to scream when she heard Oz's voice.

"I'm sorry. I didn't mean to startle you." He let her go.

"Damn it, Oz, don't do that."

He held his hands up as if he was trying to ward her off. "I'm sorry. I didn't think it would affect you like that."

"I don't mean to fuss at you. Just some shit has hit the fan, and I don't know what to do about it."

"Maybe there's something I can do?" Oz offered.

"Don't think anyone can help with this."

"You may be surprised at what I can do." His words struck her as odd, but then she dismissed that feeling. This was Oz, and he was her friend.

As they talked, she continued to put the small dildos on the shelf.

"Maybe but this is something that I don't think anyone can do. No offense to you, but yeah, this is something that will take a lot more than just being nice to get it done."

"One thing I can do is to take you from here for a walk."

She shook her head. "I can't. I promised Clay I would stick close to the house or here."

"Ah, he wouldn't begrudge you a little walk. Come on, just for a little while." The smile on his face was charming, and she found that she wanted to go. There was a park just down the street a few blocks. Why not go there and enjoy herself to take her mind off what was happening?

"Okay, okay, you've twisted my arm. Let's go for that walk." She looped her arm into his and allowed him to lead her out of the store. It was a beautiful day; she would stay optimistic and believe that Clay would find Liliana. In her haste she'd left her purse and cell phone, but she figured they wouldn't be gone long.

"So you going to tell me what's wrong?"

"Oz, you're very persistent."

"Yeah, I am. I want to know what has such a beautiful woman so upset."

She still had her arm hooked in his. They'd walked several blocks, and she could see the park in sight in the distance.

"My sister is missing."

"The sister you said you had problems with?"

"Yes, one and the same. I only have one sister."

"What makes you think she's missing?"

"She isn't the type to just leave and not say she's going. She's totally in love with her man, and she wouldn't have just left him like that. Me, she probably would have. But I deserve everything she wants to dish out."

"Ahh, I can't believe that. You've only done what you wanted in life. Nothing more."

She couldn't help but look at him funny. How'd he know what she'd done or hadn't done?

"It's just a guess," he offered.

"I have wanted what I shouldn't want and that is what I'm paying for right now. Liliana deserved a better sister than me and if she comes back, I plan to show her."

"Why don't you go tell her?"

"Go tell her? I don't know where she is."

"What if I do?"

"Oz, what are you getting at? And why would you play about something like this?"

"Who says I'm playing, Eva? I never thought you were this fucking dense. Fuck, have I been wrong about you all this time? Please don't tell me I need to spell it out for you."

She gasped. His voice sounded like the snake in her dreams. He still held on to her arm and tightened his hold like a vice. She jerked to get away.

"What the hell, stop and let me go!"

"You're not as strong as you used to be, are you, Eva?" He pulled her close, with his hands holding her arms.

"Who the hell are you really?"

"Do you really still not recognize me?"

"Oz O'Dea," she whispered. "It's you, Asmoday. The serpent in my dreams and from the garden." She began to tremble.

It dawned on her in that moment who he was and who he had been. She'd allowed the demon from her past back into her life. Now what did he want? And whatever he wanted, was she prepared to give it to him?

"Give the girl a cookie. Has the shit really hit the fan now? Or as you humans like to say, this shit just got real." His words dripped with sarcasm.

"What is it you want?" She didn't entertain his question.

"What have I always wanted?"

"I'm not sure."

"But you should be. You see, whenever you did something selfish and only for you, I got off on that. I thrive on your greediness."

"I'm not like that anymore." She didn't know if she was trying to convince him or herself that what she was saying was true.

"Oh don't I know it. Which is the reason why I want you to stop this foolishness of trying to be good and be the real you. You're not fucking virtuous, Eva. You get off on being a fucking bitch just as much as I get off on you being such."

She looked about the park, hoping to find someone who'd be able to help her, but she knew it was futile. He was a demon. How would anyone begin to help her? In that instant she thought of Clay and was just about to voice his name when Asmoday's fingernails became claws and dug into her arms.

"You call him, and I'll have your precious Liliana killed," he snarled, the calm demeanor of before gone and replaced with that of a cold-hearted killer.

She could hear the truth in those words. Asmoday, the demon of her past, had her sister. It was either do as he said or he'd kill her.

"Tell me what you want, and I'll do it."

"Oh of that I have no doubt. You always were into preserving yourself and no one else."

"Let her go. She has nothing to do with this."

He burst out laughing, causing a flock of birds to fly up and scatter at the sound.

"You know as well as I do that she has everything to do with this. You, my dear, can't help but want what she has."

"No! You're wrong! I've learned my lesson. I'm learning it. She belongs with him, and I don't."

"No, all you've learned to do is to hide what you really want from yourself. But you forget I know you better than you know yourself. You still think that she wants what you had. Has always wanted what you had, which in turn has made this a never-ending cycle. A very delicious cycle, because I feed off your greed and lusts."

"Feed off me?"

What the hell was he? Was he some sort of demonic vampire? Then it dawned on her Oz was a demon of lust and rapaciousness. He fed off her sexual energy as well as her gluttony to have what she wanted at all costs. So all of these years that she'd be torturing Lili she'd been supplying Asmoday his kicks. This was the reason he'd started coming around and invading her dreams. She'd stopped giving him his fix, and he wanted it to continue.

"I have news for you, Asmoday. You will have to look somewhere else to find what you're looking for. I'm not that girl anymore."

"I'm not giving you a choice, Eva."

"Asmoday, let me go before the shit really hits the fan. Let my sister go."

"Whoa, it's amazing to see the concern you pretend to have for your sister now. Admit it, Eva. You've only ever cared about yourself. The reason you're trying to be good now is to get back your demon. You hate what they've turned you into." His words were scathing, and she flinched.

There was one thing about demons that you couldn't get away from. They were sharp and to the point, and it didn't matter to them who they hurt when they were doing it. Asmoday was out for blood, Eva's blood. That was unless she played ball.

"That was before."

"Before what?" he goaded.

"I learned that what I was doing was wrong."

"Why was it wrong? Was it wrong since they said it was?"

"I hurt Liliana and Samael with my selfishness."

"Ugh! Don't want to fucking hear that shit! All the time that has gone by and now you want to play nice? Fuck that shit!" He grabbed her roughly, and the next thing she knew was that she was in the in between. Just as she was looking around trying to make sense of where she was, she was hit over the back of the head and knew no more.

Chapter Fifteen

When Eva awakened she was in a dark and dank cavern and shackled to the wall. She couldn't see anything, but her hearing was amplified and what she did hear was terrifying. There was a lot of screaming, growling, and other unidentifiable sounds that would have had a lesser person peeing in their pants. She wasn't a demon anymore, which meant she couldn't protect herself if one decided to do something to her. She held her eyes closed tightly, and she tried to concentrate on Clay. But she couldn't feel his presence like she had before. Something was touching her, and her eyes opened up wide. Though she couldn't see a thing it didn't stop her from trying to do so.

She heard a small hiss close to her ear and a flick of a tongue, and she shuddered.

"You can try to reach your demon, but he won't be able to find you where we have you." The disembodied voice hissed yet again and drew even nearer. So close was it, she could taste its rancid breath. Some demons were plain disgusting when they wanted to be and preferred that. She could only figure it was the same with the one that seemed intent on exploring her.

It was a voice she didn't recognize, so she could only assume it was one of Asmoday's minions. The thought that Asmoday wasn't the only one she'd have to deal with filled her with dread. She shuddered as that wet and rough tongue flicked over her cheek this time, and she turned her face away. She pressed herself against the wall trying to make herself as small as possible so whatever thing was touching her couldn't. It was all in vain. There was another swipe of a tongue and hands were groping her.

"Get the fuck away from me," she shrieked.

Her heart was racing, and it was all she could do to calm herself. It wouldn't do to lose it wherever she was, so she had to maintain calm. She took deep breaths and soon found that the racing of her heart stopped. She sensed the demon moving away, and she was left with the sound of her own breathing. She wasn't sure what made the demon leave her alone, but she was happy it did. She heard faint movement and wondered if she were already going crazy in the dark. She closed her eyes.

"Eva?" a voice said tentatively.

Her eyes shot open, and she couldn't keep the relief from her voice. She wasn't crazy. That was her sister's voice she heard. It was sort of shocking that Asmoday would put her in the same place he'd put her sister.

"Lili … yes, it's me, Eva."

"Why am I here? What have you done?" Accusation was ripe in Liliana's voice.

"I'm sorry. This is my entire fault. You're leverage." She couldn't blame Lili for thinking that she was capable of this type of deceit. She blamed herself.

"Leverage for what?" She could hear the disbelief in Lili's voice.

"Asmoday, for him to get what he wants I have to do what he wishes."

Suddenly she felt extremely tired, and it was all she could do not to just close her eyes to block it all out. She knew it was her body's way of coping. But she couldn't do that, because there was too much at stake. For the millionth time since the change she cursed her human body. If there was any time that she needed to be a demon, now was that time. Then she could save the both of them.

"Who the hell is Asmoday?" Lili's voice was higher than usual, and Eva totally understood the reason why.

"He's a demon, Liliana. He's a demon that gorges on lust and greed."

Lili began to cry. Eva pulled herself up and scooted over in the dark, tentatively reaching out to see if she could find Lili by touch. When her hand came in contact with skin she knew it was Lili and that she could get in close enough to pull her into her arms. The chains did not hinder them that much. Lili sobbed and buried her face into Eva's shoulder.

"I'm sorry, Lili. I will get us out of this." She wished she could see Lili's face, so that her words weren't just empty things echoing in the cavern.

"I just want to go home. I want Samael."

Lord, how she wished that saying their names would bring them. But knowing Asmoday, he had something set up that was cloaking them from their men.

"They'll find us, Lili. I promise you I will get you out of this, even if I have to sacrifice myself to do it."

"How the hell do you know you will get us out of this? Tell me how. What could you possibly do to appease that demon?"

"By giving him what he wants. I owe you, and the least I could do is to make amends for what I've done." Lili went silent on her, something she'd done a lot of as a child when she was scared. Eva's eyes were adjusting a bit, and she could now just see the outline of Lili's head. She laid her head atop Lili's and continued to hold her. Unable to stay silent a minute longer, she asked the burning question that she needed to know most in that moment.

"He didn't hurt you, did he?" Eva asked.

"No, they haven't touched me." The way she said it suggested that she didn't think that it would stay that way.

"I won't let them hurt you."

"You can't promise me that. The demon that brought me in here has already said his reward for helping Asmoday is me."

"Lili, you've got to believe me. I had nothing to do with this, and I won't let them harm you."

"You've told so many lies, Eva."

Eva felt the wetness of Liliana's tears slide sluggishly down her chest where Lili's head rested.

"I know and for that I'm truly sorry."

"Sorry that you got caught?"

Eva took in a sharp breath. "I deserved that. But no. I am sorry that my actions have put you into this mess."

"You're damn right about that. Now how powerful is this demon?"

"He's powerful enough that he can block out Samael and Clay as long as he'd like. He's older than we are." Her wrists were starting to cramp from the shackles, but she didn't want to let Lili go.

It was as if Lili had read her mind. "Don't let me go. Please, Eva. With you here at least I don't feel alone."

"I won't," she said with more confidence than she was feeling. This was her fault. If she'd told Clay about the dreams she'd been having along with the demonic visitation, perhaps they wouldn't be in this predicament.

"Samael won't stop till he finds me." Lili's breath was hot against Eva's skin. It was a reminder to Eva that they were both still there and alive.

"No, he won't," she agreed. "He loves you." As she talked she ran her head along Lili's curls to soothe her. Liliana had quieted down, and the soft sound of her breathing let Eva know she'd fallen to sleep.

Those words got her to thinking. Would Clay

come for her? He loved having sex with her, but was that enough to keep them together after all that she'd put them through? There were times it seemed as if he cared for her. She was too scared to latch on to that. What if it was just wishful thinking on her part? Clay was there to watch her. That wasn't a promise that he'd want and love her.

Love. Yes, that was what she wanted from Clay. She admitted it to herself for the first time in forever. She'd always wanted his approval and his love. Hopefully it wasn't too late. He'd find them, and he'd love her as much as she loved him.

In a perfect world, all she needed was her family. Clay, Lili and Samael were her family, right along with Jess and Remiel. She didn't care if she ever became a demon again. If she were human and had her family, then that was all that mattered.

If Clay didn't want her, she'd deal with that when the time came. What she needed to get a handle on was on how she was going to get out of this mess and keep Liliana safe. She'd protected her when she was younger, and she'd do so again with her own life if it came to it.

She gave a shuddering sigh as she forced herself to hold back the tears that threatened to flow. Crying wasn't going to help her. She had to be strong for Lili. If there was one thing she was determined to do it was to be strong. It was a waiting game. Asmoday had waited all this time to do what he was doing, so she didn't expect he would make any hasty moves unless something didn't go right.

She'd hold on to that belief, and she'd pray like she never had before. This wasn't her finest hour. The shoe didn't feel good on the other foot was the right analogy for how she was feeling. Payback was a bitch, and its name was mockery in the guise of Asmoday the lust demon.

****

"Clay."

Clay twisted around at the sound of his name, facing Remiel and Salathiel. It was Remie who spoke first.

"We went to check on Eva. She's gone now too."

"What? Did you check my place, her place and the shop?" Clay could hear the urgency in his own voice.

"Yes, we checked all of those places. We did find out that she had been at the shop, and she left with a guy that has been frequenting the place."

Clay frowned and then it hit him who that someone was. "Oz O'Dea."

Salathiel spoke up with his deep baritone voice. "The girl at the counter said that she left on her own. There wasn't any issue with her going with him." Clay wasn't sure what girl at the counter Sal was talking about. Not that Eva and Lili had a lot of employees, but there was more than one girl there. His face must have expressed that because it didn't take long for Remie to speak up.

"He's talking about Jess." Remie confirmed who Clay figured would be at the counter when the two had asked.

"Then perhaps she's okay, but that being said, I can't feel her anymore." That gut feeling was the main reason Clay had sent the two angels to check on Eva in the first place. Something was wrong; he could feel it. This had to be what Kam had been talking about. He'd thought the danger was to Eva alone. That was the mistake he'd made. Thinking that whoever had a vendetta against them would go directly for Eva.

Remiel took a step forward, his eyes shining fiercely. "We will find them."

"Yes, we will. I think our next stop has to be the Nether."

Samael, who'd been silent up until now, spoke. "It's the only plausible place that a demon could have taken the women. Otherwise we would be able to feel their presence."

"We will have to go into the Nether and look for them and if need be into hell," Clay stated.

"Remie and I'll have to stay behind if you go into hell." Sal's expression showed that he wasn't too happy with that idea.

"I know. In that case just having the two of you in the Nether with us is help enough. I know that you can't go any further than that, and I would not expect you to bend the rules."

"It could be a trap, Clay," Salathiel stated.

"It most likely is a trap. Whoever has the girls has planned this, and there is no way that he or she will just let them go. I'm willing to offer myself up in their place."

Samael placed his hand on Clay's shoulder. "I'm willing to do the same. Now come on, we need to get to the Nether. I am sure it is being watched."

Clay placed his hand out and the other men placed their hands one on top of the other. No words needed to be said. They stood there in unity, and then each of them faded and headed for the Nether.

Chapter Sixteen

Eva awakened at some point in the night—at least she thought it was night—to a small flickering light that was off in a corner of the room. There were also intermittent noises that she could hear. Some things were hard to understand, but she did hear a few distinct cries and screams. Some time in the night she'd been moved and placed in an actual room.

There was a small bed that both she and Lili had been placed on, the only amenity in the room. For all intents and purposes they were in a basic jail cell. The doorway was made of bars, and the walls were still the rock of before. From what she could tell, this wasn't the Nether anymore. They were in hell. The place where all a human's nightmares could happen and most likely would.

Magic. It had to be dark demon magic on Asmoday's part. She was still leaning against the granite wall holding Lili. She studied the light and held on to it as if it were a beacon. It kept her mind from racing and playing out different scenarios.

The revolting demon had come back, and she'd found out his name was Vestis. But he hadn't touched her. He'd brought food and water for the frail little beings, as he liked to call them, along with a small lamp that just barely lit the cave walls, let alone the floor.

So seeing as Asmoday fed her and Lili it meant he didn't want them dead, at least not at the moment. She held on to that fact, using it to keep herself going. The food and water had been a welcome addition right along with the lamp.

"Lover boy is taking his own sweet time to find the two of you," Asmoday said in a mocking voice.

She gulped, and her gaze traveled up Asmoday's

form. He'd scared her by just appearing suddenly. For someone who'd been a demon, it was odd to have been scared by that. She had to wonder if she were turning more and more human. Not even just day by day, but minute by minute with time clicking away, was she slipping so far into being a human that she would soon be a distant memory as a demon?

She'd spent too much time daydreaming and thinking about being back with Clay. She had to keep better watch. She couldn't let Asmoday win this. He stood before her in his demon form, as pale as the moon with eyes of red. Everything about him seemed serpentine. He even had a forked tongue; the only exception was the fact that he had arms and legs. If she'd been anyone else she'd have been scared of what he looked like. He was meant to be terrifying. But having been a demon herself, this visage wasn't difficult to take.

"Startle you, did I? So lost in thought you didn't hear me come in." He kneeled beside her, taking one of her curls in his hand, stroking the bit of hair slowly. He chuckled as if he'd made a joke.

"Fucking let me go, Asmoday."

"Oh, that dirty mouth of yours gives me a fucking hard on."

"I think saying your own fucking name gives you an erection."

"Oh baby, please keep talking dirty to me. Daddy likes," he jeered and grabbed his cock.

She rolled her eyes and tried to not focus on him gripping himself. He wanted her to see what he was doing, and she didn't want to give him that pleasure. Eva noticed that Lili didn't stir. She nudged her then regarded him with an expression of disdain. She was still breathing, which reduced some of the worry. The fact that Lili was sleeping through all that was happening was a concern.

"What did you to do Lili, you bastard?"

"Just making sure she sleeps nice and sweet until I am ready to play puppet master."

"You keep your fucking claws off her. You hurt her, and I'm going to kill you, Asmoday."

Asmoday burst out laughing. "You're in no position to tell me what to do or not to do, Eva. As for killing me, bitch please. It would take a whole lot more than you to get rid of me."

"Try me!" she threatened.

"Oh my dear, sweet girl, that's the idea. My plan is to try you in so many ways till you beg and scream for mercy and then to do it all over again." He tugged at the curl until a sharp pain generated at the roots from his pulling.

She bit her lip as to not cry out in pain. She didn't want to give him that pleasure.

"Mmm, I admire your spunk, Eva. This is the one reason I hated to see you start to act like the good little girl that you aren't."

He let go of the curl and brought a clawed finger to her chin, forcing her to have to see him. He licked his lips, his sharp teeth gnashing together.

"It is what it is. Why not get over this fucking shit of being good and come back to the dark side with me? We could rule the world."

"Rule the world? Are you forgetting that the world doesn't belong to us and never has?"

"Oh, but it could, Eva, it could. I want you by my side. I need your greed and your lusts fueling me."

"You're fucking nuts if you think that we could even begin to take over anything. Even you aren't that powerful."

"No, you're right. I'm not." An evil grin spread

across his face. "You are, though."

She knew that her confusion had to show on her face.

"What the fuck are you talking about?"

"You're the key I've been looking for, for all these years. Basically, my dear Eva, you're the yin to my yang, and the fucking chocolate in my pudding."

"My god you've freaking lost it. What kind of key are you talking about?"

"Did you know the true reason they don't want you to be a demon?"

She'd been about to say something else when his words stopped her cold.

"What the fuck are you talking about now?"

"They didn't want you to be a demon for the very reason I want you to be one. You are the key to ruling the world. Anyone that has you has the power. It's mighty great that you're fucking hot too."

He put his hand on her jean-clad leg and squeezed her thigh. She kept her leg still though the urge to puke and to jerk away was strong. It wasn't his appearance that did it to her. It was what he represented. The temptation that he was laying at her feet was beyond real. Could she resist it? She had to or she'd doom them all to an uncertain fate. *Clay, where are you? I need you now more than ever. Help me.*

She bit her lip, closed her eyes and clenched her fingers together. She sensed her own ability to be childish when she found herself wishing that if she just closed her eyes he'd be gone when she opened them back up.

When she felt she was centered again she peered through her lashes, hoping beyond hope that Asmoday had left again. She had no such luck. He was still there looking at her with such an intense mien it made her uncomfortable.

"Just let me go, Asmoday. Find yourself another puppet to play with."

"I have the one I want and using the strings that I like."

How could she have missed that he was this crazy? The answer to that was that he'd hidden it well and she'd wanted to just have fun. She'd had the urge to piss off Clay and to try to make him jealous as well.

Which she'd succeeded doing but that act had put Lili in danger. Once again she'd done something selfish and for herself and look where it got her. This was all because Asmoday was crazy, but it was also because she'd allowed greed and selfishness to rule her life.

She gawked when Asmoday stood and started to dance around the room.

"What in the world are you doing?" She frowned, watching him.

"Dancing." He did some crazy spin.

"Yeah, I got that part, but why?"

Asmoday had the most god-awful grin on his face, and she couldn't help but wonder what was going through his head.

"I have you where I want you, and I'm told that Clay and Samael have come into the Nether. That means I will have them both soon."

Eva's eyes widened, and Asmoday burst out laughing as he continued to do his strange victory dance. How would she stop him? How could she stop him? She couldn't let him hurt the others. She'd have to do what he wanted as much as it hurt to even think of it. But to protect the others was the main goal.

"If I do what you want me to do, will you leave the others alone?" She said the words before she could talk herself out of them.

Asmoday stopped dancing so quickly he almost fell over. Eva found herself wishing he had. It would have been at least a bit of humor when all she wanted to do was to scream and cry. She squared her shoulders. She couldn't let him see her pain no matter how much this all hurt. Asmoday would love to see that, and she wouldn't give him any satisfaction.

"What? You'd deny me my fun?" He had the nerve to look disbelieving.

"I want this madness to stop."

"Damn you, Eva. You wish to deny me my fucking fun!"

Blinking Eva looked at him. He was an enigma. A crazy fucking paradox, she thought. "Asmoday, you're not making any sense."

"I lied. Samael and Clay haven't been seen coming for you."

"You lied?"

"Yep, I lied. I'm a demon. Why would you presume I would give you the truth?"

He was right in this instance. Why would she have expected him to be truthful with her? He loved to toy with her. The only assumption she could truly make was that he would lie to her and that everything he said would be some form of a lie. This meant that what he said was the truth. Samael and Clay had come through the Nether. They were looking for them. She wouldn't let Asmoday on to the fact that she knew he was lying yet again.

The sad part of it was that she and Lili weren't in the Nether. This meant that Clay and Samael were going on a wild goose chase looking for them. It would be one of the first places to look for them so she couldn't fault them. One of the reasons Asmoday was so thrilled was that he had two of the strongest demons going around in circles. If Clay or Samael didn't kick Asmoday's ass, she definitely would.

"Tell me this. What will you do to them when you do have them?"

"I plan to let them both see me violate you along with that pretty little sister of yours."

"After all of that, you think I would agree to do what you want?"

"You will have no other choice."

"There are always choices."

"Hmm, and let me see, how have you been doing with choices so far, Eva?" He gave a bellowing laugh. "Yeah, you're not good at making choices. Well unless they are choices that benefit you anyways."

She'd let him think that. Perhaps that would be her advantage, him thinking that she was all out for her herself as she had been before. She had to face it; she was going to need an advantage. Human versus demon usually meant bad times for the human. However, she wasn't going down like a bitch. She would fight until the end to save Lili and herself.

****

Clay and the others moved through the Nether, searching the different caves for any signs of the women, and were coming up empty. Most of the demons and angels that frequented the place that they spoke to stated they hadn't seen any other beings besides demons and angelic beings. Nor had they sensed them in the area.

"He has to have them cloaked somehow. Making it so we can't detect them but neither can others of our respective kinds," Clay said in frustration.

"If it were going to be easy, Clay, we'd have found them already," Salathiel said in a firm voice.

"Sal, could you be any more the bringer of bad news, please?" Samael asked gruffly.

"Someone has to be the one to state the facts," Sal said in his defense.

The angel was so big that his wings brushed against the cave walls. Some of the tunnels were so tight that they had to move through it single file. They were in one such tunnel at the moment, and moods weren't the best. Clay felt his frustration building even more and just as he was about to blow, Remie's hand touched his shoulder and calmed him.

"You guys need to lighten up. We can't be tearing at each other if we want to get this figured out," Remiel stated.

"You're right—thanks, Remie. I'm sorry, Samael and Salathiel. Forgive my ill temper."

Both males chimed in. "It's okay, Clay."

His diplomacy was a reason Remiel was in the group, though it wasn't the only one. Perhaps being the 'dream angel' as some called him really was one of the reasons why he could get someone to calm down as easily as he did. Clay was thankful for him being around. If they fell apart before they even started, all would be for naught.

The men traveled for a few more hours, having completely explored the Nether, and they were now on the descent down towards hell. They were so close to the edge that one could hear shrieking and moaning and the proverbial gnashing of teeth. The path was wider than it had been for a while, so Clay turned to Remie and Sal.

"This is where you two turn back." He clasped both of their arms tightly.

"You know that if we could go farther, we would," Remie said solemnly.

"He's right," Sal agreed.

Samael walked up beside them and placed his hand on Remie's shoulder. "Yes, we both know, and we are grateful. Isn't that correct, Clay?"

"Yes, very true. Truly we can't thank you enough. It would have taken us forever to go through the Nether. Even though the girls aren't here, the two of you saved us a massive amount of time," Clay affirmed with a nod of his head.

"We will keep vigilant above and in the Nether for signs of Lili and Eva," Salathiel promised.

Clay let go of their arms, and with one last nod, he turned back to descend down into the bowels of hell in search of Eva and Liliana with Samael at his side. He would focus on Eva and think of times past when they were happy together. That would get him through this, and once he found her, he'd make sure she stayed happy. He wasn't letting her go, no matter what.

Chapter Seventeen

Asmoday had finally gotten bored and had left her and Liliana alone. In fact it had been a few days since she'd seen him. He'd done one nice thing though and that was taking off the shackles so they could move about freely. That freedom came with a warning that if they tried to escape there were worse demons on the other side of the bars than he or Vestis. The only demon she came into contact with was the vile Vestis.

The good thing was he seemed to be more interested in Asmoday than he was in harassing her and Lili. She'd heard them on the other side of those magical bars, and she didn't want to chance it. Least not yet, not until Liliana came back to her and was able to move on her own. One thing it seemed that Asmoday had forgotten—Eva had been a demon too. She knew the place like the back of her hand, and she'd use that to her benefit.

Although she thought Asmoday was crazy in even suggesting that she'd try. It wasn't an option for Eva as Lili was still out cold from whatever spell that Asmoday had put her under. Speaking of crazy, she wondered how long it would take her to get off her rocker and end up like Asmoday. No, she wouldn't think like that. Her focus should be on waking Lili up and getting them out of there. Eva sat next to her on the bed and held her hand tightly as she talked to her as if she were awake.

"Remember when we were children and we used to go into our secret hideout that we had in the hills behind the foster home?" She pretended Lili answered with a yes and continued talking.

"Those were the days, yeah? The times when we'd run around catching frogs, snakes and terrifying our foster mother with our tomboyish ways."

She watched the rise and fall of Lili's chest, hoping that by talking to her she'd snap out of it. Nothing. It was as if she was sleeping beauty and couldn't be awakened unless she was kissed. She unfortunately didn't have the right equipment to be the Prince.

She lay down beside Lili, putting her head on her chest, still holding her hand.

"I'm truly sorry, Lili, for everything. I shouldn't have ever cursed you in the garden." Her thoughts turned inward, and once more she found herself in the past as she reminisced about a time gone by.

****

At the Tigris River

She'd gone looking for Lilith and Samael. Tired of playing second fiddle to Lilith when it came to Adam, she'd wanted them to feel her pain and anguish. Eva had come upon them about to make love. She'd been furious. Not only did Lilith have Adam wrapped about her little finger, but she also had the angel Samael.

"I love you, Lilith. I would risk everything to be with you." Eva had watched Lilith smile at Samael.

"I love you too, Samael. You have given up so much for me."

"And he is about to give up so much more." They'd both gasped and pulled apart, staring at Eve as she stood above them with her arms across her chest.

"Who's this female, Samael?"

"I'm Adam's new wife, Eve. And you must be this Lilith he cannot stop talking about." She'd spoken before Samael could interrupt.

"Eve, what are you doing here? Why aren't you back in Eden with Adam?" Eva had smirked as Samael had covered their bodies with a robe, as if she hadn't

already seen their nakedness.

"Making sure you both get what you deserve." Liliana had clearly looked puzzled, not knowing what was going on.

"What we deserve? Why are you speaking such foolishness? Leave us be, and go back to the Garden of Eden," Lilith had dared to order.

"Oh, I will be going back, but not before I do what I came here to do. That would be imparting a gift to you that will ensure my happiness and give me much pleasure."

"Eve, stop before things get out of hand." She'd heard Samael's warning, but she hadn't been scared of him. His words had only fueled the fire of her anger.

"What will you do, Fallen? That's right, Samael, you will not do anything. You've been left bereft of your power for the choices you've made. So what'll you do?" Eve had laughed in spite of the anger she felt coming off Samael in waves. He wasn't going to stop her. She would continue on her path. It had been the choice she was destined to make. She couldn't hesitate, and she'd had to see it through.

"I curse you both." She'd heard Lilith gasp and watched as she pressed herself against Samael. Finish this, Eve, she'd told herself. *"I curse you, Samael, to be doomed to walk this Earth with knowledge of who you were and the awareness of the love you have for Lilith."*

"Is that all, Eve? That isn't a curse; it's what's already in place," Samael had taunted.

"Oh, don't rush me. I've only just begun." A wicked grin on her face, she waited for a moment as she saw Samael trying to soothe Lilith.

"Now let's see. Where was I? Oh, yes. You, Samael, will know Lilith and love Lilith throughout eternity. All the same, she will never know you. You can't

remind her either. *The knowledge of what she has done has to come from her."* She'd giggled and then looked directly at Lilith. *"And you, dear, get the worst of it. You will not know who you are, and Samael can't tell you. You will die, and every time you die, you will come back and be that much further from the truth. This curse will last until you remember your name and what you did to me."*

The tears that had fallen from Lilith's eyes had actually given her pause for a moment. She'd wondered if she'd done the right thing. Again that voice in her head whispered that she'd come too far. She needed to finish what she'd started, and she was right to be doing so.

"Why are you doing this? What did I do to you?"

"Do you know how hard it is to live with a man who doesn't love you? Who pines after another woman and compares everything you do to what she did? No, you don't, because everyone wants Lilith! Lilith even had an angel choose to fall just for the pleasure of being between her thighs. I was the one taken from his rib, made to be his. The perfect fit for him and yet he pines for you!"

"You must be mistaken! Stop this! Go back to him, please, Eve. This is madness!" Eve had ignored Lilith's pleading back then.

"Oh, I am going back, but I'll not stop it. The curse stands." She'd laughed, though even to her own ears it had sounded hollow.

"Eve, no good will come of this," Samael had warned her once more as he held his crying Lilith.

"Maybe you're right, but I feel better already."

****

Present time Asmoday's jail cell

She'd been such a bitch. It was no wonder Liliana didn't have much to do with her once she found out the truth, and she really couldn't blame her. That was just one example of the dirty shit she'd done to Liliana. The worst of it truly, as it had begun the vicious cycle.

She whispered softly against Liliana's chest the words that she should have uttered long ago. "I'm sorry, Lili, truly sorry, and I know I have a long way to prove it. But I will prove it to you."

She could hear the steady beat of Liliana's heart, and it was soothing music to her ears. Every beat of that very human heart reminded her that it wasn't over yet. Asmoday hadn't won as long as their hearts still beat.

If she got them out of this—no, change that. *When* she got them out of this, she'd do whatever it took to show Lili and Samael that she was sorry. The life that she'd led up until she'd been changed to human was a travesty, a complete sham of a life. She wanted to be with Clay and to enjoy what she hadn't before. No more plotting so much that she didn't have time to enjoy life. If she were given another chance after this, she'd make the most of it.

So much time spent being greedy and wanting what someone else had. Where had that gotten her? It had taken her on the track to nowhere and fast. On the outside things had seemed great, but in truth if she looked inside of herself she'd hated what she'd become. It wasn't being a demon that was the bad thing, for all demons played a part in the way life flowed.

It was the things that she'd done knowingly to her sister and to Samael. There were so many things that she missed out on because of her choices. Kamuel was right, too long had she listened to the snake. Epiphany of epiphanies, she now knew that snake in the grass had always been Asmoday and unless she made her stand this time, it would just continue to go on and on.

"You're going to lay on me all night?"

Lili! She sat up and took in Liliana's face. She didn't seem any worse for wear at all.

"How are you doing? Are you okay?" She touched her face, felt her forehead to make sure she didn't feel hot. Lili batted her hands away.

"Of course I'm fine. Still seem to be stuck in this godforsaken place with you. But I'm fine. I feel more rested than I ever have in my life."

"You've been out for a while."

"How long's a while?"

Eva didn't really want to tell her, but she couldn't lie to her. That was one of the issues Lili had with her before. Lies. The telling of lies damaged their relationship, and the kind of dishonesties that slipped so easily off one's tongue always caused so much pain that perhaps there was no return. The amount of pain she'd caused Lili was mind boggling, and she could see why she found it so hard to believe that she loved her. She did, but she was just a bitch when it came to jealousy, a mistrust that she was finding out she shouldn't have even had.

"A few days. But I've been keeping watch over you and no one's bothered you."

"No one's bothered me?" Lili placed emphasis on the 'no one'. "You mean a demon hasn't touched me? 'Cause this isn't home anymore, even I can see that."

"Yes, that's exactly what I mean. I have a confession to make."

Lili smirked. "Oh? What would that be?" She'd crossed her arms over her chest.

She wouldn't let this escalate into something that it wasn't, so she let the snide remark pass and finished what she was saying.

"I've been having dreams for quite a while. Dreams of a snake, a demon and the like, and I fear it's my fault this has happened. I should have told Clay. Shit, I should have told either you or Samael. But I thought I could handle this all on my own."

Disbelief crossed Lili's face first, and then what Eva could assume was anger did as well.

"You mean to tell me that you had some inkling about all this and you said nothing? Not even to Clay whom you're living with?"

"It's not like that at all, Lili. I mean the dreams came. I thought at first they were just silly dreams of the past and some erotic dreams because of frustration. But I didn't really think at first that it was something to worry about."

"Did you just hear yourself? You said at first. This means there was a point when you finally thought something was wrong, Eva!"

"Lili, haven't you ever done something that you regretted and you wanted to make amends? Or have you always just been perfect?" She was tired of being cut down; she'd stand up for herself. She hadn't wanted all of this to happen, but by god she wasn't going to be treated badly because of this either.

Lili stopped to stare at her, and her demeanor softened. "I've done things I wasn't proud of, yes."

"I didn't hide this with some sort of agenda in mind, Lili. I honestly believed that I could figure out how to stop the dreams. Hell, I even thought it was because I'd been a demon that the dreams were somehow just memories or subconscious … I don't know. Either way I thought I could handle it."

"But you couldn't."

She put her head down and sighed.

"Yes, I know that now and all I am trying to say is that I'm sorry and that if I can I will get you out of this. No matter what happens to me, I will get you out of this."

"Look at me."

Eva lifted her head, keeping her eyes intent on Lili. She was scared of what she would see there, but found that Lili's eyes were swarming with tears just as hers were.

"I've been angry with you for a long while. I wanted you to feel the same pain that I've felt. But that isn't right for me to feel like. I know that, and I've had to ask forgiveness for that. I don't want to fight anymore, and I'm scared of letting you back into my life."

"Lili, I…"

Lili shook her head. "No, let me finish what I'm saying."

She'd been about to apologize again, but it seemed Lili needed to get something out.

"I said all that to say this. I love you, and that hasn't ever stopped. However, it doesn't mean I will allow you to hurt me or Samael again. Please don't fuck this up, Eva. If you do I have to cut you loose. Get it?"

Oh she definitely got it. This was her last chance, something she'd known all along but now it was there out in the open. It wasn't an idle threat. It was the implicit truth.

"Yes, I got it, Lili. Please hear me out."

"Go ahead. You heard me out, so now it's my time to chill out and listen."

Lili settled her back against the wall and drew her legs up to hug them close to her body.

"I know I fucked up royally. I will get you out of this. I love you. I know it's hard to believe after the shit I pulled. I know I have a long road ahead of me for you to believe what I'm saying is true. I'm willing to do so."

Lili didn't say anything. She just took ahold of Eva's hands and squeezed gently. Eva would take that to mean Lili had heard what she had to say and that they'd take things slow.

"Now, Vestis has left us some food. You need to eat. You haven't eaten anything the last few days." Asmoday was a demon who liked the finer things that the earthly realm held, and it showed in the amenities that their "jail" held.

She reached over and grabbed the water bottle and ham sandwiches that had been left for them. She was surprised she didn't have to pull maggots off them, but again she knew Asmoday was keeping them healthy for a reason. It wouldn't do for the prisoners to get sickly before he could dangle the prize before his adversary.

Both women settled back on the makeshift bed and ate in silence. Who knew how long they were going to be there. At least now she didn't have to worry about her and Lili going at it while they were in this predicament. They were quite possibly on the road to recovery and mending their relationship.

Chapter Eighteen

Asmoday had settled in a large throne in the bowels of hell with Vestis at his feet and several other minions of hell flitting about here and there. A cacophony of sound filled the air as several of the demons fought amongst themselves. With a growl of impatience Asmoday vaulted from his seat and roared until there was utter silence, which in itself was a major feat seeing as it was hell.

Demons scattered and cowered before Asmoday, and finally when he had their attention he hunkered back into his seat. The chair was large, but even so it was dwarfed by Asmoday's large stature. It also allowed him to stare down at the others.

He'd picked each demon for the task at hand and had to say he was quite pleased with those he'd chosen. They were at attention standing in a somewhat perfect line. Asmoday smirked. *This was how hell should be—all demons should bow before his greatness. It was time to make sure that all the demons in his command were behind him a hundred percent. And if they weren't? He'd kill them.*

"Now that I have your attention, there is a matter we need to discuss. There are two demons that are looking for the women I have. I want them brought to me if you find them. Subdue them, but do not kill them. That's my job. Do you all understand?"

There was growling, snarling with a lot of bellowing, but Asmoday knew that even the dumbest of demons knew what he wanted and would follow that order. After all this was his house and what he said was what everyone did.

"But, Master, if they are demons, why would we have to fight them?"

It was the demon Abadan who spoke up. He was one of the lesser night demons of hell. The other demons backed up, leaving Abadan to stand before Asmoday, whose sharp gaze pierced the demon and made him back up in fear.

"For one, it's because you do whatever I fucking tell you to do. Secondly, they are our enemies; they are coming to take what is mine. But the pleasure of their death is all mine. Got it, Abadan?"

Abadan hissed, shifting his eyes left and right as if to see if any of the other demons would take up for him. When no one said anything, Asmoday smirked.

"And we are waiting for what, Abadan?"

"I got it … I fucking got it!"

Asmoday was on the demon quickly, his hands wrapped about the demon's neck, his face inches from the trembling fiend. Asmoday tightened his fingers on the demon's throat, watching him struggling and grabbing at his hands.

"Please, Asmo, please. I'm sorry. I won't do it again, Master," Abadan said between gargling gasps as he clutched frantically at the hands that held him in such a tight grip.

"Now you tremble in fear." He sneered at the cowering Abadan. "I will fucking rip your head from your body if you ever talk to me like that again. You'd better recognize who I am." There was a cacophony of sound as the other demons began making snorts, grunts and growls.

"I know, Master, I know. Forgive … forgive!" Abadan's dark eyes were almost bulging from his head, and he was starting to froth at the mouth as he thrashed desperately.

"I should kill you, Abadan, for your insolence."

Asmoday had the other demon up in the air with

his feet dangling off the ground, a sure sign of his power to all who wished to oppose him. He looked at every last demon in the line.

"Which one of you other motherfuckers wish to start some shit?" When no one said anything, he snapped his teeth together triumphantly and brought Abadan face to face with him.

"I will let your ill temper pass because if I were a freaking pathetic peon like you I'd be pissed too. Now shut the fuck up and get back in line." He tossed Abadan to the ground hard, hearing him cry out in pain and then scramble to his feet. Asmoday growled, giving the other demon a flash of his jagged teeth. Abadan skulked back into formation.

"Now that we got that shit straightened out, and you all know who's boss here, it's time for you to get out there and do what I need done."

Asmoday made sure he looked every demon in the eye, including Vestis, who had moved to stand with the others. They lowered their gazes either in respect or out of fear, as a demon of a lesser station was apt to do. Even Vestis lowered his eyes and cringed before him.

Asmoday couldn't stop the snigger that fell from his curling lips as no one made an attempt to usurp his power. It was the main reason that Luc had named him one of his generals. With one last look at the others Asmoday strutted back over to his throne and flounced down into it.

"Vestis, come, sit at my feet again."

Forever faithful Vestis scurried over and placed himself at his feet. Just like a good pet should. Asmoday stroked his fingers through Vestis's long hair. Not looking at the others, he barked out his next order.

"Go and find the ones called Clay and Samael. Bring them to me in one piece." In a flurry of wings the room cleared and only Vestis and Asmoday were left. Vestis put his chin on Asmoday's knee.

"Asmo, I was wondering why you didn't let me go and look for Clay and Samael like the others?"

"I wanted you here. Don't tell me you're going to make a mistake like the other devil Abadan."

"No, I would never, Asmo." Asmoday smirked as Vestis wrung his hands together.

"So that wasn't you questioning me just now, Vee?"

"Not in the way that Abadan did." Vestis's words ended with a whine.

That's a good pet. I can always count on you, can't I?"

"Oh yes, Asmo, you can. I'm always on your side and willing to do whatever you need me to do."

Asmoday could not stop the grin that crossed over his face, and he continued to stroke his fingers through the white locks on Vestis's head. "This is why you're going to be my second in command once we get rid of Eva's crew."

"Sounds like the perfect plan, Master." Vestis's rubbed his cheek on Asmoday's lap.

"It is a textbook plan. Getting rid of them will allow me to use Eva to the greatest benefit."

"But how will you get her to agree to it?"

"She will have no choice once they're dead. She will want to be with me then. Clay stands in the way of all of it, as does her sister. If they are gone, I don't have to worry about them changing her mind."

He stood, shoving Vestis off of him. Just talking about what he would do with Eva once the time came filled him with the lust for blood. The vision of Liliana's ripe body dripping with blood as he violated her over and over again was another act that he couldn't wait to fulfill.

"My taste for blood is getting worse. I must end this soon. How are our captives doing?"

"They're doing fine at the moment, Asmo. Of course Lili has woken up. I've kept the others away from them with threats and warnings."

Asmoday nodded. "I didn't expect that she would stay asleep too long. In fact her being awake is perfectly fitting, so that I can use her in the capacity that she is needed. Seeing that Clay and Samael will come looking for them here now that the Nether is no longer an option."

"But what if they're plotting?"

"What of it?" He assumed he meant Eva and Lili.

"Well you don't want that, do you?" Vestis still sat on the ground where Asmoday had pushed him, though he'd righted himself.

"Who cares if they plot?"

"They could come up with a plan to escape or worse, try to kill you."

"They can try all they want. They can't beat me. I'm unbeatable. They're all inferior to me."

He'd had such a long time to plan all of this that he was confident in his own plan and power. Screw them. He had this and did have them right where he wanted them. The others were either for him or against him, and he'd deal with them accordingly.

"Now I'm going to head back to Eva and Lili. You carry on my orders and make sure the others follow them, and you'll be rewarded quite well." Asmoday didn't wait for him to answer. He left so that the only thing that attested to his present was a swirling white vapor.

****

Vestis stared at the swirling emission that had come from Asmoday until it dissipated and he could breathe easy. He'd always wanted to please Asmoday, but now he'd realized the demon he'd admired had fully gone off the deep end. Sure they were all a bit crazy; it was inherent because of the Fall and what they were. But for Asmoday to have lost it this completely ... why hadn't he seen it? He tried to think if there had been signs, but could not come up with anything concrete.

If anyone were going to rule anything, it would be Vestis. He, after all, embodied corruption. What better ingredient to the destruction of the world than corruption? They didn't call him Vestis the Venal for nothing. He got to his feet and meandered over to the vacant throne and lowered himself into it. What a perfect fit.

"Oh yes, this feels so very right. I think Luc would rather have me sitting here. It must have been an oversight on his part to put Asmo here instead. Perhaps speaking to him and letting him know what Asmo is about will score some brownie points for me, along with this throne."

He could not help but speak the words aloud so that he could speak them into existence. He'd play along and bide his time, playing the perfect pet that Asmoday was so apt to call him, and then he'd strike. Asmoday was too caught up in himself, and that was going to be his downfall. He'd make sure of it.

Asmoday thought to give him sloppy seconds. No, Vestis wanted it all, and he planned to take it all. *Oh Asmo, if you'd only treated me as an equal today things might have been different. Right now I will let you have the glory and one tomorrow soon it will be my time to have the victory and to sit in this very throne.*

He didn't need to rule the world as Asmoday wanted. He just wanted to rule the demons that had been in this very chamber. He'd show Luc that he could do a better job than Asmoday ever had or ever would. One thing about him was that he knew how to bide his time. Rushing into this quickly could get him killed before he'd even had a chance to get word to Luc and see what he'd want him to do. Asmoday was cunning or else he wouldn't have been able to hide his intentions from Luc.

Vestis had learned from the best, and his time was coming and very soon. He'd give Asmoday time to get his plan rolling and then he would make a visit to Luc and play out his hand. One thing he was good at was a poker face. It wasn't so hard to play at that with Asmoday, seeing as his desire for him was real, but that was where it stopped. Loyalty was something that demons had very little of unless true leadership showed up.

Chapter Nineteen

Eva held her breath as Asmoday entered the room. The determination in his steps made it clear that they would not like what he was about to do. Lili shrank against Eva and held on to her so tightly her fingers bruised her skin.

"Don't let him take me," Lili whispered against her ear. "Please, Eva, don't let him take me again." Lili had already recounted the story of how Oz O'Dea had come to the shop when she'd been opening up and the next thing she'd known she'd woken up in the Nether. He hadn't hurt her, but he had terrified her.

"What do you want, Asmoday?" She tried to inject a confidence in her voice that she wasn't feeling as she held her trembling sister in her arms. She scooted up on the bed, urging Lili to get behind her as she confronted Asmoday. Lili scrambled behind her, gripping Eva.

"What do you think I'm here for, Eva?" She could hear the humor in his voice, and once again she was reminded he was crazy as fuck.

"If I could even begin to understand you, Asmoday, then I would have the answer to that question. Since I have no clue, how about you just quit beating around the fucking bush and tell me?"

"Motherfuck, girl, your anger is a sweet aphrodisiac. You do this just to turn me on, don't you?"

She sighed. "If I wanted you, really desired you, your stupid ass wouldn't have to ask that question."

"Then perhaps I will slake my lusts on your poor sister there. She looks so ripe for the taking." Lili gave out a shriek at his words.

"How many times have I told you, you will not touch her, Asmoday?"

"You've said a lot of things, dear Eva, which you haven't proven to me one way or the other. You'll have to do some proving of that to me. But for now I think I will satisfy myself in causing your sister more terror." Asmoday snapped his fingers, and two rather large demons appeared. One grabbed Eva and the other Liliana.

Liliana and Eva both screamed and struggled against their captors fruitlessly. Asmoday let out a loud bellowing hoot as he watched them fight to no avail.

"It's of no use. Your fighting only makes things harder for you. Struggle as much as you like. It only adds to my pleasure. It's time for my games to begin." As he uttered in the ancient language, the almost pleasant room disappeared to reveal that it truly had been just an illusion. The cave was dark and dank, with what appeared to be water sliding down its walls and onto the floor. The heat within the room because of all the fires was close to unbearable. Both women gasped for air as they tried to adjust their breathing to the change in temperature. The random fire here and there was what made it possible for their eyes to see.

"Asmoday! Please, I beg of you—let Liliana go, and I'll do anything you want me to."

"You're going to do that anyway, Eva. So killing your lover and the other two will be just an added bonus." Lili yelled profanities, kicking and struggling against the demon who held her.

"What could you possibly gain from all of this? Luc will kill you."

"Luc is none the wiser. It will stay that way and then when it's too late, you and I will rule all."

"I'm not some puzzle piece that will help you rule the world."

"You're wrong. You have the power to make me

strong. I've scrutinized through the years. Your greed and lust fuel me and make me stronger."

"Then you should realize what you're saying is futile and beyond crazy. Nothing I wanted came to maturity and lasted."

"That's because you didn't have me in your equation." He had an answer for everything she said, and she could tell he wasn't going to be deterred.

"Then I will add you to the equation, but you have to promise me you won't hurt Lili. Please do this for me." It was more than obvious at this point that if that demon didn't have hold of her, she'd be lying prostrate on the ground. Begging him to not hurt Lili wasn't an issue for her. If he wanted begging, he'd get it. But the bastard would pay in the end for that embarrassment.

Asmoday looked as if he would consider it. He leaned his head to the side and tapped a finger against his lips.

"Let her go," he said to the demon that held her. She fell to the floor as the demon did what was asked of him, though he did not move away.

"Strip for me, Eva," Asmoday ordered. There was no change in his tone. It was as if it were something he'd asked her many times.

She knew it was a test. She glanced once at Lili to see how she was faring. Though Liliana had tears streaming down her face, she was not as bad off as she could be. If she could get Asmoday to free Lili then all of this would be worth it.

"No, don't, Eva," Lili pleaded with her.

"Stop, Lili, I have to. If it makes it easier for you to close your eyes, then close your eyes. But I have to do this." Something in her voice must have registered with Lili that she was serious, and she calmed down. Eva nodded at Lili, and then squaring her shoulders, she faced

Asmoday.

Walking closer to Asmoday she unbuttoned her blouse slowly then parted it until she exposed her bra. The shirt slipped off her shoulders as she shrugged out of it. She unsnapped the front bra clasp and opened the bra, letting it hang to the sides.

She'd try to make as if she were enjoying it. She was going to do anything to get him to release Lili. As vain as Asmoday was, if he thought she were enjoying giving him a show, then he would be rather thrilled. The clue that she was right was the lustful grin he had spreading across his face as he beheld her breasts.

"Ahh, now that's pure beauty, Eva. You have such lovely breasts."

Eva dropped her hands to her sides, not continuing till he told her to. He'd told her to strip, but she knew he liked to give orders and tonight would be no different.

"Carry on, Eva. I didn't tell your sexy ass to stop."

"Just making sure you didn't want to just ogle at my breasts some more." She couldn't help that snide remark.

"Oh I'm going to do more than that. So much more than that to you and you'll love every fucking bit of it."

Shit, this sucker really was all about himself. If there ever were a more narcissistic male she didn't want to meet up with him. Asmoday was enough. She'd heard that Luc was narcissist, but then he was supposed to be glorious to behold. She'd never had the pleasure or displeasure to meet up with him.

After taking her bra off the rest of the way, she worked off her pants and underwear, tossing them to the floor as well. Her body held a fine sheen of perspiration because of the heat. Asmoday's gaze traveled up her body, slowly taking in every nuance of her bared flesh.

"Turn around slowly."

She did so even with all of the eyes taking in her every move. The slow turn was almost a dance with the added music of her sister sobbing in the background and the snarls coming from the other two demons, along with the general sounds of the underworld.

She turned her thoughts inward and thought of Clay. How he held her and made her feel safe. He was her safety and with an assurance born of the love she would not deny anymore. If she ever got the chance to tell him she'd let him know it. Even if it never was returned, she had to tell him. She'd let him know she'd been lying when she said that all she wanted was a fuck from him. She would love to be able to experience that and more with him. Though as time went by with Asmoday that seemed like a distant dream that would never happen.

She completed the turn and came face to face with Asmoday. He moved his clawed hands to cup her breasts. She could not suppress the shudder that went through her. It was one of revulsion.

The gleam in his eyes told her he figured that shudder to be something akin to pleasure. It was in that moment that the thought of him raping her became a reality. That's what it would be if he even tried touching her in that way. She didn't want him. The one she wanted was somewhere searching the inferno for her and Lili.

"We have the two you seek."

Asmoday's clawed hands tightened on her breast, and he uttered a curse. She'd heard the words just as he had. There was a brief second she didn't think he was going to let her go as his grip tightened yet again and then finally he removed his hands from her breasts. She kept her eyes tightly closed, biting her lip to stop crying out from the pain that radiated outward from his claws digging into her tender flesh.

The words sank in, and she opened her eyes. Asmoday clapped his hands in excitement. He grabbed her by her arm and pulled her along with him. She clawed at his hand trying to free herself to get back to Lili, who had heard the words as well and had begun struggling.

"Rahab, keep her here and don't let her free and by any means don't leave her. If you do I will violently end your life. Do you get that?"

"Master, I am yours to command. I've been in your legion since the beginning. I wouldn't ever perceive to go outside your rule."

Asmoday got Eva under control and drug her from the room kicking and screaming. She could hear Lili crying her name. The sound was heartbreaking. They were being separated, and she'd lost control.

"Asmoday, where in the hell are you taking me now? You have to let me stay with Lili."

"A very special place where I should have put you in the beginning," he growled out.

He thrust her into another area. This time it could literally pass for a hole in the wall. She fell to her knees only to scramble quickly up and try to rush back out, but it was too late. Asmoday had already shielded the room with his magic so she could not leave. Asmoday was gone, and there was no way out for her unless another demon knew how to scry away the spell.

She couldn't hold out hope for that so she moved about the tight space, investigating it and inspecting to see if there was a way out. Nothing. Not even a small crevice she could squeeze through. Asmoday was running worried. Clay and Samael must be close. Who else could the other demon have been speaking about that would cause Asmoday to drop everything he was doing?

Dropping to the ground in frustration, she wrapped her arms about her legs and sat her chin on her knees. *Think, Eva. What can I do to save my family? What could you give Asmoday to appease him and in the long run save the others?* The only thing she could possibly do was to give herself fully to Asmoday as a sacrifice. The others would not die because of her past mistakes nor would they die because of anything else she did in the present.

The issue at hand was that Asmoday was off his rocker and went back and forth on what he truly wanted from her. He'd said he wanted her but when she offered herself up in return for the freedom of the others, then he'd flip flop around on it. Perhaps the real deal was that he wanted her and wanted to kill them anyway.

Her eyes went wide at the thought. *That's it! That's what he wanted. The sick fuck wants me, but he wants to kill the others too.*

She'd have to get him to believe it was what she wanted too. He could lie. Well, then so could she. She was going to turn herself into an actress and give him what he wanted. She'd spent most of her life lying—what would be the difference now? The difference would be saving Liliana, Clay and Samael and defeating Asmoday.

Chapter Twenty

Clay and Samael had been so busy working their way through the labyrinth of tunnels in the abyss they didn't see the ambush. They'd fought long and hard, but the legion of demons kept coming until they were subdued. Clay was angry with himself for allowing complacency, which he contributed to having spent too much time above and away from the Netherworld.

Clay and Samael were tethered and upside down with their hands and legs bound by demon magic that glowed as it held them fast. He turned to see how Samael was faring. Besides the big scowl on his face, he appeared fine.

"Well I'd say struggling isn't going to help us," Samael uttered.

"Yeah, every time we do, the binding spell makes it even harder to move."

Besides the spell, they were surrounded by at least twenty demons though it was hard to count them when one was upside down. They'd been going through the maze of tunnels and had gotten comfortable with the fact that no one had stopped or opposed them coming in. That's when a horde of fiends had subdued them and bound them in the ancient trusses.

"Well I guess we will soon find out who put this plan into action," Clay said simply.

They'd been hanging upside down for about an hour. Though time was really relative down there, it let them put what was happening into perspective. Once they'd figured out they should stop struggling so the bindings would stop pulsating and hurting them, it was all a matter of just getting used to seeing their world from a different vantage point.

"Yeah, I expect we will. Whoever this bastard is,

we need to rip him or her to shreds for taking Lili and Eva."

"The odds aren't in our favor, being tied up as we are. Still I can't help thinking where there is a will there is definitely a way. But yes an ass whooping is in order. Though we shouldn't be surprised if whoever has them fights dirty."

"Oh but I'm expecting it."

"As am I, Samael, as am I."

"Just be prepared for anything to happen," Samael warned.

"I didn't come this far not to be, and I'm sure you didn't either. I'm sorry, bro. I should have heeded Kamuel and had someone watching both Eva and Lili. I didn't think Lili would be used to get to Eva. Though in retrospect when I think about what Kam said, I should've." He truly was sorry.

"No, there's no time for recriminations or being sorry. We got in this together, and we'll save our women together."

"Agreed and I think someone's coming. Have you noticed that our hosts have stopped all their growling and posturing?"

Both men turned their heads toward the entrance. The other fiends had quieted, though some of them were shifting nervously.

The demon that stepped into the room put a frown on Clay's face. He recognized this demon out of all legions that filled hell. It was the same demon that had made trouble for him and Eve in the garden. He'd whispered words of dissention in Eve's ears, told her she wanted things that she shouldn't. Letting her prescribe to wanting knowledge and power for things that they didn't need in the garden, this demon had been their downfall. This was the warning that Kamuel had given him, about an enemy of old.

"Clay, I can see you recognize me by that look in your eyes. Glad to see you brought along a friend to join in your demise. It's a win-win situation for me. Seeing as I plan to kill the lot of you anyways."

"I see nothing has changed in all the years that we've known one another. You're still hiding behind women," Clay jeered.

"I have to admit to a little bit of disappointment though, Clay. You had Salathiel and Remiel watching me when I was Oz. Yet none of you pieced anything together. I'd thought you would have been here long before now. You forced my hand, and I had to change my plan of attack."

"So it takes a legion to capture us. Once again you prove you have to hide behind females and a whole slew of others to do your dirty work."

"What's the point of being a leader if you can't have others do shit for you? Fuck yeah, I got others to do my shit, and I will continue to have others to do my dirty work." Asmoday began to pace back and forth in front of them, the excitement in his eyes evident. Clay didn't know what was going to happen, but he could only hope that he was there when this asshole died.

"Where are Eva and Liliana, and what have you done to them? You'd better not have done anything to them."

"I second that," Samael said through his teeth.

"You two are in no position to make any kind of demands. But in answer to your question, Clay, I have each of your females in a safe little hole designed just for them."

"What are your plans for us, Asmoday?" Clay had an idea, but he wanted it from the demon's own mouth.

"What's my plan for the lot of you?" Asmoday looked only too eager to tell and in fact he settled down on the floor with his hands on his knees to continue.

"I plan to kill you, Lili and lover boy over there. Eva I'm keeping for my own." The gleam in Asmoday's eyes spoke volumes to Clay. For one, he recognized the true craziness that existed in him, and two, this demon thought he had them over a barrel. All they had to do was play their cards right and perhaps, just perhaps, the four of them could get out of this unscathed.

"Oh and tell me what does your boss Luc say?" Samael asked Asmoday. Asmoday made a strange face and didn't answer.

He's off his bloody rocker. Clay peered over at his friend as Samael spoke in the way that fellow demons could to each other without others being privy.

A skill that apparently Asmoday had forgotten they possessed in his haste to subdue them. Clay's words informed him that he saw through Asmoday's façade as well. One thing that Clay was hoping for was that Asmoday would underestimate who he held captive and his own ability to conquer them.

He's forgotten we can talk to each other like this, Clay stated.

Yes, we need to make sure we use what we've got to destroy this fool.

Asmoday let out a noise, and Clay turned his attention back to him.

"Luc knows what he needs to know. This is my time. This is for me. It has nothing to do with him. All I have to tell him if he does find out is that you and Samael had plans to take over my legion. He'd understand fully and let me have my way and say I was justified in my actions."

"So you think that Luc, being who he is and as

powerful as he is, would fall for something like that?" Clay asked.

"Luc has problems of his own and is too busy to watch what the left hand is doing, let alone the right."

Asmoday snapped his fingers, and the world spun for a moment as he righted both him and Samael. The bindings that held their feet went away, making it possible for them to walk. Both he and Samael were propelled forward by a push to their backs from the demons that followed behind.

"It's time to take a walk, my fellow devils. I will let you see your women one more time. Never let it be said that I wasn't a generous individual. One last time with the one you would die for. Quite fitting, I think."

With their hands still bound behind and several demons surrounding them, they were led out into the web of adjoining tunnels, he hoped towards Eva and Liliana.

****

Eva heard the commotion outside of her cell and stood quickly, looking towards the entrance. When Clay was thrust into the room bound and fell to the ground, she let out a cry and ran over to him. She saw the strange bindings holding his hands behind his back and could feel the strange pulsing magic that lived within them. Kneeling over him she cupped his face, never so happy to see him in her life.

"Clay!" She pressed kisses to his face over and over again, only pulling back away when she realized there was someone else in the room. Asmoday.

"Aw, look, the reunited doomed lovers. Isn't that special? Enjoy him while you can, Eva, for soon I will kill him. I will even be nice and let him touch what is mine for a little while longer. Oh and don't get any bright ideas. Though the bindings are gone this area does basically what the straps did. You see, I thought of everything" He tapped his head with his finger and laughed. Then he waved his hand and the bands that held his arms disappeared. Turning on his heels he left them there alone. Glancing back down at Clay she could not hold back the huge smile that spread across her face. Before she could say anything his hands were stroking into her hair and tugging her head down towards his.

"Where are Samael and Lili?"

"A few tunnels back as far as I know. He pushed Samael into a room first. Asmoday basically said she was alive." She nodded and held on to him.

Clay's arm wrapped around her, and his kiss was hot and heavy. Parting the kiss he placed one last gentle kiss on her lips.

"I'm sticky and hot. It's so hot in here, though I think he is keeping it at a certain temperature just for me."

"It's okay. I'm not going to stop holding you because you're sweaty."

She giggled. "I've seen better days."

His countenance turned serious. "I'm going to get you out of this somehow, Eva. I don't know how, but I will."

"I'm so sorry, Clay. This is my entire fault, all of this. I should have told you about the dreams I was having and that I was being visited by the serpent." She rushed head first into her apologies, wanting him to know that she messed up and she knew it.

"Stop, baby. We have time for all that later. Right now I want to hold you and to figure out a way for us to defeat him."

"I already know a way and you're not going to stop me."

"When you say it like that, that tells me it's going to be something I don't like."

"It probably is. But I can't tell you what it is. It has to be done and it has to be my sacrifice, not yours. All of this is happening because of me, and I must end it."

"No! You're not going to play the fucking martyr." He'd stood and she fell to her butt. Clay paced back and forth in the small area, his eyes wild.

"Kamuel told me that I needed to be who I was meant to be. I also think he wanted me to truly feel remorse for the things I've done and to walk in a human's footsteps."

"That didn't mean you had to sacrifice yourself."

"Tell me how you know that, Clay? Perhaps the moral of this story is for me reap what I've sowed."

He stopped his pacing and pulled her up into his arms, burying his face into her neck. She held on to him, trembling. It was so good to see him again and to have him hold her.

"Why would they give you another chance if but to take you from me?" He took his face from her neck and asked in a gruff voice so full of emotion.

"That's the mistake I made before. This isn't just about you and me." She searched his eyes, hoping he could tell that she was determined to do this. His shoulders sagged, alerting her to the fact that her words hit home.

"I don't want to lose you, Eva."

"I can't promise that this won't be my end. I don't know what's going to happen and neither do you. But this is a path that I have to take."

"He plans to kill us and to keep you."

"I know, but I will die before ever letting him touch me," she vowed.

"There's so much I want to tell you."

"It's enough that you're here. It speaks volumes.

You didn't have to come after me."

"There shouldn't have been doubt in my coming to look for you. As for not having to come after you, no, I had to. There was no other choice."

She kissed the side of his mouth and pulled back. "He didn't hurt you, did he?"

"I think I should be asking you that. You're naked. Why are you naked?"

"He didn't try anything if that's what you're wondering. He made me strip I think just to prove to himself that he could."

"He's fucking crazy."

"Yeah I think we've already established that fact, Clay."

Gripping the edges of his t-shirt she lifted slowly to take it off of him. He held his arms up, letting her remove the shirt.

"What are you doing, Eva?"

"What does it look like? You're way too over dressed for my liking."

"Baby, we don't have to do this; you know Asmoday is probably watching." He had his hands at the button of his pants, pausing.

"That's okay. He can watch all he wants. He will never have anything even close to this with me." She kissed his chin, then his throat. "So come on ... undress all the way," she whispered softly.

The speed with which he finished undressing all the way made her smile. He grabbed her quickly and pushed her up against the wall, his hands at her waist. He stroked his thumbs across her lower belly, though his eyes never left hers. His touch made her whimper.

"I've missed you, Eva.

"I've missed you as well Clay."

He kissed her then, roughly, no tenderness, but

she didn't mind at all. He bruised her lips, and she moaned.

"Fuck, baby, I'm sorry."

"No, don't be. We both want and desire the same thing—each other." He kissed her bottom lip. Tugging at it with his teeth then sucking on it before letting go.

"I think it's more than obvious. Now pick me up so I can wrap my legs around you and we can do this right."

"You're fucking bossy, but I love it." He picked her up, and she wrapped her legs tight around his waist, rising so he could thrust into her. When he did she let out a deep moan of pleasure, pressing her forehead to his as he muttered an expletive. They stayed still for a few moments, the only sound their heavy breathing.

"Are you ready, baby?"

"More than ready. Fuck me, Clay."

He pushed forward, and she pressed down to meet his thrust. Soon they were gliding together in a sensual dance. When she sped up his hands went to her waist to still her.

"No, Eva … nice and slow like this. I want to savor you." With his hands at her waist he taught her the rhythm that he desired. Then he bent his head to kiss the tops of her breasts, and she arched her back to give him better access.

She was so wet she could feel the juices coating her inner thighs. He did this to her, no one else. He made her crazy with need. Even in the midst of what was happening, she wanted him. She always would. She gripped the back of his head as he took a nipple into his mouth, rubbing gently as he teased that sensitive nub with his teeth and tongue.

"Damn, you're tormenting me." White-hot need coiled deep in her lower belly. She felt the telltale tremble of her legs—a sure sign she was close to orgasm.

"It's only right. You've tormented me since the beginning of time." He growled low, his hands caressing along her sides. She leaned up, licking his throat, then nipping him.

"Mmm, damn you taste so good. Now fuck me like you mean it."

She wanted to savor every part of him. Who knew if this would be the last chance she got. Nibbling a path up his throat, she kissed him hungrily, as she started to ride him faster. She wasn't going to let him tell her no this time. She wanted to come, and she wanted him coming with her.

"Like this?" He plunged into her harder and harder, rolling his hips in a circle.

"Ohhh, yes, just like that. I'm going to come, Clay." She could hear herself whimpering.

"Then come, come all over me." His words released her. She let out a loud wail as she came hard, flooding him with her juices. It wasn't long after that he was filling her with his cream, marking her as his forever.

When the fever for each other had finally calmed, they lay huddled together just talking and enjoying what little time they had together. Nothing was certain for them, but what they could hold on to, they held on to tightly, not about to let each other go until they absolutely had to.

Chapter Twenty-One

She was cocooned pleasantly in Clay's warmth when she was ripped out of his arms and pressed against someone else. She let out a terrified scream. That something else breathed hotly against her ear as she writhed in its arms.

"Eva!" Clay called out, trying to reach for her as she held out a hand to try to grip his.

"Enough with the kicking and shouting, Eva, or I will have Lili killed right now." Asmoday's words sent coldness through her body, and her struggles immediately stopped.

"You too, Clay. Stop it or all you hold dear will die even more quickly and I will make you see it all. Now we are going to go and play a little game. All four of you will be playing. Your judgment has come, and I am so ready to hand out your fates."

A loud humming began pulsing in the air around them, and that was when her arms were pulled behind her and she was led out of the cavern, propelled by Asmoday. She looked frantically back, searching for Clay. He was farther behind with a strange pulsing collar that had been placed at his neck.

Lili and Samael also marched behind all of them. Demons pushed them to walk. Samael had that band about his neck as well—one of the ways Asmoday could control them. They were demons just like he was and if he didn't pacify them, they'd be able to kill him.

She was shoved so hard by Asmoday that she almost fell to the ground and would have had he not grabbed her and held her up by her wrists. He forced her forward again.

"Keep going. Don't worry, you'll get to see them all one last fucking time."

NIKKI PRINCE

She didn't try to look back anymore. She didn't want them to get killed because of some stupid mistake she made. They walked for a while until Asmoday stopped her inside a large room that held a throne. He pushed her in front of it as he sat.

"Kneel, Eva, and do it quickly before I do something you don't want me to do to that dear sister of yours." Eva knelt before him.

"Ahh, just how I like to see you, laid bare before me, ass in the air ripe for the taking."

He gripped her by the hair, forcing her to turn so that she could see Clay, Samael and Lili. All three of them were on their knees as well. It also allowed her to see the wall to wall demons that filled the place. Asmoday's army of fiends snarled and growled, bowing before him as well.

"Do you comprehend all of this, Eva? Do you get it? Really see what I've been telling you all along? This is what you could have. All of this could be yours to rule with me. Right along with us ruling the world. We could have it all."

"Yes, I understand Asmoday," she purred softly. "This is what I've always wanted." Clay's head shot up.

"Eva, what the fuck are you saying?" His dark gaze met hers and even though it hurt she held it. She'd save them at all costs. She'd be the lamb to the slaughter.

"No, Clay, he's right. All along since the garden I wanted everything. Wanted to have the understanding of why I couldn't have certain things that were due me."

She turned to stare at Asmoday. Placing her hand on his thigh, she squeezed.

"I was changed into a human because they're all afraid of what I can do as a demon. They're afraid of me and the power that I hold." She laughed.

Asmoday's face lit up, and he clapped his hands.

"Yes! Fuck, it's about time you became enlightened to that fact. I saw it in you in the garden. I groomed you for this, for us!"

She heard Lili sobbing in the background, but she forged on. If in letting down the others she saved them, then that was all that mattered.

"I'm so sorry, Asmoday. You did, you tried telling me through the years that I was better than this and that I could have more. I should have heeded your call sooner. But I'm here now, and I am so ready for this." His hands eased from her hair and she rose leisurely.

"Yes, yes you are."

"I want a throne next to yours."

"It's done. You will be my queen and shall rule with me. We will even take over Luc's dominion!"

"I can see you thought of everything, Asmoday."

"Of course I have. This has been the plan all along. You just needed to heed my words and listen. I will forgive you for fucking that shit up for so long."

"I know I've been a bad girl."

With a sway of her hips, she walked to Asmoday and settled in his lap. She steadied herself so that the revulsion she was feeling didn't show. Asmoday ran his hands up her legs and gripped her at the waist. Heated lust was unmistakable in his eyes and in his touch. Eva stayed on the path to getting them free.

"How will we do this?"

"I will make you a demon again; there is no way you can rule with me as a human."

"You have that power, Asmoday?"

"Yes, I have the power to make you my demon queen." He kissed her shoulder. Clay growled, and for show, she tossed him a look of contempt. She curled her fingers into Asmoday's hair, stroking the locks.

"I grow tired of this human body. I would love to be what I was truly meant to be. Kamuel had it wrong. What does he know about who I am and what is best for me?"

"Exactly," Asmoday hissed.

"I want to kill them when you're ready," she stated calmly though her stomach was churning.

"Kill who?"

"Lili, Clay and Samael, you know the three who hold me back in this world. Will you give that choice to me?" For effect she stood and moved to the others, circling them as she spoke. She rubbed her hand over Lili's head as the other woman sobbed. Samael, though bound, tried to reach her to push her away, and she jumped out of his way with a laugh.

"How about I do you first, Samael? You've been a thorn in my side for far too long."

"Fuck, girl! Own this shit!" Asmoday sidled next to her.

"I can, and I will. You just have to give me the tools and the means to do it."

"Damn, when you get bloodthirsty you get motherfucking bloodthirsty. This is better than I'd even thought you'd be."

"Fuck you, Eva, have you always been this fucking crazy?" Clay yelled out, and she ignored him. She couldn't let her smokescreen break down. If she looked at him it would.

"Don't do this!" Samael voiced loudly.

"Show me!" she demanded. "Show me what weapon you'd use on them to end their pitiful existences."

"No, Eva! If you ever loved me you wouldn't do this!" Lili screamed. None of them realized that this was the only way. She had to do this to correct all of the mistakes she'd made.

Asmoday tugged her close, and in his other hand he produced a crystalline dagger that sparkled with a strange purple hue. It was the demon lance she'd heard whispered about. It was as if it was alive. It pulsed and as she reached for it, it got brighter.

"She likes you," Asmoday said. "She wants you to take ahold of her and to let her power free."

"She?"

"Yes, she." He raised the dagger. "It's alive, don't you know. It identifies who should wield it. It discerns whose life it will take and why."

"What else can she do besides take a life? Can she give it as well?"

"Most definitely, Eva. Whatever is in the wielder's heart, she will perform it. This same dagger can make you a demon again, give you back what was taken, and it will win us the war against Luc."

"So I could use this to kill them. And then?"

"We could use it to kill them and as many others as we wish. Though I must warn you, in doing so we will set about an apocalypse like never before seen. It will pit angels and demons against each other."

She had to ask because she was curious. "How did you happen to get this, Asmoday?"

"Luc entrusted me with it."

Those words gave Eva pause. Why in the world would Luc give Asmoday this kind of power? The king of all demons didn't see the craziness that was standing before her? If she could see it, why couldn't he?

"He knew just who to give the job to—he picked the best demon out of the bunch." She fed his ego; he loved that shit and would eat it up.

"Girl, words like that make me hard, and you know it. Stroking my ego is like giving me a fucking blow job."

"Can I hold it, Asmoday?" She batted her lashes at him and tossed him a wink.

"What—the dagger or my cock? I have to say I am hoping you will want to hold on to both."

"I want the dagger right now and your cock I will hold as much as you like later. Once this is all said and done we will have an eternity, won't we?"

Asmoday let her go and walked a few feet away, as if he were in deep contemplation. "Are you sure you're ready for such power?"

"Isn't this what you wanted? The reason that you've done all that you have? This instance, this solitary flash in time when we are together and we both get what we want?"

"I've always wanted you, Eva. You just refused to see it."

"I know I was blind and in denial. You're what I want, you and that dagger. I'd be lying if I didn't say that I want that blade. I want the supremacy that all of this will give me. I want to be a demon again."

Asmoday's eyes were wild, and he'd even started drooling. His craziness and his need to be master of all was going to be his downfall, and she was going to make sure of it. She just needed him to put that weapon of destruction in her hands. She waited with baited breath.

"Come on, Asmoday. Why are you hesitating? We've won. Give me the fucking blade so I can end this shit once and for all." She held out her hand to him. "Well?"

Edging close, he tentatively held out the blade to her, and she knew she'd obtained his trust. When the blade was placed in her hand, she closed her eyes as its dark energies waxed and waned in a continuous stream. She had him now in a position that even he would not be able to get out of. There was no turning back.

"Who will you kill first?" She didn't acknowledge his question yet. It was too soon. The darkness in her was fighting the light. The battle between the two parts of her wasn't something that she could conquer easily.

There was pure unadulterated excitement in Asmoday's voice as she turned her back to him and looked at her family. For a moment deep, soul-reaching blackness clutched at her soul, and she heard those whispers of temptation yet again. It was Asmoday of old and new, telling her that this was what she craved. Her hand shook as she fought that darkness.

"Yes … yes … yes!" Asmoday screeched behind her. "You can feel it. I can see your evilness. It's all around you!"

She wondered if he were right. If he could see how evil she was, did that mean all of the good that she was had been swallowed up and was no more? Had she just been deluding herself? It was then that she heard another whisper in her mind. It was Salathiel.

Do you remember how brave you were when I forced you to leave the garden?

She closed her eyes and let those words flow through her.

Yes, you stood at the garden so that we could never enter it again.

Right, yet there was still promise in that. There is always going to be evil that men and women do. It was prophesied, but you have the right of choice. What will that choice be, Eva? Good or bad?

Good, I will do good! she answered Salathiel back.

It was as if the scales fell from her eyes, and she could fully see all that would happen if she'd turned toward that darkness that ate at everyone's soul.

Eva knelt quickly on the ground and held the blade to her own breast. Asmoday let out a horrible hissing sound as he ran to grab the blade. "Nooooo! You will not take away my victory! I will kill you first before I allow that."

A struggle ensued, and they wrestled on the floor to the roar of the other shades that were in the room. Lili, Samael and Clay's screams and shouts also joined the discord. The prick of the blade hit her chest, and she gasped as pain shot through her whole body. Her eyes locked with Asmoday's as he plunged the blade into her heart. She sensed she was floating in a pain-filled haze then struggling to keep her eyes opened. Her head fell to the side as she gasped for breath, the blade still within her chest as her life's blood pumped out around it and stained the ground. She was dropped to the ground, and Asmoday made a shrieking sound.

"This isn't how it's supposed to be!" he screamed, spittle flying from his mouth. She was losing the battle. Her eyes would close soon, and she'd be no more. She needed to see Clay one last time. Clay ran to her, and it was then she realized he was no longer bound by Asmoday's chains and neither was Samael.

She looked just behind him and saw a plethora of angels who had all the demons of Asmoday's legion at the sword.

"Eva, just hold on. You did it. You beat this. Please don't leave me."

"Don't worry about me. Help Lili, help the others."

He reached for the sword that protruded from her chest, and she grasped his hands weakly. "No, this is the only thing keeping me alive right now. You must kill Asmoday." She was slipping away, a blessed peace filling her. "Take care of Lili for me and let her know I did love her." The sounds of the chaos in the room disappeared into nothingness as she took her last breath.

Chapter Twenty-Two

Clay gave a roar of pain and was off his feet in an instant, his hands at Asmoday's throat and his powers fully restored. Asmoday's eyes began to bulge from his head as Clay squeezed.

"No! Stand back, Adam of old." Turning to see who'd dared to tell him to stop, Clay saw Luc in all of his glory. He was still as beautiful as ever and just as regal. The blond-haired demon in his human likeness strode forward. The sea of demons and angels parted as Luc made his way to Clay and Asmoday.

"Free him. he is mine to deal with. Not yours. Take your angels and humans from this place. Now is not the time for war. I decide that. Not you, not Kamuel and most definitely not the dog of a demon you hold in your hands." Luc's voice was calm and even.

"See, Master? I told you Asmoday was up to no good!" Another demon called from the crowd.

"That you did, Vestis, and you will be rewarded accordingly for taking care of this snake in the grass." Luc turned his gaze back to Clay.

"That is an order, Clay. I rule here and no one else."

Clay dropped Asmoday and hurried back to Eva.

"The blade, Luc, what about the blade in her chest?" He tossed Luc a glance.

"What blade?" Luc said simply.

"The fucking blade in her chest." He all but screamed at the Prince of true darkness.

"There's no blade. Now run on home before I change my mind."

What the hell was he talking about no blade? He stared at Eva's breast. There was a mark where the blade had been, yet no blade. He clutched her to him.

"Let's go, we need to get the women to safety." He heard a loud screech of terror and pain and knew that Luc was sufficiently dealing with Asmoday.

Most importantly, Eva was so still it worried him. His words were no sooner from his mouth than they were crossing the Nether over into the heavenly realm. Kamuel led them to a room of all white, and Clay laid her on the bed. Several angels surrounded Eva, cleansing her of blood and filth and when they moved away she was covered in a robe of purest white.

A hand was placed on his shoulder. "We'll do all that we can to make sure she lives, Clay. She sacrificed her life for all of yours. That counts for something in this realm. The blade was her way out, and she took the right path. She didn't commit the highest sin by killing herself. Asmoday took on that evil burden. Let her rest. She needs to heal."

With a sob of relief Clay left her in the very capable hands of the angels of healing. He needed to check on Samael and Lili.

****

Eva awakened with a gasp. Everything was so white. Why was everything so white? She was dead, wasn't she?

"Ah, you have awakened. It's been quite a journey," a soft voice spoke. Turning her head, Eva was faced with Kamuel.

"Am I in limbo, Kamuel? How long have I been out?"

"Yes, I suppose you could call this limbo. You've been out for a good month."

"Are Clay, Lili and Samael safe?"

"They're doing rather well. Though they've been a bit worried about you sleeping for so long. It's been hard to keep them out of here."

"Sleep? You mean I'm not dead?"

Kamuel let out a snort of laughter. "Dead? By no means are you dead. You're perfectly healthy. You've paid your debt. Are you ready to see them?"

"Oh yes, yes I am. I just hope they can forgive me."

"Clay has been by your side through all of this. I just tossed him out of here a little while ago. He's waiting in the wings. Do you need help sitting up?" She shook her head in the negative as she gingerly sat up in bed, propping herself on the pillow.

As she adjusted herself the door opened and Clay sprinted into the room. He pulled her close, and she snuggled into his warmth.

"Eva, it's so good to see that you're awake."

"Clay, I thought never to hold you again." He kissed the top of her head.

"You can't get rid of me."

"I wanted to say that I'm sorry for everything."

"I wanted to say that I'm sorry as well and to say thank you. You freed us."

"My actions of the past hurt us all. You and the others were right. I'm just glad to have made amends."

"Lili wants to come in."

"She's here?"

"Yes, they've allowed her to stay while you were healing. Do you want to see her and Samael?"

She swallowed back the tears and nodded frantically. The door opened once more, and both Lili and Samael entered. Lili rushed to her side as Clay took a step away.

She was enveloped into Lili's arms, and both of them began to sob. "I'm sorry, Lili, more sorry than you'll ever know."

"Sister dear, you don't have to apologize. I know

that your words ring true as your actions proved. I love you. I forgive it all, and I want you in my life." Tears streamed down her cheeks hotly, and she let out a sob, overcome with emotion at Lili's words.

"Thank you. I love you. I've always loved you. I just allowed temptation to get in the way."

"I love you too. Samael and I've forgiven you. So don't fret about that anymore." She leaned in close and kissed her cheek, but before she pulled back she whispered softly into Eva's ear. "Fight for your demon like I fought for mine."

Lili got up and Samael came over and kissed her forehead. He didn't speak, but words weren't needed. She already had confirmation from Lili that he'd forgiven her. The two left the room, leaving her with Clay.

"I need to say something, Clay."

"You don't need to apologize anymore." He shook his head.

"Not an apology. Sit next to me and listen." He sat on the bed next to her. She held out her hand, and he took it within his own.

"I love you. I should have said it long ago. But I was too stubborn. I love you, and it's okay if you don't love me too."

"Stop right there, Eva." His words gave her pause. What had she done now? He kissed the back of her hand and just let silence fill the room. She could hear her heartbeat.

"I love you too. I have since time began for us. I should have made sure that you could feel it. I failed to do that, but I promise that isn't how it will be for us from now on."

"From now on?" Once again she was mimicking words, and she sounded like a parrot.

"Yes, from now on. Kamuel has said that you are allowed a clean slate. You've paid your debt. He also said you have your choice of being a demon again or human."

"But if I chose to be a human that means I'll die."

"Yes, that's what it means, but we have also been given our own curse in a way."

"What do you mean our own curse? Clay, you're talking in riddles."

"Well just as you cursed Lili with reincarnation, if you choose to stay human we have been granted the same. You will be human, and we will have each other for an eternity. But this time I'll know you and you'd know me."

"I'd have the same choice if I stayed demon, right?"

"Yes basically, if that is the choice that you want to make."

"I just want to be with you and either choice gets me that."

"Right."

"Well I'm ready to make that choice. I want to be human again. This is my second chance at living the blessing I was given, and I want to do that. I don't want or need any powers. What I want I have already. You, Lili and Samael are all I require."

"Fantastic!" He kissed her hungrily then pulled away.

"Thank you, Clay, for keeping at me and believing that I'd make the right choice when it came to what to do."

"Anything for you, baby.

He kissed her again, and she wrapped her arms around his neck, drinking in that kiss and his love. She'd won. She'd beat the demon of temptation at his own game. She now had the spoils of her victory, and life was good.

The End

EVERNIGHT PUBLISHING ®

www.evernightpublishing.com